A CENTIMETER AT A TIME, CHEKOV'S ARM DISAPPEARED INTO THE WINDOW . . .

He could still feel the arm, could feel the weight of the tricorder in his hand, but all he could see in the window was the view of the rolling plain that the alien device had shown them since they had first released it from its protective walls.

The pull on his arm increased sharply as his elbow disappeared into the window. Startled, Chekov jerked back, and his boots missed their footing on the loose gravel. Unbalanced, he pitched forward toward the window, drawn in by the pressure on his arm. The alien scientist's hold on his waist slowed his movement, but his momentum pushed her arm against the surface of the window. The field caught her, and both of them fell inside. . . .

Look for STAR TREK Fiction from Pocket Books

Star Trek: The Original Series

Star Trek: The Next Generation

Star Trek: Deep Space Nine

STAR TREK®

WINDOWS ON A LOST WORLD

V. E. MITCHELL

POCKET BOOKS

New York   London   Toronto   Sydney   Tokyo   Singapore

This book is a work of fiction. Names, characters, places and incidents are either products of the author's imagination or are used fictitiously. Any resemblance to actual events or locales or persons, living or dead, is entirely coincidental.

An *Original* Publication of POCKET BOOKS

POCKET BOOKS, a division of Simon & Schuster Inc.
1230 Avenue of the Americas, New York, NY 10020

ISBN: 0-671-79512-0

First Pocket Books printing June 1993

10 9 8 7 6 5 4 3 2 1

POCKET and colophon are registered trademarks of
Simon & Schuster Inc.

Printed in the U.S.A.

To my parents,

Leslie and Virginia Mitchell,

*for teaching me
that anything worth doing
is worth doing right*

WINDOWS ON
A LOST WORLD

Chapter One

Captain's Log, Stardate 5419.4:

The *Enterprise* is approaching the Dulciphar star cluster, once the most densely populated region in this sector of the galaxy. Our mission: routine archaeological inventory of the ancient civilizations in the cluster. To that end, ship's personnel has been supplemented by a twenty-person team of researchers from the University of Nexqualy on Perren IX, led by Dr. Abdul Ramesh Kaul. Dr. Kaul is the Federation's foremost authority on the Meztorien culture, whose ruins are widely scattered throughout this quadrant. It is a distinct honor to be associated with such eminent scholars as Dr. Kaul and his team.

"WHY ME?" Ensign Pavel Chekov demanded, breaking his stride to lift his arms toward the ceiling as if imploring some unseen deity to answer his question. "Why do I have to be the person who gets stuck with the Djelifan? To listen to her talk, you would think that God Herself was from Djelifa and that She used that planet as Her base for creating the Universe."

1

Lieutenant Hikaru Sulu ducked his head to hide a grin. "Do you have proof She didn't?" Turning the last corner to the turbolift, he glanced at Chekov from the corner of his eye. As he expected, Chekov still hadn't gotten the joke. While Chekov claimed half the Federation's technology was invented in his native Russia, the matriarchal Djelifans *knew* that everything in the Universe came from their planet. Whoever paired the visiting archaeologists with "buddies" among the *Enterprise*'s crew had obviously been thinking of Chekov's Russian provincialism when assigning him to work with the Djelifan post-doctoral researcher, Talika Nyar. As they reached the turbolift Sulu gave an apologetic shrug. "Besides, I didn't get teamed up with any prize. Meredith is so shy she's hardly spoken three words to me."

"At least she's attractive." Chekov stepped into the turbolift. He glanced toward the intercom receiver.

The orangish-yellow star grew larger and brighter in the viewscreen, its attendant planets gleaming like diamond chips in their sun's reflected light. Captain James T. Kirk studied the image, trying to guess what discoveries they would make here. The familiar rhythms of his ship flowed around him soothingly—Uhura's voice directing intraship messages, Chekov and Sulu adjusting the ship's approach, Spock at his station correlating the sensor readings as they came in. He let his anticipation build until he *had* to know what this solar system held for them. "Report, Mr. Spock."

The Vulcan raised his head from his scanner display and faced Kirk, his movements controlled and economical. "We are approaching the Careta system. The star is classified as F9 and has been fading gradually for the last 500,000 years. It is orbited by ten planets, most of them small, and has a broad zone of widely scattered asteroids between the fifth and sixth planets. The third and fourth planets are currently in the habitable zone, although the climates of both are marginal. At present, neither shows long-range readings that would indicate the presence of intelligent life."

"In other words, two possible choices for us to explore." Kirk glanced at the viewscreen, trying to guess which planet was the more likely candidate before Spock launched into another round of statistics.

"The possibility also exists that artifacts remain in the asteroid belt." Spock's voice held a note of reproof, as if chiding Kirk for jumping to so hasty and unscientific a conclusion. "The Meztoriens often established orbiting habitats in remote sections of systems that they did not otherwise occupy. A detailed survey would be required to establish whether such habitats were present in this system."

Knowing he would regret it, Kirk took the bait. "How long would it take to perform such a survey?"

"It will take 7.25 days to scan the asteroid belt with sufficient resolution to insure that we have not missed any potential Meztorien artifacts." Spock paused, raising one eyebrow. "We should, in any case, conduct such a survey. If we confine ourselves to investigating only the planets, we risk overlooking significant discoveries. This quadrant contains an anomalously high number of 'orphan' archaeological sites for which we have no context. It is possible that the smaller planetary bodies or the asteroid belt may contain information that will allow us to determine predecessor or successor cultures for some of these isolated remains."

Kirk suppressed a groan. By now, he thought, he should know when to keep his mouth shut. "I'll make you a deal, Mr. Spock. You can survey all the asteroids you like if we find something on one of those planets to keep our passengers busy in the meantime. They're getting anxious to do some serious work."

"Agreed, Captain, although I recommend that we conduct the asteroid survey regardless."

"We'll see, Spock. First, let's see what's on the planets." *And hope it's big enough to keep the archaeologists busy for a while!*

"Yes, Captain." Spock turned back to his sensors. Kirk watched him for a moment, then shifted his attention to the main viewscreen. *Third planet or fourth?* Which would it be?

By late afternoon the verdict was in: the fourth planet. After listening to Spock's summary, Kirk scheduled a briefing for the *Enterprise*'s researchers and the visiting archaeologists to plan their investigation.

Kirk, Spock, and McCoy took seats on one side of the table and waited for the archaeologists to sort themselves into their places. Each had brought a personal datapad and several data tapes, as if unsure what information they needed for the briefing.

"Forgive our disarray," Dr. Abdul Ramesh Kaul said with an apologetic smile. "We try always to be completely prepared." Kaul was a short, wiry man with teak-colored skin darkened by the recent weeks of fieldwork. He was bald except for a narrow fringe of silvery-gray hair, and he regarded everything with an impish twinkle in his eye. His two chief assistants for this system—selected by lot, Kirk had been told, to rotate the work and the experience among the team— could not have been chosen to provide a greater contrast to each other or to their leader.

One glance at Dr. Talika Nyar identified her as a native of a high-gravity planet. She was short and wide, with mousy brown hair and a huge beak of a nose; her sturdy bones and powerful muscles made Kirk feel frail in comparison. Her planet, Djelifa, had recently joined the Federation, and Talika's assignment to this expedition was the first contact anyone on the *Enterprise* had had with her people. So far Kirk had heard mixed reviews about Talika's interactions with his crew. Djelifa was a strongly matriarchal society—the strongest in the Federation, if the sociologists' reports were true—and Talika was having trouble accepting the equality that prevailed on the *Enterprise*. The glare with which she answered Kirk's scrutiny did not convince him of her willingness to cooperate with his officers.

In contrast, Dr. Meredith Lassiter was delicate and willowy, with luminous white-blond hair and sea-green eyes. Her physique suggested that she had been raised on the Moon or a low-gravity orbital habitat, but she had not volunteered any information about her background. The few times Kirk had seen her with other people, she had avoided all eye contact and had only spoken when asked a direct question. Lassiter slid into her seat and began fiddling with a data tape, staring at it as if it would vanish if she looked away. She seemed as out of place on the archaeological team as the Djelifan.

When everyone was settled Spock called up his scans of the planet. "Careta IV is a class-M planet, with a gravity 0.85 of Earth. The oxygen content of the atmosphere is below optimum for humans, although it is well within the range tolerated by Vulcans. The climate is cool to cold at most sites, due to the cooling of the star in this solar system. Preliminary scans have identified a number of sites worthy of exploration."

Kaul nodded at Lassiter, who looked up from the

data tape and stared at the wall behind Spock. "We have run analyses on the five largest sites to select our initial survey target." Her voice was soft and whispery, like the rustle of dry leaves in a forest. "Each site has unique characteristics that should be explored, but we feel that Site J3 is the best choice for our first look at the Caretian civilization."

Talika requested a closer view of the site. The screen zoomed in on the area, a rolling flood plain below columned cliffs carved from dark, fissured rock. Low mounds marked the ruins of several large structures. Shadowed lines, enhanced by the ship's computer, formed a broken grid across the site. "Sensors less weathering, more shelter at Site J3 show. Better preserved should artifacts from destruction by natural causes be." Talika's voice was low and gravelly, a match for half the baritones in the ship's glee club. Although her command of English was excellent, her sentences were heavily influenced by the rhythms of her native language. "Small burial of major structures later abandonment than elsewhere suggests."

Spock focused the screen on a large mound near the cliffs. "This structure was one of the last built on the planet, judging by the thickness of the soil covering and the spectral analyses of the quarries in the vicinity. From the readings it is impossible to determine when these structures were abandoned, but we estimate an age in excess of 100,000 years."

Kaul leaned forward, drumming his fingers against the table. His skin was almost as dark as the pseudowood finish. "A hundred thousand years is somewhat younger than we would expect for Meztorien ruins in this sector. By then the Meztoriens in the nearby clusters had succumbed to the Darneel invasion, and the surviving fragments of their empire had fallen into a dark age from which they never emerged. Construction on even such a modest scale as the ruins we see here would have been beyond their capabilities."

Kirk nodded to close down the scientific speculations. Clearly they were not going to get any answers without going down to the planet. "Mr. Spock, what's your recommendation?"

Spock glanced at his display. "The extreme antiquity of these ruins makes it virtually impossible to date them from orbit. To obtain precise information we will have to beam down to the planet. I concur with the recommendation of Dr. Kaul's team to study Site J3 first. In addition to the scientific reasons they have already cited, the location offers a sheltered area to set up a base camp."

McCoy nodded. "The vegetation is sparse in this area due to a combination of low rainfall and cool temperatures. This minimizes the chances of running into dangerous native life-forms. About all we'll have to watch out for is this world's equivalent of poisonous snakes or insects. Beyond that, the biggest danger is going to be tripping over ourselves and our equipment."

"Does anyone else have anything to add?" Kirk checked the group's reactions. The archaeologists appeared eager to get down to the planet, and Kirk saw no reason to deny them their wish. "Very well. We'll run detailed sensor scans of the site while Dr. Kaul's people work out their excavation plan. The survey team will beam down at first light. Meeting dismissed."

Kirk made his escape before anyone dragged him into the detailed planning. As the door whisked shut behind him, he heard Spock launch into a technical discussion of the types of sensor information he could obtain for the archaeologists. Grinning to himself, Kirk headed for the relative peace of the bridge, where he could decide who from the *Enterprise* was joining the landing party.

"It's not fair!" Chekov grumbled, staring at his landing party assignment. He deactivated the screen and turned away, Sulu falling in step with him as they left his quarters and headed for the recreation room. "Why do I have to accompany her to the planet, just because I got assigned to show her around the *Enterprise?*"

"Some people have all the luck." Sulu's expression was bland, disguising his relief at missing this particular planetside excursion. Although he couldn't justify the feeling, he was glad he had been assigned to supervise the comprehensive sensor scans Spock had ordered of the planet and the solar system. "Besides, weren't you the one who was talking about specializing in the sciences? Maybe even trying for Mr. Spock's job when he gets promoted?"

"Me?" Chekov's voice cracked on the rising note. "I have just decided to change my specialization. To something safer, like security."

"Then you could beam down to Careta to help muscle the equipment into place." Sulu chuckled and waved to some friends who were hurrying to catch the turbolift. "I don't think you're going to win this one, Pavel. The gods seem to want you on that landing party."

"While you get to stay on the ship, doing all of Mr. Spock's sensor scans. This time I envy you. Normally I would prefer being in the landing party, but this time I do not." He gave Sulu a rueful grin.

Sulu nodded, his expression gone sober. "I know what you mean. I can't put my finger on it, but I wish we'd given this planet a miss." He clapped Chekov on the shoulder. "If it's any consolation, I'll be riding herd on the sensors the whole time. If you get into any trouble, we'll beam you up in a flash."

"That is very reassuring." Chekov's tone said differently. A lot could happen in the time it took to realize someone was in danger. "I would find it more reassuring if you would tell me what trouble we should expect."

"Isn't that Mr. Spock's department?" The recreation room door opened for them. They stepped through and Uhura waved for them to join her. Sulu acknowledged her signal, and went to get himself a cup of tea. "I mean, knowing everything *before* we need the information?"

"I suppose." Chekov looked glum. "But this is one planet I think the *Enterprise* could do without."

"Are you sure about this mission, Jim?" McCoy asked, sliding lower in the chair in Kirk's cabin. "Is it just me, or is there something strange about this planet?"

Kirk fiddled with his coffee cup, lifting it, then returning it to the table without tasting the tepid beverage. He glanced toward Spock, who was studying the edge of the table with a look of intense concentration that triggered warning bells in Kirk's head. "Would you be more specific, Bones?"

"Oh, that's right. You missed the discussions this afternoon." McCoy knocked back the remains of his coffee, grimacing at the taste. "I listened to Dr. Kaul and his people, and the longer I listened, the more nervous I got. There's something decidedly odd about this planet, and no one quite knows what to make of it."

"Spock? What's this about?"

Spock straightened, shifting his attention to Kirk's face. "Some of the survey results are inconsistent. For

9

example, there are distortions in the planet's magnetic field near several of the major sites. Also, the grid patterns associated with the buried cities do not match anything left by the Meztorien civilization, although Dr. Kaul has not acknowledged this."

"That's understandable, Spock." Laughter pulled up the corners of McCoy's mouth. "He's spent the last fifty years studying the Meztoriens. Do you really expect him to jump with joy at the thought that these ruins *might* have been built by someone else?"

"Continue, Spock. What else should I know?" Kirk gulped the last mouthful of his coffee. It tasted as terrible as he had feared.

"Our scans revealed several other anomalies that I am unable to explain at this time. The civilization on this planet appears to have disintegrated rapidly and completely, with few or no survivors. On the other hand, for their apparent age the ruins are remarkably well preserved and are surprisingly close to the surface. One would expect considerably more destruction after a hundred thousand years."

McCoy grimaced, as if the discrepancies left an unpleasant taste in his mouth. "Or new colonists to take over the abandoned real estate. It isn't *natural* for a habitable planet to be this deserted."

Spock nodded. "That was the other peculiarity that everyone noticed. I have ordered a detailed inventory of the planet's natural resources to determine if a crucial deficiency prevented another race from colonizing this planet. It is unlikely that all those passing through this sector missed the Careta system in the course of their explorations."

"What you're saying is . . ." Kirk paused, fiddling with his empty cup. The facts kept pointing to the same conclusion. "There is no obvious reason to avoid this planet, yet everyone who has come through here in the last hundred thousand years seems to have done exactly that."

"We better watch our step down there, Jim," McCoy said, finishing the thought for Kirk. "Whatever scared everyone else off might still be waiting for us."

"Warning noted, Bones. Do you have any suggestions on finding out what this is *before* we beam down?" Kirk paused for McCoy to answer, but got only the silence he expected. "In that case, gentlemen, we will have to be very careful until we find out what surprises the inhabitants of Careta IV left behind." He couldn't quite keep the grin of pleasure off his face. Archaeological missions were usually dull and slow-paced, much too tame for his liking. A mystery promised to liven this one up. The last few weeks had been peaceful and relaxing, a restful change from their previous assignment, but now Kirk was ready for some action. The grin widened as he considered doing a little investigation of his own. Yes, perhaps Careta IV wouldn't be so boring after all.

Chapter Two

THERE WAS SOMETHING ABOUT materializing on a new planet, Kirk thought as the transporter beam released him—a special zip in the air, a distinctive shiver in the ground beneath his feet. He had never been able to define, even to himself, why the first few seconds on any planet seemed so charged with hidden potential. It wasn't because he was the first human to stand on a particular world, because he had experienced the same feeling his first time on such long-established human colonies as Deneb II or Rigel IV. And it wasn't because a planet deviated from the Earth–normal conditions of the *Enterprise*. Any of the differences on Careta IV could be programmed into the ship's environmental controls. After running through all the possible explanations yet again, Kirk was left with the last and least satisfying answer—that the brief, charged excitement just after he materialized occurred because this was the first time that *he,* James T. Kirk, had stepped onto this particular world.

Kirk moved away from the beam-down point to let

the next group materialize. Spock followed him, activating his tricorder to scan the area for the fine details the ship's sensors could not detect. The four security guards fanned out to confirm the landing site for the *Columbus,* checking the terrain and other site factors against the *Enterprise's* sensor readings. *Columbus* carried a cargo of excavating tools, power packs, and other heavy equipment, and the archaeologists wanted the shuttlecraft close to their working site without having it on top of any important artifacts.

Talika, Chekov, Kaul, and three archaeological technicians materialized next. The scientists unlimbered their tricorders and began an in-depth site survey. Chekov joined Kirk, watching the archaeologists with a wary expression on his boyish face. "What is our plan, Captain?"

"Right now we wait for the experts to tell us." Kirk looked around. From the ground the site appeared larger and more desolate than it had from the crisp, impersonal reports of the ship's sensors. Immense walls of fissured basalt, fractured into columns, reached for the sky like a staircase designed for giants. The thousand-meter vertical sweep of the cliffs was interrupted by irregularly spaced ledges covered with shattered rock. More talus had collected below the towering basalt walls, burying some of the ruins. A fast-moving river, as wide as the two kilometers of flood plain between it and the cliffs, swept past. Its surface was ruffled to white-crested waves by the stiff breeze blowing up the canyon. A hundred-meter-long tree, stripped of foliage, revolved lazily in the current as it raced downstream. Closer to them, sparse blades of dried grass and a few sagebrush-like bushes rustled in the wind.

Spock rejoined Kirk and Chekov, studying his tricorder with an air of intense concentration. "This is most unusual. My tricorder readings suggest that these ruins are almost twice as old as we originally estimated."

Chekov whistled. "That would make them over two hundred thousand years old." He shook his head in disbelief.

"I take it that our friends will have some trouble dealing with that age?" Kirk frowned, trying to remember the history of this sector. He wasn't sure, but he *thought* that the Meztorien civilization had risen about 150,000 years ago. If Spock's newest readings were correct, these ruins were far too old to belong to any known civilization. They might belong to one of the "orphan" cultures that Spock had mentioned earlier, but most of those ruins were even older than two hundred thousand years.

"That is correct, Captain." Spock adjusted his tricorder and scanned the area again. "The earliest known Meztorien ruins are dated at 172,500 years before present. It is possible that these structures come from an earlier period of the Meztorien civilization, but that would require a drastic revision of our current theories concerning their expansion into this part of the galaxy."

"As I recall, the Meztorien expansion is one of the better-documented events of that era." Kirk scanned the desolate landscape around them. It seemed an unlikely place to discover anything that would destroy the Federation's painstakingly reconstructed history of this sector. "I should think that would be an enormous obstacle to any major reinterpretations."

"Rather." Spock consulted his tricorder screen. "However, we must consider that each new piece of information we discover contains the potential for rendering inoperative all our previous assumptions about a given situation."

Chekov scuffed a rock toward the archaeologists. "I

predict that our 'friends' will be most unhappy when they discover that this planet does not fit any of their grand theories."

Glancing toward Kaul's team, Kirk saw that they were huddled in a group, arguing about something. "It looks like you're right, Mr. Chekov. Shall we see what they've found?" The breeze shifted, blowing the sound of angry voices toward them. The captain exhaled heavily. *"Before* they kill each other."

By the time the three *Enterprise* officers reached the archaeologists, the argument had escalated almost to the point of blows. "It is quite impossible to have so ancient a date for Meztorien ruins." Kaul's voice was soft, but his tone was implacable. "Your sensor readings must be in error."

"I not mistake make!" Talika's voice sounded like the growl of an approaching thunderstorm. "Five times checked I readings to confirm. Inferior Federation machine indefinite results gives. Djelifan equipment would with one reading clearer answers show. Ruins for Meztorien too old are. Therefore from more ancient civilization must be. Perhaps remnant of 'orphan' predecessor of Meztoriens is."

"There *are* no older civilizations than Meztorien in this quadrant," said Kordes, a post-doctoral researcher obviously trying to gain points with Kaul. "In two hundred years of intensive investigations, no one has turned up the slightest evidence that anyone was here before them. The so-called 'orphan' cultures are sensationalist media reports created by publicity seekers who use improper excavation techniques and careless data analysis."

Spock stepped forward to interrupt the argument, holding out his tricorder. "My tricorder also reports extreme age for these ruins, Dr. Kaul. It would appear that we are dealing with a find of extreme importance.

V. E. Mitchell

May I congratulate you on your good fortune in discovering these ruins?"

Kaul turned toward Spock, blinking rapidly. Kirk could almost hear the relays snapping in Kaul's head as he tried to shift his processing circuits. *Who says Spock doesn't understand human psychology?* Kirk thought, hiding a smile. "I beg your pardon, Mr. Spock?" Kaul said, his face reflecting the ongoing reorientation of his thoughts.

"I said you were fortunate to be the first human to discover this site. Surely a previously unknown civilization of such antiquity is a find of tremendous importance. Such a discovery will revolutionize our perception of the history of this quadrant."

"That is true." Kaul's expression settled into a mask that matched Spock's for blandness. He focused his attention on Kirk with such intensity that the captain knew what Kaul wanted before he spoke. "To catalog a find of such magnitude will require additional time and manpower. I hope, Captain, that you will consider the difficulty of this task and assign me the resources necessary to conduct the research. If we are dealing with a previously unknown race, we will require several weeks to determine the nature of their civilization and to recommend the follow-up studies required to do this discovery justice."

"I understand, Dr. Kaul." Kirk finally let his grin out. If Kaul realized how well Spock had manipulated him, he showed no signs of it. "I'll assign extra crewmen to help with your preliminary investigations, of course. To extend our stay here, I must consult with Starfleet Command. However, if the results of your preliminary survey support your findings so far, there should be no difficulties."

"Very well, Captain Kirk. When can I expect the additional men?"

"I'll have the duty officer request volunteers with the appropriate experience. You should have them by the time the shuttlecraft arrives with your equipment."

"Thank you, Captain Kirk. That is quite acceptable."

"I'm glad, Dr. Kaul. I'll make the arrangements." Kirk turned away, feeling a sudden need to put some space between himself and Kaul. The last few minutes had made him wonder if he really wanted anything to do with Careta IV after all. Maybe they would have been better off if they had not found the ruins. Inexplicably the image of an ancient plague ship floated into his mind, a galleon that drifted across the ocean, majestic and serene, abandoned by all except the rats.

Kirk pushed the image away, wondering what had brought it into his mind so forcefully. Careta IV must be getting to him. He looked around, checking the desolate landscape for visible threats, but saw only his own people. There was no obvious explanation for his reaction. Wondering what unconscious games his mind was playing, Kirk reached for his communicator to ask for the extra help that Kaul had requested.

Why do I have all the luck? Chekov wondered as he followed Talika along the base of the cliffs. He would have been perfectly delighted to coordinate the *Columbus*'s landing and to set up their base of operations, making sure the equipment was accessible and ready for use. Instead, he had been assigned to help Talika survey the ruins for the most promising sites at which to begin their excavations. She skipped across the hexagonal plates of loose rock as if they were minor annoyances, little larger than pebbles. Her life on a heavy-gravity world had given her a massive

17

strength in her lower body, and the power of her muscles let her bound over obstacles that Chekov had to strain to surmount.

"Why did not Kirk to me someone competent assign?" Talika demanded as she paused yet again to let Chekov clamber over a pile of loose rock. "Why feeble male who barely on two feet stays?"

"Just because you are used to twice this much gravity—" Chekov tested a large boulder for stability, felt it totter and then settle more firmly into a cradle of smaller stones. He eased himself onto the boulder while he caught his breath, thinking *perhaps* Mr. Spock could match Talika's physical prowess. "Everybody on the *Enterprise* would have trouble keeping up with the pace you are setting. What is the hurry?"

"Hurry is assignment with distinction to complete. Although *how* to work am I, with flimsiest of Federation devices and only most substandard assistance, know I not. On Djelifa, such obstacles to accomplishment we permit not."

Her words stung Chekov into replying before he considered how many misinterpretations she could find for his words. "This is not Djelifa! And we are not obstructing your work!"

She looked him over with the impersonal expression of a buyer in a meat market. "Then what explanation give you for assigning assistant—and male one, at that—so weak he barely his own mass supports? How carry you samples or move rocks?"

"Sorry I asked," Chekov muttered, probing his right ankle. He had turned it on the last stretch when a rock had rolled beneath his boot, but he found no swelling or tenderness in the joint. This time, at least, he had been lucky. Still, he wasn't sure which rankled more—Talika's condescension or his own inability to measure up to her standards.

"That my meaning is! You Federation-*tska* all weaklings are. You like little girls behave who have not to ritual house gone for duties and responsibilities of adults to learn." A scowl twisted her face, deepening as she watched Chekov check his ankle. "How like boy-child, whimpering and crying because rocks in path are. Why not back to ship go and let me without interference to work finish?"

Because my orders require me to keep you *out of trouble,* he thought. Chekov bit his tongue to hold back the angry reply. Talika's greater physical strength, combined with her reluctance to pay any attention to him, made it almost impossible for him to do his job. The worst of it was that her impatience could easily send her charging into danger. Whatever else she knew, Chekov could see that she was ignorant of the basic rules for surveying unexplored planets. "I would be glad to let you do your job without interference," he said when he had gotten a grip on his temper. "However, I ask that you grant me the same courtesy. I am to assist you with your exploration and, specifically, to watch out for any unanticipated dangers. We know nothing about this planet. Therefore, the chances are very great that we will not recognize something dangerous until it attacks us."

Talika snorted, a sound that reminded Chekov of the large draft horse he had seen in the Moscow animal preserve when he was a child. "What possible danger could there on deserted planet be? Weaklings like Federation-*tska* might for worry find reason, but as Djelifan, nothing to fear have I."

"I suppose the mountain will *ask* if you are a Djelifan before it falls on you?" Chekov levered himself to his feet, moving cautiously until he was sure the ankle would hold his weight. "Or perhaps the snake will request an introduction before it strikes?"

"I from non-Djelifans such cowardice expect. However, to such whinings I will listen not." Talika started off without waiting for Chekov, moving at a rapid pace despite the irregularly shaped blocks of rock beneath her boots. Dislodged by her movements, several fist-sized chunks bounced down the hill, collecting others as they went. The slide gathered volume and momentum, but fortunately the top of the slope where Chekov was standing remained stable.

He watched the moving carpet of rock, his fists clenched tight with nervousness until the slide began to slow. How long, he wondered, will Talika get away with such carelessness? When the dust had settled and he judged it was safe, he picked his way cautiously across the loose rock. They had been moving along the cliffs for the last hour, chasing ephemeral signs of the alien ruins, and the talus piles had grown larger and more unstable. Looking at the fissured wall, Chekov wondered if the rubble was deeper here because the rocks were naturally more broken or if someone had blasted the cliffs to bury something. He paused, trying to remember where Spock had suggested possible tunnels in the cliffs. Could something be here, its entrance covered by the rocks that had fallen from above? He activated his tricorder and began scanning.

The cliff was webbed with fissures and cracks that ran in all directions through the rock. At first, Chekov had trouble distinguishing the dominant vertical fractures, which broke the cliffs into columns all along the valley, and the less prominent but no less pervasive horizontal fracture set that separated the vertical pillars into the plentiful hexagonal plates. In this area the rocks were honeycombed with randomly oriented cracks. Chekov scratched his head, trying to remember his basic geology courses. In rocks like these basalts the joints were formed by the cooling and contraction of molten rock, with one set of cracks more or less parallel to the ground's surface and a second, vertical set forming hexagons as the rock cooled. The patterns in nature were never perfect, but neither were they as chaotic as these readings. After a hundred thousand years he could not prove that the rocks had been blasted, but Chekov doubted that even Spock would dispute the probabilities. Someone had tried to bury this area so deeply that no one would ever find it.

"Would you your boots quit dragging and over here get?" Talika bellowed, her voice as loud as though she were standing at his shoulder.

In spite of himself, Chekov jumped. Angry at himself for letting her startle him, he snarled his reply. "Why don't you be a little more polite? At least *ask* why I've got my tricorder out before you start yelling insults!"

She started back toward him, a puzzled frown on her face. "For what reason should you your tricorder have out? Our scans nothing here showed to investigate. Why time waste?"

The shock almost made Chekov miss his footing. Talika—curious? It was the first emotion besides scorn that he had seen from her. He gestured toward the cliffs beside him. "The rocks are all shattered here, as if someone tried to blow up this entire cliff. I would guess that whatever they wanted to bury, we would be interested in finding it. The question is, how big is this object, and how well is it hidden?"

Talika surveyed the talus, worrying her lower lip with her large, square teeth. He watched her expression, hoping that he had finally made a favorable impression on her. It would make the rest of this assignment much more pleasant if they could work together as a team. At last she grunted and activated her own tricorder.

With a sigh of relief Chekov resumed his scanning. That she had accepted his idea gave him hope that he could eventually break through her armor. With that thought came the knowledge that he was not the only person in the Federation who would have to deal with this problem. Thousands, perhaps millions, of other men were going to have to convince the Djelifan women that they were as capable as the Djelifans. It wasn't going to be easy, he concluded, but beginnings seldom were. Still, it was encouraging to know that Talika could unbend enough to listen to him. Maybe, someday, he would forgive the person who had teamed him up with her.

They worked their way back and forth across the hill for the next half an hour with no results. Talika was becoming restive and irritable, muttering to herself in her own language, and Chekov was beginning to doubt his hunch when his tricorder gave him a flicker of an anomalous reading. "I found something!" He pointed toward the spot to give Talika the bearing.

She swung her tricorder around, sweeping the general area. "Nothing!" she growled after the fifth sweep. She fiddled with the controls, and her frown deepened.

Chekov adjusted his tricorder, and to his dismay, the anomaly disappeared. He shook the device and still got nothing. Puzzled, he swept the scanner across a wider area. Twice the readings flickered, then smoothed to the expected background values. "If I did not know better, I would think that someone was jamming us," he muttered. Hearing his words aloud, he felt an idea explode in his mind. Maybe something *was* aware of them. On occasion they had encountered alien devices that still functioned after exceedingly long periods of time. Given the age of the artifacts they had already found on Careta IV, it was more than reasonable to assume that any surviving technology on Careta no longer functioned perfectly. *But where does that leave us?* he asked himself. Chekov gestured to Talika, signaling for her to wait while he picked his way across the talus to join her.

"If there is a device down there, it must still be operating at a very low level. It seems able to detect us when we make enough noise, but if it does not know our location, it apparently cannot lock on to the radiation from our tricorders." He swiped a hand across his forehead, pushing his hair back. "Do you have any suggestions for dealing with such an object?"

"How know you this?" Her tone wavered between curiosity and her previous contempt. "This impossible is, unlike completely anything known."

"I agree that it does not act like anything I have seen before, but that does not make it impossible. Perhaps we are seeing a defense mechanism designed to protect whatever is here. If someone wanted to hide an object or if they wanted to protect it from destruction, they would not want it to register on anyone's sensors." He pointed his tricorder hopefully at the talus. As he had expected, the readings remained unchanged. "If someone had placed a jamming field generator at the base of these cliffs, it would prevent us from detecting anything beneath the rocks. Or if someone was being very tricky, he might want us to think that something was here so that we would not look in another place for the thing that they really did not want us to find." He shrugged, grimacing with frustration. "I could design a device that did any of these things, but that does not tell us which of these situations we are dealing with here."

Talika nodded. "What is object? Where is object? Does object in truth exist?"

Chekov nodded. "If we assume that it *does* exist, we still have to answer the other two questions."

"Job to find artifacts is. Therefore, as working hypothesis, assumption that object exists is made."

Talika nibbled on her lip, her eyes darting back and forth as she studied the loose rocks below them. "If I down hill go, making much noise, perhaps sensors think both away have gone. You here wait, being very quiet, and when I hand raise, both of us for object in area scan. Do you other way to solve problem see?"

What were their options? Chekov fiddled with his tricorder while he reviewed the facts. The radiation put out by their tricorders was either too weak or at the wrong frequency for the artifact to detect it without other clues. However, voices and movements on the rocks above it apparently were enough to pinpoint their location and trigger the jamming. The stronger signal of the *Enterprise*'s sensors would be easier for the ancient equipment to detect, and the sensors would probably be jammed if he had Sulu run a quick sweep around his coordinates. Talika's plan had the best chance of succeeding. "Let's do it," he said. "Good luck!"

"And to you."

Chekov settled himself onto a boulder and deactivated his tricorder. Nodding her approval, Talika started down the slope, picking an area covered with fist-sized rocks and slithering down it as though she were skiing. Watching her, Chekov was not at all sorry to have been cast in the role of "weak male." That trick looked like more of a challenge than he really wanted to try.

Talika reached the bottom of the slope, surrounded by a moving, clattering, grinding mass of small rocks. She stopped, letting the stones flow around her until they buried her ankles. The last rocks tumbled and clacked themselves into a charged silence. One minute, two minutes, three. Finally Talika pointed her tricorder toward the talus slope and signaled for Chekov to activate his.

He hit the switch and was rewarded immediately.

Low-level power readings were coming from beneath the pile of shattered rock. The source was small, less than three meters in any of its dimensions. Struggling to control his excitement, Chekov repeated his scan, both to confirm the existence of the artifact and to check his bearings. Anything that small, buried under so many tons of rock, would not be easy to excavate, even with the best location they could get.

Chekov eased himself to his feet and picked his way along the hillside, his tricorder still aimed toward the mysterious power source. After almost five minutes of cautious movement, coupled with constant readings, a rock slipped from beneath his foot. At the first clatter from the bouncing stone, the power readings terminated. "Damn!"

"Ah-ii-ya!" Talika's scream of triumph ripped through the valley. "Alive it is. After so much time, it still working is. Ah-ii-ya!"

Only then did Chekov realize Talika's strongest motivation. Given her culture's overweening sense of their own superiority, it rankled her to take second position to a man on the archaeology team, even to someone with Dr. Kaul's decades of experience. This discovery would give her the status within the Federation to dictate her own terms from now on. Shaking his head at the scope of her ambition, he started for their base camp to help bring back the necessary equipment so they could excavate their find.

Chapter Three

EVEN RUNNING THE EXCAVATORS NONSTOP, it took almost twelve hours to remove the rock that had been blasted from the mountainside to bury the artifact. Chekov alternated between impatience to learn what he and Talika had discovered and an equally strong desire to abandon the planet without ever seeing what the excavators would uncover. At first the work went quickly, with the excavator technicians locking onto the large boulders and transporting them beyond where Kaul's team planned to work. Even so, with the large volume of rubble, the operation required skill and precision to keep additional debris from sliding down and burying the site more deeply.

As the sun slid below the rim of the canyon and the shadows deepened, Kirk ordered Sulu to beam down half a dozen high-powered floodlights, and the digging continued. The first landing party returned to the *Enterprise* for the night, but they were replaced by a second shift of technicians and archaeologists. The majority of the work was still concentrated at the primary site, where Kaul believed they were most likely to find critical information.

Chekov spent the evening regaling Sulu with his morning's adventures, including comparing Careta IV's barren landscapes to the desolate sweep of Russia's northern steppes. At first he was relieved to be on the ship, warm and far from the bleak, eerie planet. However, the longer he thought about the artifact, the more curious he became. What had they found? How could it possibly be active after all these millennia? As often as he pushed the thought away, it returned. He wanted to be there when the excavators removed the last debris from the object. Finally, he surrendered and requested permission to return to the planet.

"Everyone else in the landing party has already asked." Kirk's voice held an unmistakable note of laughter when he came on the intercom. "You're the last. Be ready to beam down in fifteen minutes."

"Captain, message coming in from Starfleet." Palmer, the communications officer for the evening shift, turned away from her board to face the captain. Her expression registered surprise, as though the message was something completely unexpected. "It's Admiral Komack, sir."

"On screen, Lieutenant." Kirk smoothed his face into a neutral expression, wondering what the admiral had in store for the *Enterprise* this time. With Komack it was never safe to assume anything; one had to be prepared for unpleasant surprises concealed by the admiral's bland delivery.

Komack's tanned face, topped by close-cropped white hair, filled the viewscreen. His mouth twisted into a tight smile as the communications link closed. "It seems congratulations are in order, Captain Kirk.

Your passengers have unearthed a find of considerable importance. The experts here are eagerly awaiting your reports."

"Thank you, sir." Kirk straightened in his chair, waiting for Komack to drop his bomb. With an opening like that, Kirk could bet that he was being softened up before Komack handed him an unpleasant assignment.

"From the preliminary reports that you sent us, we believe that this is the most significant find in the last three decades. You have permission to take as much time as you need to explore Careta IV, and to use every available means to investigate this civilization. Our experts are extremely eager to know why we have found no evidence of these people before. Please inform Dr. Kaul that I have instructed you to allow him to call upon the complete resources of the *Enterprise* to assist in his investigations."

Kirk clenched his hand on the arm of his chair. He should have known that Komack's orders would give the archaeologists carte blanche concerning his ship and crew. "I understand, Admiral. We will do our best."

"Very good, Captain Kirk. Starfleet out." On the last word Komack's image winked out.

"Kirk out," he muttered to the already blank screen. Komack's order extended Kaul's control over their mission, though the archaeologist already had enough authority to make the *Enterprise* little more than a glorified taxi for his team. Shaking his head, Kirk signaled for the duty officer to take over the conn. Whether he liked the orders or not, it was time to beam down to the planet and see what the excavators had discovered.

By the time Chekov reached the transporter room, most of the people had beamed down. Kirk, McCoy, and two security guards entered the room while Chekov was deciding whether he had been made the victim of an elaborate practical joke. Still, if someone was playing a joke on him, it was the unknown aliens who had lived on this planet so many millennia ago. It was their buried artifact that exerted such a powerful attraction that he was willing—indeed, eager—to give up the warmth and companionship of the *Enterprise's* recreation lounge to see the excavators remove the last rubble from the mysterious object.

Kirk grinned when he saw Chekov waiting by the transporter. "Not quite your idea of the best way to spend the evening, Mr. Chekov?" he asked as he stepped onto the pad.

"No, sir. I'm not really sure why I feel that I should beam back down." Chekov took the station behind Kirk while the others moved into position. The captain signaled for the transporter chief to energize.

"Because we're all a bunch of damned fools," McCoy said, resuming the conversation when they materialized. He pulled his jacket tighter to block out the sharp wind. A tiny speck of a moon rode high overhead, emphasizing the bleakness of the scene with its weak light. "At this hour we should all be sitting in our quarters, with our feet up, a good book on the screen, and a little nip of something to warm the soul."

"I suppose there's something to that idea." Kirk shot the doctor a speculative grin and started across the empty ground that separated them from the excavators. The work area was awash with a brilliant flood of white, casting workers and equipment into harsh relief against the surrounding darkness. "But after a couple of nights doing that, I'm ready for something else. What about you, Mr. Chekov?"

After considering the best answer, Chekov gave a diffident shrug. "I was thinking about doing what Dr.

McCoy suggested, but I was curious. After all, it is not often that we can discover a new piece of history."

McCoy chuckled. "Very diplomatic. It might even save you from my worst on your next physical."

They stepped into the circle of brightness cast by the floodlights. Chekov examined the cliff face, looking for the spot where he and Talika had crossed the talus slope that morning. He couldn't find it; the area had changed too much. Where the artifact had been covered by a hundred meters of broken rock, only a small mound remained. The rest of the rubble had been moved by the excavators, one boulder at a time, exposing the sharp line of the cliffs.

Spock returned from talking to the technicians. "Captain, the excavation is proceeding according to schedule. We should reach the artifact in approximately 1.35 hours if the work continues as anticipated."

"Then can we go home after that, Spock?" McCoy asked, his eyes dancing at the prospect of baiting the Vulcan. "Some of us can't stay awake all night like machines."

"Indeed, Doctor. It is fortunate that some people are better equipped for unforeseen circumstances." He turned to Kirk. "Since most of the day shift has beamed down to observe, I recommend that we take advantage of this opportunity to scan the base of the cliffs for further artifacts. The floodlights produce sufficient illumination to allow several teams to examine the rock surfaces. We should, in any case, make a detailed scan of the nearby area, since it appears that the cliffs were demolished to produce the rubble that covered this object."

Kirk tallied the number of people in the area. If he had been operating the excavators, he thought, having that many spectators would have made him too nervous to do his job properly. Spock's suggestion would clear the area until most of the rubble was transported away from the site. "Putting all the sightseers to work sounds like a good idea to me, Spock. I'm sure the technicians don't need the audience."

"I would like to have a closer look at those cliffs anyway." Chekov activated his tricorder and started toward the wall of rocks exposed by the excavators. Dozens of meters of rock had covered the area when he and Talika had examined it that morning. Now it was stripped of cover for the first time in millennia, its mysteries waiting for him to unravel them. It was a heady thought, to be walking somewhere that no living creature had been for thousands upon thousands of years.

He programmed the tricorder to cycle through all the sensor bands with each pass. As he approached the cliffs, Chekov felt as though the rocks were tilting over him, waiting to crash down and bury him. He shuddered, feeling the weight press against him, blotting out all light and air, enclosing him in a suffocating blackness that went on for all eternity.

Chekov pulled himself back to the present. His tricorder gave no indication that the cliffs here were any less stable than were those above the rest of the site. He mustn't let his imagination run away with him, regardless of the hour or the enigmas surrounding the vanished civilization on this planet. Forcing his attention back to his work, he began the detailed scans that Spock had requested.

The next half hour went quickly. Buoyed by the hope that he would find more information about the as yet unknown civilization that had occupied the planet, Chekov scanned the cliff face and the surrounding ground a meter at a time. The semicircle of loose dirt and rubble that had been covered by the deepest talus confirmed, to Chekov's mind, that the rocks had been deliberately blasted loose to cover something. Someone had not wanted this object found, *ever*.

Before Chekov could work through the implications of that thought, his communicator signaled him to return to the excavation site. The artifact should be freed from its rocky cocoon within the next fifteen minutes, which barely gave the farthest people time to get back.

By the time he reached the brightly lit area around the site, Chekov could see that something had gone wrong with the timetable. A substantial pile of rocks still covered the presumed location of the object, and the knot of people around the technicians moved with sharp, jerky motions. Kirk's face looked grim and tense in the harsh light, and a deep frown creased McCoy's forehead.

Chekov slipped in beside McCoy. "What is wrong, Doctor?" he asked in a low voice.

"They can't seem to find the dratted object with the sensors," McCoy answered, keeping his voice down. "One minute it was there, the next gone." He shook his head. "It's got to be operator error. Things don't just disappear from sight."

"Normally that is correct, Doctor. However, this object refuses to act in a normal fashion." Remembering how the artifact had pulled the same trick on him and Talika that morning, he started forward to see if he could help. As he did, the air shimmered, and Scott materialized.

"I told you to take care of your equipment, Terrensen," Scott said as he closed the distance to the technicians. "You canna expect it to work properly if you do not make the calibration runs every hour."

"We did that, Mr. Scott," replied the younger of the

two technicians, a bean pole of a man with a tousled shock of brown hair. "We haven't been taking any shortcuts, I promise you. We were picking up an anomalous *nothing* in the middle of that pile of rubble, but the readings disappeared from the scanners."

"Let me see what you've been doing, then." Scott pushed between the technicians and bent over the control panel, punching in the diagnostic sequence. As he read the numbers, a frown crept across his face. He entered more commands. After a long pause, during which his scowl deepened, the results from the second group of tests appeared on the screen. "That's not possible," he said, shaking his head. "The diagnostics program reports that the anomaly never was there. Even when I order the computer to correlate all sensor readings for the last twelve hours, the programs maintain that only a pile of rocks is there and that *that* is all that ever *was* there. The diagnostics and the scanners aren't agreeing on what they're seeing."

Spock joined Scott, skimming the diagnostic reports on the displays. "If we believe the current readings, we have been pursuing a mirage. However, up to five minutes ago our analysis showed that an anomalous object, possibly of considerable antiquity, was buried beneath that pile of rubble."

Wondering if he could see any resemblance between the present sensor readings and the ones from that morning, Chekov stepped forward. "May I examine the sensor logs from just before and just after the readings changed? Dr. Talika and I had similar difficulties this morning, but at the time we thought they were caused by the rubble piled above the artifact."

Terrensen hit the playback switch, and the records scrolled down the screen in parallel columns. With the advantage of a larger power supply and stationary operation, the scanners on the excavating equipment were far more sensitive than the tricorders and could record a wider range of readings simultaneously. It took Chekov a few moments to sort through the data, but when he found it, the anomaly—a thirty-cubic-meter space for which the sensors reported *no* data—stood out like a beacon. He paged backward through the readings to confirm his suspicions. "Here, just before the sensors begin reporting only more stones in this place. There is a major spike in the lower frequencies, almost like the power absorption curve of a biaxial shield generator."

"Is that true, Spock?" Kirk asked as he joined the group. "And what does it mean in connection with all this?" He waved his arm to encompass the cliffs as well as the heap of rubble spotlighted by the circle of brilliant light.

"The second occurrence of this pattern in the readings greatly increases the probability that it is not caused by random fluctuations in the energy output levels of the device we are attempting to locate." Spock examined the data. "Mr. Chekov's inference that the effect is caused by a biaxial shield generator may be correct. However, if so, it is a device of completely alien manufacture, a supposition supported by the rest of our findings on this planet."

"But what's the purpose of the shield, Spock? Why is it here?" Kirk gestured sharply toward the displays as if expecting them to show him the answers in block capitals.

"Unknown, Captain." Spock, too, glanced toward the screen, as if to discover whether Kirk had found something of importance. "Either someone is taking great pains to conceal an artifact from us, or they are trying to make us believe that something is hidden in this area when, in fact, there is nothing."

"And we have no way to tell which is the correct answer." Kirk shivered and pulled his jacket tighter around himself. The air temperature had dropped several degrees in the last half hour, and a sharp wind had come up. Before long the cold would become decidedly uncomfortable.

"Not without removing the rest of the rubble to see what lies beneath it." Spock glanced again at the screen, looking for clues to how the unknown aliens had thought. Unfortunately, with so little to go on, the facts could be interpreted to support many different conclusions. "When we have finished the excavation, logically we will either find an artifact, or we will discover that someone created conditions that were intended to convince us that an artifact was present. The null sensor readings support either hypothesis."

Kirk nodded, even though Spock had told him little that he didn't already know. With the sensors reporting only rocks and more rocks, they would have to operate the excavators blindly, increasing their chances of accidentally damaging anything that was buried beneath the pile of rubble. "What is your recommendation, Mr. Scott? Can you adjust the scanners on the excavating equipment?"

Scott shook his head. "There isn't a thing more we can do, Captain. The equipment was designed to compensate for most types of interference because many of the civilizations in the Dalreth sector routinely screened their important monuments with shields or scramblers. If these sensors canna do the job, nothing can."

Kirk weighed his options. Without the excavators they would have to move the rest of the rocks by hand, a slow and labor-intensive process that no one would like. "Let's see if we can finish clearing the area using visual cross-checks, then."

The technicians started working again, referring back to the earlier scans for reference to prevent them from accidentally catching a piece of the artifact with their transporter beams. After moving five boulders in fifteen minutes, they gave up. "I can't do it," said the older technician, a short, wiry man nearing retirement age. "I don't know which is rock and which is artifact, even extrapolating from where we thought the earlier scans told us the object should be. I'm just not sure what's real and what isn't."

Terrensen nodded his agreement. "At this stage we dare not make any mistakes—and suddenly we're working blind. Even after looking at twelve hours of anomalous sensor data, there's too much guesswork in this one."

"Very well. You did your best." Kirk turned to the crowd that had gathered expectantly around the console. "You heard them, everybody. We're reduced to old-fashioned methods to get the job done."

With surprisingly few protests the twenty-five crewmen fell to, lifting the irregular blocks of basalt and shifting them a dozen meters from the artifact. Once the rocks were clear of the area where they thought the artifact was, the technicians locked on to them and beamed them to the pile of excavated rubble. In a surprisingly short time, the broken rock had been cleared away, revealing four huge basalt slabs standing on their edges, capped by a fifth. The stone cube was twice as tall as Kirk, and the edges of the stones fit tightly together, as though they had been ground to form a tight seal.

Kirk shook his head, marveling at the perversity of the universe. Such huge sheets of stone, balanced in such a position, could not be natural, even though they also could not be the source of the power readings Chekov had first noticed, nor could they have caused the total absence of sensor information they had been tracking earlier. Also, unlike the boulders they had moved, the standing rocks could not be shifted by a few crewmen. "Spock, what do the sensors say now?"

"Absolutely nothing, Captain." Spock adjusted a lever and repeated his readings. "The scanners report that the object we are looking at does not exist."

Chapter Four

FOR A FEW SECONDS thirty pairs of eyes stared at Spock in utter disbelief. "What do you mean, Spock?" Kirk asked when he found his voice. The object *had* to exist. They could see it, they could see the inky shadow it threw across the uneven ground, and most of them had touched it as they removed the boulders that had covered it.

Spock stepped to one side so Kirk could read the displays. "I mean, Captain, that despite the evidence of our senses, the object does not register on any of our detectors. I would surmise the presence of a class-B jamming field of an unknown and extremely sophisticated design, probably controlled by a biaxial shield generator as Mr. Chekov suggested. The logical corollary is that we will be unable to detect any other protections the artifact may possess."

"How likely do you-all expect that to be?" McCoy strolled over to join Spock and Kirk. Leaning against the console, he crossed his arms over his chest. "This object is hundreds of thousands of years old, but you're saying it's protected by some of the latest and most sophisticated technology known to *our* science."

"That is correct, Doctor. Many civilizations have attained a high degree of technical expertise. I see no reason for you to doubt the authenticity of the artifact simply because it does not conform to your preconceived notions of the way things should be."

"Enough." Kirk gestured both men to silence. "What I need are solid recommendations on how we should proceed. Ideas, anyone?"

Kaul, who had been summoned from the primary site, pushed his way through the crowd. "What's this about an object that doesn't exist?" he asked, breathless from his hurry. "If the object is that well protected, its significance is incalculable. This find merits our most careful attention."

"See for yourself," Kirk said, pointing to the readouts. "And while Dr. Kaul is checking that, does anyone have any ideas on what to do next?"

Scott glanced from the displays to the artifact, as if to assure himself that the object really was there. "A class-B jamming field renders most of our tractor beams and antigravity lifters inoperative. However, mechanical methods should serve to open the structure."

"Then you believe something is hidden inside those slabs?" Kirk asked the question mostly to hear their reasoning. After the trouble someone had taken to conceal the stone cube, something had to be inside it.

"It would be illogical to expend so much effort to conceal an object unless it was extremely dangerous." Spock studied the black cube, his face taut with concentration. "However, at the moment, we possess no information to indicate why the object is dangerous."

Kirk felt the decision click into place. Given the *Enterprise*'s assignment and Admiral Komack's restatement of their orders, his next words were inevitable. "Nor will we know anything until we open the cube. Taking risks is our business, gentlemen. Let's find out why someone worked so hard to hide that thing from us. Mr. Scott, beam down the equipment you need to open it."

"Aye, Captain." Scott stepped away from the group, pulling out his communicator.

After several minutes of spirited discussion, a pile of equipment and three more technicians materialized a dozen meters from the artifact. Scott hurried to the new arrivals, waving his hands broadly to show where things should go. He promptly drafted any spectators who got too close, and before long a spidery construction of poles and braces took shape over the black stone cube.

Kaul scurried around the workers, poking his tricorder against the artifact, demanding that they hurry so he could proceed with examining what was inside the cube. Talika followed behind him, her bulk dwarfing Kaul's slight frame. Occasionally, over Scott's shouted orders and the clanks and bangs of the construction, Kirk made out snatches of Talika's sharp-toned monologue. She was arguing with Kaul over the significance of the find and disputing his proposals for studying the object.

"Some things never change, do they, Jim?" Shaking his head, McCoy chuckled at the sight of the massive Djelifan shadowing the slight Indian.

"What's that, Bones?" Kirk, who had been watching Scott oversee a tricky connection between three crossbeams, turned his head to follow McCoy's pointed look. The mismatch between the two archaeologists could not have been more incongruous.

"How these young upstarts always get so wrapped up in their own ideas that they can't see beyond the ends of their noses." He shot Kirk a sideways look.

"Although you have to admit that, in Dr. Nyar's case, she has a decidedly longer view than most."

In spite of himself Kirk smiled. Like the rest of her physique, Talika's nose was not small. "Now, Bones, you know the Djelifans consider a long nose to be a sign of beauty."

"I suppose the next thing you're going to tell me is that she's the pan-Djelifan beauty queen or something." McCoy rolled his eyes upward. "Her voice reminds me too much of my ex-wife."

Kirk shrugged, unsure how seriously he should take McCoy's words. "I can't help you with that, I'm afraid, but I'm told that Dr. Talika is a very attractive woman, according to her people's standards." Pulling his jacket tighter around himself to ward off the sharp breeze blowing down the canyon, he started toward Scott. The night air was dry, smelling of dust and of ozone from the hot lights. "By the way, didn't you read the briefing on Djelifan customs?"

"I skimmed through it, but there's a lot of technical material there." McCoy fell into step with Kirk, shaking his head in perplexity. "I'm just an old country doctor, Jim. It seemed to me that the person who wrote that briefing went out of his way to use the most obscure jargon he could possibly find."

Spock joined them, his long legs easily matching Kirk's unhurried pace. The lower oxygen content of Careta's atmosphere was slowing the humans down, but the air and temperature reminded Spock of a winter day in the L-Langon Mountains. "What the captain means is that you should have paid more attention to the section on Djelifan naming customs. Each woman, when she reaches her age of majority, earns the right to her own *unique* personal name. Males and female children who have not proven their worth to the society are known by their clan name and group designator."

McCoy shot Kirk an annoyed look. He didn't think the captain had found any more time than he had for unraveling the report, but Kirk and Spock were acting as though everyone should have gleaned the one important fact from the briefing. "Does his lecture have a point, Jim? That section was the worst part of the entire report."

"I'm afraid it does, Bones." Kirk gave the doctor a rueful grin. The loose rock crunched beneath his boots, the sound surprisingly loud in a brief lull in the work noises. "What he's trying to tell you is that buried beneath the technical jargon was the crucial fact that it is considered exceedingly rude to address an adult Djelifan woman by her last name."

"Oh." McCoy frowned, trying to remember what he had deciphered from the report's deliberately obtuse language. "How was I supposed to know that's what it said?"

"I guess that's why we keep Mr. Spock around to translate." Before the doctor could reply, Kirk shifted his attention to the construction. The framework over the artifact was complete, and several crewmen were reinforcing the joints while others hoisted into position the metal plates that would form the work surface. "How long before you're ready, Scotty?"

"How long?" Scott stepped back, surveying the scaffold with a proprietary air. "It shouldn't be more than five minutes before we get everything locked down and the winches secured to the decking. But if you wouldn't mind, Captain, I would prefer to have everyone except the lads helping me stand back a wee bit when we make our try at the cube. Until we lift its top off, we won't know why someone thought it was necessary to seal that beastie up so tightly."

"Good thinking. We'll start clearing the area now, so we won't have to waste time when you're ready."

"Thank you, Captain. We'll give you enough warning, in case everyone hasn't moved back." He checked the workers who were wrestling the winches into place. Two teams had their first units securely fastened and were climbing down to get their second, while a third team was hauling its second winch up to platform level. The fourth team had gotten a unit onto the decking but was struggling to maneuver it into position.

After watching them briefly, Scott bounded up the ladder. "Here, lads. Let me show you how to handle these darlings."

With a grin of amusement, Kirk turned away. "Come on, gentlemen. Let's get the sightseers back to a safe distance."

Scott's five minutes stretched to fifteen, but Kirk barely noticed. It took that much time to convince everyone to retreat to a safe distance and remain there. The archaeologists in particular were hard to persuade. Kaul wanted to be near the artifact when it was opened, fearing that the sensors would still be jammed and that his skills as a trained observer would be needed to record the details of the scene as the huge basalt slabs were lifted from their positions. Finally, to end the argument, Kirk agreed to a compromise. Since they did not know what a safe distance was, he allowed the archaeologists to station themselves halfway between the artifact and the designated perimeter. He suspected that if the unknown aliens had intended to leave a lethal trap around the artifact, everyone would need to be much farther away. Kirk frowned, wondering if he should order his people back to the *Enterprise*.

Spock raised an eyebrow at Kirk's expression. "Captain, you seem concerned about the possibility of unanticipated defenses associated with the artifact."

"The thought had crossed my mind, Spock." Kirk

glared at the artifact, willing it to surrender its secrets. Scott and his crew were anchoring the last cables with suction grapples, the final step before lifting the upper slab of dense black basalt. "If you have any thoughts on the matter, I'd appreciate hearing them *before* Mr. Scott lifts the top off that thing."

"My analysis of the defenses we have encountered so far indicates that they are intended to disguise the presence of the object and to render it difficult to approach. I would conclude that this pattern will continue and that nothing contained within the enclosure will prove more than incidentally lethal."

"'Incidentally lethal'?" McCoy asked. "Is that something like 'accidentally dead'?"

Kirk decided to interrupt before the doctor launched into a full tirade. "You mean something like being caught under one of those slabs when it falls?"

"That would be a prime example. The intent of the aliens seems to be to render this artifact inaccessible, not to deliberately injure anyone who seeks to discover what is here."

Scott turned toward the captain and raised his hand, signaling that the last cable was secure. "I hope you're right, Spock. Here goes the test." Kirk ordered Scott to activate the winches.

The motors hummed to life, first drawing in the slack on the cables and then pulling against the weight of the slab. At first nothing happened. Scott increased the power to the winches, and still the slab refused to move. The humming rose to a shrill keening as the motors labored against the weight.

"That is most unusual." Spock moved to the excavator's console and rerouted the power supplies for the digging equipment and the floodlights. "Any two of those winches should have been sufficient to lift that mass. The others were to insure control over the slab once it was raised."

Kirk reached for his communicator. "Are you sure those slabs weren't bonded together?"

"Visual inspection showed no signs of any bonding compounds. Of course, we were unable to obtain any meaningful results with our tricorder scans." Spock flipped the last relay, and the floodlights dimmed to half intensity.

Kirk activated his communicator. "Scotty, the power supply from this station is available to you."

"Thank you, Captain," Scott's voice replied from the communicator. He moved to his controls and tied the extra energy into his power grid. The shrill whine of the winches climbed in volume and became harsher, the overlapping sounds beginning to pulse in rising and falling beats. Several people covered their ears to block out the noise. A deep, irregular groaning joined the din, its unevenness more disturbing than the steady shriek of the motors.

Everyone held his breath, waiting. The winches could not withstand much more stress, and Kirk was surprised that Scott, usually so protective of his equipment, had not shut down the motors already. He grinned. Like everyone else, Scott was determined to solve this mystery, even if it meant spending the next three days reconditioning the overtaxed equipment.

The groaning became louder, and Kirk realized it was the sound of the basalt slab scraping against the walls of the cube. With a loud crack and a final shriek of protest, the near end of the slab pulled free. The cube shuddered and came apart, the vertical slabs tilting outward under the pull of the guide cables attached to them. The slabs toppled in slow motion, as though they were falling in microgravity, but the shock waves rippled outward from their impact. A cloud of dust billowed up around the slabs, obscuring their first sight of the artifact.

The whine from the winches dropped to a normal

pitch, although Kirk thought the sound was a little ragged. Then from the work crew on the platform came the sounds of retching and gagging. Before Kirk could wonder what was happening, the dust cloud reached them. A heavy, nauseating smell permeated the air. Before he had consciously identified the suldanic gas, Kirk was on the ground, retching.

A communicator chirped nearby. "Spock to *Enterprise*. Emergency beam-up. All personnel on the planet. Repeat, emergency beam-up. Now." The Vulcan's voice sounded strained, as though he were barely controlling his own response to the gas.

Mercifully, the technicians in the transporter room worked quickly. They beat the ship's record time for recovering that many people under field conditions by a full minute. Even so, Kirk thought as he left sickbay after receiving his antidote and antinausea shots, there were going to be a lot of people under the weather on the *Enterprise* tomorrow. Someone had truly *not* wanted that artifact to be discovered.

Chapter Five

HE HAD BEEN RIGHT about the "morning after," Kirk thought grimly as he surveyed the group around the briefing table. Even though he had been treated promptly, the brief exposure to the suldanic gas had left him with a headache of monumental proportions and a stomach that felt as though he were coming down with a case of the Bilindian flu. Judging from McCoy's complexion, the doctor felt as bad as he did, while Kaul and Talika, who had been stationed closer to the artifact, looked even worse. Chekov was holding himself together mostly by youthful enthusiasm for the mystery presented by the artifact, and Spock's Vulcan control was standing him in good stead, but they both were obviously fighting the aftereffects of the gas. The only person in the room who looked halfway human was Meredith Lassiter, who had monitored the artifact from the safety of the *Enterprise,* but even she had dark circles under her eyes from working all night to process the scanner data on the artifact.

"This, apparently, is what someone tried so hard to keep us from discovering." Lassiter cued the image onto their screens.

The object was about two meters high and four meters long, but only ten centimeters thick. The back side was a metallic blue-gray, with no scratches or tarnish to mar the finish. The other side reminded Kirk of a pair of plate-glass windows enclosed in a flat black frame. The illusion was enhanced by the lifelike landscape on the left, showing a rolling plain covered with knee-deep grass. However, the right side of the object was blank. The glassy sheen of the windowlike surface was the only thing that differentiated it from its background.

"What is it?" Chekov asked, his expression reflecting the bewilderment everyone felt. "Is that what we almost got killed for?"

Lassiter nodded. "What it is, we're not yet certain. However, it appears that the safeguards connected to the stone cube were intended to prevent us from gaining access to this object."

Spock put a list of numbers on the screen. "This object is definitely the source of the power readings first detected by Dr. Talika and Ensign Chekov. We surmise that the barrier surrounding it contained a dampening field. However, in the time since the field was activated, it had become defective. Stray energy fluctuations escaped the containment field and permitted us to detect the object. The shielding also produced a jamming field that completely blocked our sensors when it detected our scanning beams. However, this function of the containment field operated with much impaired efficiency. Our preliminary analysis of the emissions from the artifact show that its major mode of energy release is at a subharmonic frequency that has been shown to produce feelings of extreme uneasiness in some humans. As a final note, the power levels emitted by the object climbed steadily for 7.3 hours after we removed the barrier and have remained constant since then."

"Almost like it was charging up its energy cells for something," Chekov murmured. "But what is it waiting for?"

Kirk nodded. "That's a good question. Any ideas, Mr. Spock?"

"None at present, Captain. Dr. Lassiter and her team have accumulated an impressive amount of data, but as yet we have no clear idea of what the object is or what its function might be."

Lassiter twisted her fingers through a lock of her pale gold hair. "We don't even know *who* left the object here. Nor who walled it off like that. The stone slabs and the protection fields are far younger than the artifact they concealed. We surmise that the Meztoriens were responsible for camouflaging the remains of a much older civilization, although we do not yet have any incontrovertible evidence for this conclusion."

"Recommendations?" Kirk looked toward Kaul to see if he had any suggestions. His face gone waxy, the senior archaeologist swayed in his seat. His eyes fluttered closed, and beads of sweat sprang out on his forehead. McCoy shoved himself from his seat, his movements less steady than Kirk would have liked, and hurried to Kaul's side.

Spock hit the intercom switch. "Medical emergency. Dr. M'Benga to the briefing room."

McCoy checked Kaul's pulse and breathing. "Secondary reaction to the suldanic gas," he said. "We were hit by a particularly nasty variant. If Dr. Kaul's reaction is typical, I recommend that everyone report to sickbay for another round of mylezan."

"I'll make that an order, Bones," Kirk said. "When this briefing is over, everyone gets a second round of shots. We don't need people falling over at critical moments."

The door opened, and M'Benga entered, followed by two orderlies and a stretcher. The orderlies lifted Kaul's limp body onto the stretcher and headed for sickbay, while M'Benga stayed to hear McCoy's diagnosis. "I will have the mylezan shots ready by the time you're through with the briefing," he said, heading for the door.

"Now, where were we?" Kirk asked as the door closed behind M'Benga. He gave the group a moment to settle down after the interruption. Talika and Lassiter were engaged in a staring contest to decide who would direct the archaeological efforts in Kaul's absence. Kirk shuddered, thinking he wouldn't want to get between Talika and something she wanted as strongly as she wanted to vindicate her theories about this planet. Lassiter apparently reached the same conclusion. She broke eye contact and stared down at the table, her face screened by the silver-gilt curtain of her hair.

"We must with greatest care artifact study." Talika's voice was heavy and measured. "Because of danger, I will explorations personally conduct, using assistant for supplemental data recording. Others will from safe distance investigations observe."

At her announcement, Chekov's face went white. For a moment Kirk thought he was suffering from a reaction similar to Kaul's, but then he stiffened his back as if accepting an impossible assignment. Suppressing a grin, Kirk asked, "Are you volunteering, Mr. Chekov?"

Chekov's mouth twitched as if he wanted to refuse, but his sense of duty won out. "I would be honored to assist Dr. Talika in investigating the artifact."

"Thank you, Ensign. Your enthusiasm is commendable." Kirk turned back to Talika. "When do you propose to begin your work?"

"We will in half hour commence. Dr. Meredith and I must sensors recalibrate for reporting significant data now missed. If Mr. Spock assists, we will much sooner finish. However, time is to administer medication needed, for those to harm on planet last night exposed." She shrugged her massive shoulders. "On Djelifa everything more efficiently handled is. Since crew of *Enterprise* Djelifan is not, schedule to innate weakness of humans must concede."

Kirk bit his tongue to hold back an angry reply. He seriously doubted that a team of Djelifans could get things done any faster than the crew of the *Enterprise*, but he knew anyone who heard Talika's unfair comparison would go out of his way to see how slowly he could do what she asked.

Spock, guessing that Kirk was struggling to avoid an undiplomatic response to Talika's arrogance, answered her. "The sensors have already been recalibrated, Dr. Talika. The job was completed an hour ago, and it remains only for you to specify which bands you wish to analyze."

"Thank you, Mr. Spock." Kirk couldn't quite keep the smug look off his face. "If no one has anything else to add, this briefing is dismissed. The landing party will beam down to the planet in half an hour."

The morning light didn't improve the planet at all, Chekov thought as he and Talika started toward the artifact. His pounding headache, a reminder of the suldanic gas attack the previous evening, only made the scene less appealing. The landing party had beamed down next to the control console, hoping it was a safe distance from which to detect any more surprises either group of aliens might have concealed to discourage people from investigating the artifact. Privately Chekov wondered if any distance, even that of the ship's standard orbit, would be enough if someone *really* intended to prevent later explorers from gaining access to the artifact. The closer they got to the object, the less reassured he felt to have Spock and his team of scientists watching their efforts from the "safety" of the console. Either they were too close and would be injured in the next attack, or they were too far away to save Chekov and Talika from a localized assault.

Talika seemed unaffected by any second thoughts. After surveying the artifact and comparing her visual results with the data on her tricorder screen, she motioned to Chekov. "You to the right circle, I to the left. We inward spiral make, scanning object, until we at center meet."

"Whatever you say." Chekov activated his tricorder and started walking, splitting his attention between Talika and the black object. The artifact was still surrounded by the spiderwork of Scott's scaffold; the fallen slabs of basalt that had imprisoned it for so many centuries had been pulled off to the sides. If Talika truly wanted him to run his traverse as a mirror image of hers, Chekov thought, she should have given him more specific instructions. At the very least, she could have told him how far apart to space his circuits. However, precision *before* the fact did not seem to be a Djelifan characteristic. Talika, at any rate, preferred lecturing after he did something wrong to explaining what she wanted beforehand, even in response to direct questions. *Maybe she thinks I can read her mind,* he thought sourly. Certainly that would explain why she consistently acted as though he were deliberately misconstruing her requests.

For once Talika seemed in no hurry to reach her destination. Chekov easily matched her pace, timing his circuits to cross her path within seconds of when she reached the overlap points. His tricorder readings remained unremarkable, showing only the steady power output from the artifact. Nothing else registered—no hidden devices beneath the rubble-strewn ground, no scanners buried deep in the cliffs above them, no clues about the origin or the function of the object they were examining.

Four revolutions on their spiral path brought them to the front of the object. The air near it seemed cooler, almost as if the object contained a low-level refrigeration field, and Chekov shivered involuntarily at the sensation. Refrigeration fields that produced such external leakage had not been in use in the Federation in over fifty years, and even then they had been restricted to specialized functions such as long-term storage of biological materials. Either he was misinterpreting his sensations or something else was happening here.

Chekov took three steps backward and pivoted slowly, watching the temperature readings on his tricorder. They climbed steadily until his back was toward the artifact, then began falling as he completed his rotation. Next to the artifact the temperature was almost ten degrees lower than it was on the flood plain upriver from his location. Frowning with puzzlement, he extended his tricorder toward Talika so she could read his results.

She shrugged. "It in shadows freezes. So what?"

He shook his head and scrolled through the temperature scans. "You do not get so drastic an effect just from the shadows. Something about the artifact is creating this temperature differential."

"Why should that to me important be?" She turned her back on him, deliberately moving toward the black object.

For a moment Chekov stared at her, wondering how

she could dismiss the anomaly so easily. To him the temperature readings spoke of ancient equipment of strange design and unknown purposes still functioning after millennia, of enigmatic aliens with incomprehensible motives and mysterious purposes, and of unsuspected dangers lurking at the edge of possibility. Dismissing any clue to the puzzle seemed criminally irresponsible, but Talika acted as though she already knew all the answers. Somehow Chekov didn't think being Djelifan, her standard reason for ignoring suggestions, would convey any immunity to the dangers of an unexplored planet.

Rather the opposite, he thought sourly as he stepped in front of the object and ran his tricorder over the smooth, windowlike surface that formed the object's right side. The device reported only the object's presence, which was less information than he would have gotten if he had pointed the tricorder at a mirror. It should have told him the composition of the artifact, located the power generating equipment around the site, and given him a dozen other useful facts. At the very least he should have gotten readings characterizing the type and strength of the shields that prevented him from obtaining any other information.

Tentatively Chekov reached toward the object. About a centimeter above the surface, he felt a faint tingling in his fingertips. When he pulled his hand away, the sensation stopped. He tried again at a different spot and got the same result. Slowly he moved his hand over the artifact, tracing the field that clung like an aura to its surface. The tingling stopped at the edge of the glassy surface, and Chekov wondered if the black frame was the source of the field or if it inhibited the field from expanding further.

All the while he was tracing the extent of the field, Chekov kept one eye on the tricorder screen. To his surprise, the readings remained absolutely unchanged. Most force fields registered at least minor power fluctuations when someone or something probed their perimeters, no matter how slight the challenge. Something was not right here. Finally, with no other tests he could do, Chekov spread his fingers and pushed his hand firmly into the force field.

The next thing he knew, he was lying on the ground two meters from the object, gasping for breath. His right arm was completely numb, and the shoulder blade felt as though it had been dislocated. Awkwardly he levered himself to a sitting position, hampered by the useless right arm.

"What silly game this is?" Talika glared down at him. "Sleeping on job?"

Chekov groaned and tried to stand. Not surprisingly, his legs were too unsteady to lift him, and he dropped back to the ground. "It threw me away. When I tried to touch the object."

"Can you not *believable* excuse invent?" She scowled, the expression twisting her face into a grimace that reminded Chekov of the Hag Mask from the Creation Play on Deveron 5. "Djelifan assistant would not so stupid be."

Chekov felt his temper unravel. "You try it! See if you have any better luck."

"Already have. Hand through surface of window reaches." Her scowl darkened. "Stupid male! Why think you that catching lies so hard would be?"

"Maybe it recognizes Djelifan superiority," he snarled before he realized the importance of her words. Talika had been exploring the left side of the artifact, with its beautifully detailed scene of some other place or time. That side had allowed her hand to penetrate the surface, while the blank side he was examining had actively rejected his attempts to reach below the field on its surface. Clearly, although they had many features in common, some basic differences distinguished the two sides of the artifact. If Talika's hand could reach into the window, could something else also pass through it?

He levered himself to his feet, noticing with relief that most of his shakiness had passed. For the first few steps, the muscles in his legs twinged and pulled, telling him how hard he had landed on the rocks, but moving worked out the discomfort. Taking his time, Chekov approached the artifact, studying it with great care.

The object did not yield its secrets to his scrutiny this time either. Whatever it was hiding, it was doing a good job of it. Finally he stopped in front of the windowlike panel, glancing between his tricorder and the artifact. The tricorder reported the same readings as it had earlier on the blank right panel, and the scene in front of him showed no signs of changing in response to his examination.

He inspected the scene more closely, thinking how much it looked like the Russian steppes. The rolling surface of the land sloped away into the distance, with knee-deep grass rippling in the breeze, and the late afternoon sunlight laced long shadows through the golds and dull greens of the vegetation. The view was so realistic and so lifelike that Chekov was certain he could step through the window and walk across the open plain.

After several minutes of careful observation, Chekov extended his hand toward the artifact. He had hoped he could find the answers without risking another attack from the object's defenses, but the tricorder readings were still suspiciously minimal. If he wanted to learn anything, he would have to take another chance.

Slowly Chekov extended his hand toward the artifact, anticipating the tingling resistance of the force field. Instead, when his fingertips were about a centimeter from the surface, a soothing warmth began to envelop them. Without thinking he reached forward, grateful for the heat to counteract the chill of the air near the artifact. Before he realized how far he had gone, his hand had disappeared up to the wrist.

Shocked, Chekov tried to pull his hand out. At first it felt like the arm was encased in a block of plastiseal that prevented him from moving it. He braced himself and pulled harder. Straining every muscle in his body, he finally broke the hold on his arm. Before he could catch himself, he stumbled backwards and sprawled in an undignified heap at Talika's feet.

"Stupid!" she said in a disgusted tone. "Said I that you could it touch."

Mustering what dignity he had left, Chekov clambered to his feet and looked for something to use as a probe. Several lengths of cable left from building the scaffold lay around the area. Except for that, the ubiquitous rocks were the only tools that came immediately to hand. Chekov picked up a fist-sized chunk of rock and lobbed it toward the artifact. It traced a lazy arc into the air, intersecting the artifact's surface while at the top of its trajectory.

Instead of passing through the window as he had expected, the rock came whizzing back at Chekov. He dropped to the ground, barely in time to escape being hit. Talika wasn't so lucky. Chekov heard a dull thud, followed by a grunt of pain, as the rock hit her in the shoulder. He braced himself, waiting for her to start yelling at him for his carelessness, but to her credit she did not.

Chekov scrambled to his feet and turned to face her. Perhaps he could forestall her temper tantrum. "I apologize for not anticipating that reaction from the artifact, Dr. Talika. I did not think I had thrown it so hard."

She frowned and ignored the apology. "You did not. Artifact threw back rock."

"Very interesting." Chekov frowned, trying to decipher the significance of her observation. The artifact had liked his arm and had tried to pull him into it, but it had actively rejected the rock. Still frowning, he picked up several small pebbles and one larger rock from the ground.

Taking the rock in his left hand, he reached toward the window. Again a sensation of warmth started in his fingers and traveled up his arm. He tried to release the rock inside the field, but his fingers were immobilized. Quickly, before his arm could be drawn further into the artifact, he jerked it clear.

"It does not seem to have any absolute prejudices against rocks," he said, staring at the artifact in bewilderment. He had expected it to push the rock away, repulsing his hand at the same time.

Spock joined Chekov and Talika. "It would appear that the device has a decided preference for materials of organic origin. With Dr. Talika's permission, I propose that we conduct more extensive tests."

"What tests?" Talika pulled her attention from the artifact to look up at Spock. "If object organics wants, send organics. Worthless male flunky Federation must have to investigation do."

Chekov ground his teeth to suppress an angry protest. There was no doubt in his mind that Talika's preferred course of action would be to send him into the artifact in hopes that he would learn something useful.

Spock, however, ignored her remark. "I would recommend a more conservative approach than sending someone into the artifact. First, I propose that we confirm our preliminary deduction that the artifact can distinguish between organic and nonorganic materials."

A stubborn expression settled on Talika's face, twisting her mouth into an unpleasant frown. "What proposals you have?"

"Our first priority should be to determine the exact parameters of what the artifact will and will not allow to penetrate its surface. At the same time, we should take more extensive sensor readings to determine what effects, if any, our investigations are producing on the energy output of the object or the scene projected onto its surface. Only after we have analyzed the data collected from these tests should we consider allowing a person to investigate the artifact."

Talika raked a hand through her mousy brown hair, the jerkiness of her movement betraying her annoyance. "Proposal unnecessarily timid is, but of Federation obstructionism typical. You will faster work if we your suggestions follow rather than proper Djelifan investigation run?"

Spock's face assumed its most bland Vulcan mask. "Almost certainly, it will take less time to do as I have suggested than it will take to convince Captain Kirk to do it your way. The probabilities suggest strongly that we will have to send someone into the artifact at a future time. However, the preliminary tests will enable us to equip that person to obtain the maximum amount of data with the least amount of risk."

"Very well." Talika's scowl gave the lie to her words. "In interests of Djelifan-Federation cooperation, things will we do your way."

"Thank you, Dr. Talika." Spock turned to Chekov. "I noticed that you had collected a handful of rocks. When Dr. Talika and I have removed ourselves from the artifact's line of sight, will you toss the pebbles at various parts of the object's surface?"

"Of course, Mr. Spock." It was difficult to put any enthusiasm in his voice, Chekov thought, but at least he kept most of his irritation to himself. Junior officers expected to draw the hazardous assignments, and this one didn't seem overly dangerous. It wouldn't have bothered him at all, except that Talika kept treating him as incompetent because he was not Djelifan and as expendable because he was male. *From her tone, you'd think that Djelifans created the Universe and are subleasing it to the rest of us so they don't have to run the whole show.*

Shoving his rebellious thoughts aside, Chekov stationed himself about five meters from the artifact along its center line. He lowered himself to the ground and piled his handful of pebbles where he could reach them. Dozens of other suitable rocks lay within easy reach. When Spock signaled that he and Talika had reached a safe distance, Chekov picked up the first stone and lobbed it toward the artifact.

Fifteen minutes and four dozen rocks later, all they knew was that rocks rebounded from the artifact with more kinetic energy than had been used to throw them. The energy for the recoil had to come from inside the object, but its shields were impenetrable and interfered with all their instruments.

Frustrated, Chekov removed his uniform tunic and wadded it into a ball. If the artifact would only accept organic materials, perhaps they could get some useful information when the carbon-based polymer fabric penetrated the field. Scrambling to his feet and moving closer, Chekov tossed the shirt into the center of the windowlike panel.

The shirt rebounded and unrolled, wrapping itself around his face. Startled, Chekov stepped backwards, tripped, and fell on his rear. As soon as the fabric came free in his hand, he relaxed. It *was* just his shirt. To make sure, Chekov retrieved his tricorder and scanned the shirt. As expected, it was no different from any other garment synthesized by the *Enterprise*'s equipment. He was shrugging back into the shirt when Spock and Talika rejoined him.

"It would seem that our hypothesis was in error." Spock ran his tricorder over the artifact yet again. In a human, the gesture would have suggested deep frustration at the inability to obtain results. "The artifact appears to know when a higher life-form wishes to penetrate the field."

"It allowed me to put a rock into the field as long as I physically held it in my hand." Chekov glared at the object, as if to demand the code that would unlock its secrets. "Will it allow anything to penetrate it, so long as it is being held by a person?"

Spock picked up a five-meter length of cable from the ground. "Please test your theory, Mr. Chekov. This cable is sufficiently long to permit us to see what will happen when the cable reaches the other side of the artifact."

Chekov took the cable and gingerly poked the end at the artifact. Despite Spock's apparent confidence in his suggestion, he more than half expected the object to throw the end of the cable back at him. When nothing happened, Chekov pushed a little harder. Ten centimeters of the cable disappeared into the unwavering scene on the window.

"The sensors still detect no changes in the artifact's status. The reverse side remains unaffected by our activities," Spock reported. "Continue with the experiment."

Twenty centimeters, thirty centimeters, forty. Chekov felt a slight, tingling warmth spread up the cable to his hands, so weak that he might have been imagining it. He wiped one hand, then the other, against his pants legs to remove the nervous perspiration and continued to feed more cable into the window.

One meter, one and a half. Chekov could no longer ignore the heat traveling through the cable, although the source of the energy did not register on Mr. Spock's tricorder. Neither did the free end of the cable appear in the scene they were viewing. He released his hold for a moment to wipe both hands. With a sizzle and a pop, the cable dropped to the ground beside the artifact, its end neatly sheared off. At the same time, the other end of the cable dropped into the scene in the artifact.

Spock picked up the cut end of the cable. It was fused to a mirror finish so perfect that Chekov saw a tiny image of himself when Spock turned the cable for him to examine. "How did the object know I had released the cable?" he asked, shaking his head in bewilderment. The thought of such power was frightening, especially when no one knew how to control it. He shuddered, wondering what would happen if the artifact lost interest in a person when he was partway through the window.

"I would surmise that we are being scanned, although I am unable to detect any radiation leaking from their sensors." Spock paused to consult his tricorder. "I suggest that we attempt to place a tricorder inside the field."

It took them fifteen minutes to secure the tricorder to the end of a metal rod and to locate a pair of gloves to protect Chekov's hands from the heat generated by the artifact. Spock gave the settings on the device one last check before signaling for Chekov to proceed with the experiment. Slowly he pushed the rod toward the artifact. At first, nothing happened. It felt to Chekov as if he were shoving against a solid wall. He centered the tip of the rod against the window and pushed harder. Again nothing happened.

Scowling with the effort, Chekov leaned against the rod with all his weight. The tricorder broke free of its fastenings and catapulted down the rod toward Chekov. At the same time, the rod penetrated the field with an abruptness that caught him off guard. He staggered, trying to keep his footing, and sprawled on the ground.

For a moment he lay still, catching his breath. As he rolled to his feet, he heard the sputter of the rod being cut into two pieces.

Spock reached past Chekov to retrieve the tricorder. The silence stretched as he examined its screen, one eyebrow raised. "This device recorded no significant information during its contact with the artifact. That result leads us to an inescapable conclusion." He paused, waiting for Chekov and Talika to catch up with his reasoning.

Chekov sighed, knowing what was coming next. "If we cannot send through a tricorder rigged for remote telemetry, we will have to have someone hold it in the field. However, that person may have difficulties maintaining his position, since the artifact exerts a pull on anything within its power."

Talika grunted. "Typical human whimpering. You tricorder in field hold, I you hold. Nothing on planet can Djelifan in proper stance move."

"I hope the artifact knows that." Chekov took the tricorder from Spock, checked the new settings that the Vulcan had programmed into it, and swung its strap around his neck for extra security. Talika braced her feet and one heavily muscled arm against the frame of the artifact while wrapping the other arm around Chekov's waist. He wasn't sure it was the position he would have chosen, but it did feel secure. It would take a great deal of force to budge Talika.

Slowly Chekov extended the tricorder toward the window. As it encountered the edge of the field, it gave off a low whine, but its screen remained blank. He extended his arm further, feeling the tingling warmth travel up his arm. As the pull increased, he had to fight to keep from jerking clear of the field. To get the data they needed and to discover what lay on the other side of the window, he needed to get the tricorder as far into the artifact as he could.

A centimeter at a time, Chekov's arm disappeared into the window. He could still feel the arm, could feel the weight of the tricorder in his hand, but all he could see was the view of the rolling plain that the alien device had shown them since they had first released it from its protective walls. The idea that his arm might end at the edge of the window was extremely disconcerting.

The pull on his arm increased sharply as his elbow disappeared into the window. Startled, Chekov jerked back, and his boots missed their footing on the loose gravel. Unbalanced, he pitched toward the window, drawn in by the pressure on his arm. Talika's hold slowed his movement, but his momentum pushed her arm against the surface of the window. The field caught her, too, and both of them fell into the window.

Chapter Six

"EXPLANATION, SPOCK?" Kirk's question was more order than request. The five security men who had beamed down with the captain fanned out, surrounding the artifact and covering it with phaser rifles. The whine of the transporter signaled the arrival of six more guards, who promptly joined the cordon around the artifact.

Spock's eyebrow rose. "Are the security men necessary?"

"Two people disappeared." Kirk glared at the object. The left window, which had swallowed Chekov and Talika, was now as blank and featureless as the right-hand window. "Can you explain what happened? From the ship's scans, it looked as if the artifact dragged them inside itself."

"That is essentially what occurred, Captain. Ensign Chekov reported that the artifact exerted pressure on his arm when he extended it into the object. Apparently he stumbled and inadvertently pushed Dr. Talika's arm into contact with the protective field that overlays the surface of the artifact. Before either of them could recover, they were dragged inside."

"Why? For what purpose? Where are they now? Are they still alive?" As the questions bubbled to the surface of Kirk's mind, the featureless panels of the object took on a dark and sinister appearance. "There isn't enough room inside that thing for it to be holding them captive."

"That is correct, Captain." Spock glanced down at his tricorder, as if hoping he could read Kirk's answers from its screen. Apparently it told him nothing new, although he scanned the object again before responding to the captain's questions. "However, I have a theory. I believe the artifact is a relay station for a matter transmission device. The most logical assumption would be that we are looking at a portion of the aliens' planetwide transportation network. If that is the case, Ensign Chekov and Dr. Talika have been transported to some other location on this planet. All we need to do is locate them and beam them back to the ship."

Kirk flipped open his communicator. "Kirk to *Enterprise*. Uhura, have the ship's sensors located either Ensign Chekov or Dr. Talika yet?"

"Negative, Captain." Uhura clipped her words short, betraying her frustration at having no information to help them locate the missing people. "We've detected no signs of them or of their equipment. There's no change on any of our scans of the planet, either."

"Thank you, Uhura. Kirk out." He turned to Spock. "Do you have any other suggestions, Mr. Spock?"

"Not at the present time." Spock studied his tricorder screen with concentrated intensity. "Unless they were transported to a location directly within the *Enterprise*'s line of sight, it may take a little time for the ship's sensors to find them. Although it is a reasonable hypothesis that the scene we saw through the device is their destination, particularly since the light spectrum and the vegetation correspond to what we have observed on this planet, other possibilities do exist. At the moment we have insufficient data to construct a valid model of how this device operates."

"And how soon do you expect to have *sufficient* data?" Hearing the sharpness in his tone, Kirk paused to rein in his impatience. It wasn't Spock's fault that they knew so little about the artifact. "What recommendations do you have for 'persuading' the object to give us some answers?"

"At the moment I am uncertain of the best method to employ, Captain. I am considering—" Spock broke off, his words interrupted by a shout from one of the security guards.

On the left side of the object, bands of color were flickering across the windowlike surface in spectral sequence—shifting from violet through red and back with an irregular, pulsating rhythm. Kirk felt his stomach twisting to the tempo of the erratic cycle, and he looked away before the nausea built to uncontrollable proportions.

When he glanced back, the window had cleared and was again showing the rolling, grass-covered plain. In the nearest foreground a length of cable, a piece of metal rod, and several familiar-looking objects were scattered across the trampled grass. Kirk moved closer, even though he was certain he would recognize *Enterprise* equipment anywhere.

Chekov's tricorder and communicator lay to the right of the scene, at the start of a wide swath of flattened grass that traced a drunken course down the hill and out of Kirk's line of sight. Talika's communicator and the ceremonial Djelifan dagger she kept holstered in her boot lay several meters from Chekov's equipment at the head of a second strip of trampled vegetation. There was no sign of the missing people.

"Fascinating."

Kirk jumped, startled to hear Spock's voice at his elbow. He had been so absorbed in studying the scene that he had not heard the Vulcan come up beside him. "What is it, Spock?"

"That path through the grass. It is far too wide for Mr. Chekov to have made unless he laid down and rolled."

"Hmm. I think you're right." Kirk examined the track carefully. The abrupt zigzags in the band of broken grass would be difficult for a rolling human to produce. "I don't know why he'd want to roll down that hill, but he'd find it virtually impossible to follow *that* course. He should have gone straight down the slope."

Spock nodded. "You are correct, Captain. I submit that we are seeing evidence that our people found traveling through the artifact to be a disconcerting experience."

"Could you be more specific, Spock? We need something more definite to go on if we're going to get them back." Something about the scene in the window nagged at Kirk. As they watched, the setting sun spread a wash of crimson and orange across the rolling hills and painted the shadows a deep, velvety black.

Sunset! Kirk felt his thoughts snap into focus. He reached for his communicator. "Kirk to *Enterprise.*"

"Uhura here," came the immediate response.

"Uhura, tell Mr. Sulu to search along the sunset terminator. We believe Ensign Chekov and Dr. Talika were transported elsewhere and released by another artifact onto the surface of the planet in an area that is . . ." He paused, glancing at Spock for a better estimate of the time in the scene they were seeing through the artifact.

"I estimate that the second artifact is approximately thirty-five minutes on the sunward side of the terminator. This assumes that we are viewing a location in the middle latitudes. I could give a more precise estimate if the scene contained any information that would allow me to estimate the distance and direction from the equator."

Sulu's voice answered, "I got that, Captain. I'm shifting orbit now to put us directly over the sunset terminator."

"Very good. Keep me posted. Kirk out." He snapped the communicator closed and returned it to his belt. "Any other suggestions, Mr. Spock?"

"I would like to record more data on the artifact, using every tricorder available. I will need approximately twenty minutes to adjust them to scan slightly different but overlapping bands and to station people all around the artifact. Logic dictates that a shield generator of such extreme antiquity should have developed leakage somewhere in its operational range. However, the fact that we have not detected it yet suggests that we must look outside the frequencies we normally search."

"Assuming the leakage is there," Kirk muttered in disgust. Until now, the aliens' technology had seemed so far in advance of the Federation's that Kirk was starting to feel like a preindustrial savage. Shaking himself to break the mood, he nodded to Spock. "See what you can do. It sounds like our best chance."

"Yes, Captain." Spock ordered one of the security men to collect everyone who had tricorders, both in their area and at the primary excavation site. By the time Spock finished adjusting the instruments, he had thirty tricorders to station around the artifact.

"While each of you scans the artifact from your

designated position," he told the combined group of crew and archaeologists, "I shall attempt to cause the artifact to respond to my presence. Given the results we have obtained so far, analysis from the *Enterprise's* computers may be required to obtain any meaningful results. However, I cannot overemphasize the importance of keeping your tricorders pointed at the artifact, whatever happens."

"That was quite a warning." Kirk, watching the group disperse to their assigned locations, kept his voice low so no one would overhear him. "What do you *really* expect will happen?"

Spock raised an eyebrow, as if to ask why Kirk should be worried about such things. "Logically, Captain, we must be prepared for every possible outcome. However, the probabilities distinctly favor an anticlimactic resolution to our efforts."

"In other words, you don't really think it's going to do anything."

"Correct, Captain." Spock checked to see that everyone was in position. "However, I intend to do my best to produce a response. Therefore, my actions introduce an element of uncertainty into my ability to predict the outcome."

"Of course, Spock."

"I am glad that you appreciate the dangers inherent in the undertaking." With his eyes on the ground, Spock started toward the artifact, pausing to pick up every fist-sized rock he saw. When he realized what Spock was planning, Kirk began collecting rocks, too. Before long, they had assembled a sizable cache of ammunition.

Spock stepped back from his rock pile and studied it with a critical eye. Even the smallest chunk massed several times more than the pebbles Chekov had thrown at the artifact. Among the miscellaneous supplies that had been beamed down but not used for building the scaffolding above the artifact were several half sheets of decking material. Choosing one, Spock hauled it back to his pile of rocks and crouched behind it, using the metal plate as a shield.

Seeing what Spock intended, Kirk knelt beside him. "If I hold it, that will leave you both hands free. That should make things easier."

"I appreciate the help, but I would prefer that you not expose yourself to needless risk, Captain. It might be advisable for you to remove yourself to a less dangerous location." Even as he said the words, Spock shifted his position to give Kirk more room behind the metal plate.

Grinning at how well the Vulcan knew him, Kirk maneuvered himself into the crowded space. "I may be mistaken about this, Spock, but I suspect that this is one of the safer locations in the area. So if you don't mind, I'll stick around and try to keep you from getting hit when that thing returns your presents with interest."

"I appreciate your concern, Captain." Spock's tone was even more neutral than usual, but he pulled several rocks behind the shield. Weighing the first two in his hands, he peeked around the metal plate, calculated the distance, and hurled the rocks toward the artifact. Moving swiftly, he grabbed two more rocks off the pile, tossed them, and followed them with two more before ducking behind the shield. The rocks hit the upper edge of the window with sharp cracks that sounded like the detonations of a string of firecrackers. Moments later, the first rock crashed against the metal plate with a bone-shaking reverberation. Before Kirk could recover from that impact, the other five rocks pounded against their shield.

"Fascinating," Spock murmured when the metal had quit vibrating. "It returned all of the rocks to their point of origin."

"So?" With his ears still ringing, Kirk failed to grasp the significance of Spock's words. The loud noise at such close proximity had triggered the headache that had been threatening to return all morning.

"A projectile thrown at a flat surface should rebound at its angle of incidence, reflected around a perpendicular line that intersects the surface at the point of impact." Spock pulled another handful of rocks behind their shield. "The probability of any *one* of the rocks returning to its point of origin, much less all of them, is so slight that—"

"I get the picture." Kirk shuddered. Between the aftereffects of the suldanic gas and the onset of the headache, he wanted Spock to finish his experiment so they could return to the *Enterprise*. "Just get on with your test."

"Yes, Captain." Spock pitched the next group of rocks toward the artifact. They, too, were returned, bouncing off the metal shield with more force than the first batch.

Kirk gritted his teeth. The noise was so loud that it felt as if each rock had hit him directly on the head. "Quit dawdling, Spock. If it's going to do that on all of them, just get it over with so we can go back to the ship!"

"As you wish, Captain."

A grin flickered across Kirk's face as he realized that Spock found the artifact's return salvos as unpleasant as he did. In fact, he thought as the next rocks crashed against the metal, Spock with his Vulcan hearing probably found the noise more intensely painful than Kirk, with his pounding headache, did.

Spock reached for more rocks, and Kirk braced himself. The artifact returned the missiles with still greater force. Kirk stumbled backwards under the assault. Groaning with the effort, he dug his feet into the loose rock. Spock must know what he was doing, he thought, and that left it to Kirk to see that he got the data he needed to determine what had happened to Chekov and Talika.

Four sets of rocks later, Kirk was less sure that Spock had thought his plan out carefully. The artifact returned each group of rocks with increasingly greater force, and Kirk was staggering under the pounding. The throbbing in his head expanded with each trial, and his entire body ached with the effort of keeping the metal sheet upright while the alien device tried to flatten them with its return fire. It was almost as though something inside the artifact was becoming annoyed at their attempts to investigate it.

"This is the last group," Spock said, his voice harsh with strain. He sidearmed the rocks toward the artifact in rapid succession and then moved to help Kirk support their shield.

For an awful moment there was total silence, but before Kirk could wonder what it meant, he had his answer. All six rocks slammed simultaneously into the decking with enough force to dent the metal. Even their combined strength was inadequate, and Kirk and Spock were thrown to the ground. Dimly, through the thunder in his head, Kirk heard someone shouting for emergency beam-up.

Kirk surveyed the subdued group of senior officers around the briefing room table. From their expressions, no one was eager to report the results of the last four hours of work. All bad news, then—or, at least, no unqualified good news, he thought, although he knew that no one would have held back something favorable just to report it at the briefing. "Mr. Sulu, what's the progress with the search for Mr. Chekov and Dr. Talika?"

"So far, not much, Captain. We located their equipment near another of the windowlike artifacts at Site

N4. Neither the communicators nor the tricorder were functional, so we beamed them back to the *Enterprise* for analysis." Sulu frowned, not liking the idea that something could damage the equipment. "Since then we've concentrated our search near the second artifact, with no success. They shouldn't have wandered far, but we haven't detected any human or Djelifan readings within fifty kilometers of Site N4. The only life-forms in the area that are larger than a rodent are two solitary crablike animals, both about five kilometers from the artifact and moving on different headings."

Lassiter looked up from her datapad, frowning. "But our previous scans didn't reveal any such indigenous life-forms," she said in her soft, whispery voice. "How large are these creatures?"

Sulu called up the sensor data. "One is about seventy-five kilos and the other is closer to a hundred, as best we can tell without closer examination. Both seem to be traveling in random patterns, with no discernible purpose to their movements. Beyond that, we don't have sufficient scanner resolution to give us detailed information. We would have to send a reconnaissance probe down to the area if we wanted to study them more closely."

Kirk nodded his approval. "Do it. If our previous surveys missed something as large as these creatures, we need to know how and why."

"Right away, Captain." Sulu relayed the order to the bridge.

"Also, can anyone explain why the second artifact was not hidden in the same manner as the first?" He glanced around the room, looking for someone who wanted to answer the question. When no one volunteered, he turned toward Spock.

"We have no explanations at this time, Captain. However, the sensor readings from that region of the planet altered when we released the first artifact from its shielding." Spock called up the data on the screen. "Some of the effects are quite subtle, but as a working hypothesis, we are assuming that the shielding around the first object somehow inhibited the functioning of other, similar objects elsewhere on the planet."

"I see, Mr. Spock. What luck have you had analyzing the data we collected down on the planet?"

"Our results are, of course, preliminary, Captain. However, I have located several frequencies that show large fluctuations in the energy output and through which it may be possible to penetrate the artifact's shielding with our sensors. I recommend that we position several arrays of scanning equipment around the object before we conduct more tests on the artifact."

Kirk nodded. "Tell Mr. Scott what you need after this briefing. By the way, what tests do you propose to conduct?"

"Logically, we should repeat the tests that Mr. Chekov attempted after we get the more sensitive scanner arrays into position." Spock glanced at his screen. "However, the computer reports only a 2.35 percent chance that we will obtain any new information if we repeat the rock-throwing experiment. Therefore, I recommend that we omit that test and that I have the computer reprocess the data we obtained this morning after we have analyzed the later information for the appropriate correction factors."

"I'm all in favor of that." Kirk rubbed a hand against his temple, thinking how little he wanted to repeat their earlier adventure and how reluctant he would feel to order someone else to submit to the same punishment. For that matter, if the artifact's data processors decided that the second set of tests were a continuation of what he and Spock had done, it might start escalating the force from where it had left off with them. That could quickly become lethal for the people receiving the artifact's return fire. He shook himself to break that train of thought and turned to his chief engineer. "Scotty, have you determined what's wrong with the communicators and the tricorder we recovered from the planet?"

"In a manner of speaking." Scott shrugged, an eloquent summary of his frustration with the alien technology. "The damage resembles that found in objects sent through a transporter where the reintegration beams are misaligned. Everything is just a wee bit off, but I canna find any definite pattern to the damage. My lads are still working on it, trying to get a handle on that alien contraption, but for the moment I canna tell you more. It's unlike anything I've ever seen before."

"Does this mean that you can't predict when—or if—you'll be able to protect our equipment when it passes through that object, Scotty?"

Scott's face went glum. "Aye, Captain. That's what it means."

"Very well, gentlemen. Mr. Spock will conduct his tests, and we'll hope they give us some answers. However, regardless of the results, if we have not located Ensign Chekov and Dr. Talika by local dawn in the area where we think they disappeared, I am leading a security team through the artifact to find them."

Spock straightened in his chair, his back rigid. "Captain, may I protest this hazardous course of action? You must not jeopardize yourself in this manner. I am the logical choice to lead the security team, if such an attempt becomes necessary."

"Objection noted." Kirk drew in a deep breath. "However, I'm the person who will go. If something goes wrong with our rescue attempt, we'll need you here to figure things out."

"I see." Spock's flat tone said that he disagreed with Kirk.

Kirk ducked his head to hide a brief grin. Who said Vulcans had no emotions? Spock's disapproval was so strong he could almost touch it. He glanced toward the Vulcan. "With luck, Mr. Spock, we'll find the missing people, and this discussion will be academic. I'm not sending anyone through that artifact simply for the sake of satisfying our curiosity about its function. It's far too dangerous."

Spock raised an eyebrow. "Perhaps the danger to people entering the object is why the artifact was buried in the first place, Captain."

"Aye," Scott murmured, half to himself. "That *would* explain why it was so difficult to locate."

Nodding, Kirk pushed himself to his feet. "Regardless of why it was hidden, we have to get our people back. Unless someone has something more to add, this briefing is over."

Spock's science teams worked feverishly to force answers from the artifact, but the alien device remained an enigma. The sensor arrays showed minuscule energy fluctuations at certain frequencies when lengths of cable were pushed through the window or when someone came into contact with the protective force field. However, none of the leaks in the shields around the artifact were sufficient to give Spock precise information about how the artifact functioned or what had happened to Chekov and Talika. The *Enterprise*'s sensors continued to report the two alien life-forms near the second artifact, and the probes following the two creatures recorded no significant information about them.

As dawn approached at the second site, Spock drove his people harder to solve the mystery. Kirk watched the frenzied activity with curious detachment, waiting for Spock to concede that the artifact had evaded analysis. He *knew,* without being able to say why, that he would have to go through the windowlike transporter to rescue the missing people.

Full daylight had spread itself across the rolling hills in the "window" when Spock finally admitted defeat. "Captain, I regret to inform you that we have been unable to produce any significant information about the object. However, I strongly recommend that you postpone passing through the device until we have breached its shields and determined how it operates. The risk to your life is too great when there are so many unknowns in the equation."

"Risk is our business, Mr. Spock. You know that as well as I." He turned toward the mysterious object, studying its uncommunicative exterior. "Besides, we owe it to Mr. Chekov and Dr. Talika to do everything in our power to rescue them. Since we aren't getting any results from here, I'm going after them."

"Yes, Captain." Spock gestured for several of his scientists to join him. While he briefed them on what to do when the captain and his men entered the artifact, Kirk summoned his volunteer security team.

Ten minutes later Kirk and the three guards were standing in front of the artifact, ready to pass through it. The *Enterprise* had stationed probes near the second artifact to record what happened when the men emerged from the "window" on that side, and Spock had teams positioned around the first artifact, ready to record every detail.

Kirk checked one last time to see if his men were ready. As the last man nodded, he started forward. "Let's get this show on the road."

Centimeters from the window, he slowly extended his arm. A soothing, gentle warmth climbed upward from his fingers, pulling him toward the artifact. Before Kirk realized what was happening, his arm was inside the window up to his shoulder. Beside him the security guards also had their arms inside the force field. The pull was irresistible, and Kirk yielded to it.

The "window" engulfed the four men and went dark, swallowing them without apparent effort. Spock moved from group to group, checking their results, but to no avail. Once again the sensors had not detected any changes in the energy output of the artifact. They had no clues as to what had happened to Kirk and the security guards.

Chapter Seven

IT HAD BEEN a jagged transition, he thought, struggling to get all eight appendages beneath his carapace. The old relics in Maintenance were putting less and less into keeping the equipment in any better condition than their own decrepit and fading carcasses. Soon the transit frames would be as useless as the ancient matriarchs who ran the ceremonies, protected by the residual shreds of prestige they drew about their discolored shells. With those antiquated and bloated relics remaining in control of the Kh!lict worlds, it was little wonder that everything was falling down around them. Something should be done, someone ought to do something, maybe he would do something . . . but later. There was something important he must do first, if he could only remember it through the tidal crash of the blood past his tympana.

His senses reeled with the ebb and flow of disorganized perceptions. The light was wrong, too red and too weak, adding to his disorientation. Where was he, then, if he had been sent so far from home? Which cool, fading star was this the matriarchs had exiled him to, what world gone sere and lifeless beneath its dying sun?

He looked behind him, saw the transit frame on the hill far above him with its *pyar*-runes fading as the power drained back into the grid. The patterns proclaimed the glories of the homeworld, the center of Kh!lict civilization. Such praise was embedded only on the transit frames of the homeworld. That meant he had been sent to a region where no one usually went. The penal zone at the southern pole, perhaps? Even that did not explain the too-cold temperature or the strangely reddened sun. Both were mysteries he could not solve at present unless he assumed the matriarchs had installed a new class of force field around the penal zone. If that was indeed where he was, he needed to put as much distance between himself and the transit frame as he could.

He staggered forward, surprised at the tremors that ran up his appendages. The Kh!lict form was perfectly designed, its eight limbs providing the ideal combination of strength and agility, balance and power. Every hatchling in its first soft shell knew how to coordinate its appendages for maximum speed or to gain the power and leverage needed to destroy a rival. A Kh!lict who staggered was as alien as—as this desolate landscape filled with the ocher whisper of the grasses and the dry beige rattle of the bitter-leaves that grew in the dark, secret hollows of the land.

He strained to move one appendage, then another, needing all his concentration to force his legs to do what instinct should have directed them to do without any intervention from his conscious mind. If the matriarchs had sent him here for a reason beyond malicious whim, he must escape the range of their surveillance before they carried out the next murky phase of their plan.

A broad swath of trampled grass led downhill, away from the transit frame. In his current abnormal condition, the thought of following someone else's pre-broken trail was immensely appealing. After he put some distance between himself and the frame, he could prepare countermeasures for whatever surprises they planned to spring on him. With an effort he urged his leaden appendages into motion and started down the hill.

He hadn't felt this bad, Kirk thought, since that three-day shore leave on Argelius early in his first deep-space tour of duty. Kirk hadn't believed the old hands, had thought they were pulling his leg when they cautioned him against mixing Argelian ale with *anything* else. From the smug "I-told-you-so" expression on the *Farragut's* doctor's face when she had given him the shot for his hangover, he realized that he had fallen victim to a long-standing ship's tradition—delivering an honest warning about the deceptively mild ale in such apprehensive tones that no junior officer would take the advice seriously.

The ground lurched beneath him as his body struggled across the irregular terrain. He tried to focus his eyes on his surroundings, fighting against the growing disorientation. The scene twisted and blurred, shapes stretching and contorting into impossible angles, colors pulsing between gloomy drabness and hallucinatory brilliance. His perspective was wrong, distorted, his eyes too close to the ground and responding to his commands as though they were no longer firmly anchored in his eye sockets. Kirk thought that was impossible until he looked down at his feet.

Instead of his familiar boots, a long, pincerlike appendage stretched into his field of view. Shock jolted through him, scrambling his thoughts and locking his muscles. His legs froze in midstride, but his momentum carried his body forward, and he overbalanced. He flopped on his belly, skidding on the dry grass. The land dropped away beneath him, and he continued to slide downhill, his body picking up speed as the slope steepened. Dizziness and extreme disorientation overwhelmed him, making it impossible to interpret what he was seeing. Finally, in self-defense, Kirk surrendered to the madness and let his consciousness escape.

His carapace scraped against a rock and spun, careening off at an angle from its previous trajectory. Anger washed through him, anger and shame at his clumsiness. No Kh!lict past his first molt *ever* tripped over his own claws. With eight appendages one could always keep enough pincers on the soil to avoid falling down hills. What had the matriarchs done to him when they forced him through the transit frame? What damage had they done to his mind and his body that he could no longer perform the most basic acts of living? Perhaps this was his punishment—this incapacity and lack of coordination. Perhaps he did not need to worry about further punishment.

The spinning slowed his forward momentum, and gradually friction brought him to a stop near the bottom of the hill. A wide, greenish-gold swath of flattened grass marked where he had descended, a clear beacon to anyone who was trailing him. If the matriarchs sent out a squad of enforcers to see that the terms of his punishment—whatever they were—were observed, the young females would have no trouble locating him. As long as he remained in this grass, he would find it impossible to hide from pursuers. Somewhere there must be a safer place for him to wait until he could devise a way to turn the tables on the matriarchs.

Cautiously he pulled each limb beneath his carapace, flexing the joints and testing for injuries as he did. A severed ligament could explain his fall, but nothing seemed obviously damaged. For all their apparent malice, the matriarchs had not left him incapacitated beyond the disorientation and the huge gaps in his memory. He should know why he was here, but he didn't. Who he was, his color-grade in his cohort, or even which cohort claimed his participation were also mysteries. Only an elementary outline of his life remained, consisting mostly of facts known to every Kh!lict who survived past the larval stage. The details, the colors and textures of his individual life that would shape his passage through the Final Transition, were missing as though they had been buried under a thick dun coat of mud.

When he was sure his body was undamaged, he levered himself off the ground. For a moment everything wavered, flickered to blackness, and then resumed the disquieting ruddy shades that distorted everything in this strange place. He took one step and then another, testing his coordination and balance to rule out any unsuspected injuries. When he still could find no apparent cause for his awkwardness, he began moving faster, hoping to put some distance between himself and whomever the matriarchs had sent to follow him. Clearly, the best and most obvious explanation for his disorientation was to make him vulnerable.

Again a tremor of uneasiness rippled through his neuroprocessors. If his punishment was to have any meaning, he should know his crime and the rules governing his sentence and probable execution. Even with the entire Kh!lict totality watching the proceedings via the remote viewers, the punishment would be worthless unless he also knew what offense had earned him so dreadful a penalty as isolation from all his kind and death in a place whose naming-colors he would never learn.

He headed downhill, away from the transit frame, although he knew that direction was the most predictable. Still, the dark, rocky gullies tucked between the beige and dusty green folds of the land offered some slight hope for confusing his trail. The grass there grew in irregular patches, giving him the hope of choosing a route where he did not flatten a wide swath behind himself and where his claws did not leave sharp impressions on the boulder-strewn surface. With luck his executioners would be fooled by his apparent blunder into the obvious. They would not expect it when he doubled back onto the first strip of rocky ground and circled around behind them.

The first two spots he investigated were disappointing, with the grass coming in thick and tall within easy view of the gully. The third rockslide was more promising, although he had to watch his step to avoid triggering a new slide, which would alert his pursuers by the russet freshness of the disturbance. In a way, he was relieved that the slope was so unstable. If he succeeded in conquering it before anyone located him, he stood a fair chance of evading them. The difficulty of the ascent would convince them that he had continued down the gully, hoping to float himself to safety in the cloudy waters of the river that must lie farther in that direction. If the enforcers could be misled for only half a day, he could hide himself so thoroughly that no one would find his location unless they had watched him through a viewer perched on his carapace. And that, he knew, was unlikely; he could not feel the telltale weight or the unbalanced pull when he moved, either of which would have alerted him to an object anchored to his carapace's crest.

The climb was slow and exhausting work, with the difficulty compounded by the need for extreme caution. Even so, he saw no signs of pursuit as he mounted the pile of loose rubble. At the top he paused, checking his back trail for the bright flash of color that would signal the enforcers' location. Nothing except the grass moved anywhere in the bleak, empty land. He wasn't sure whether the desolation was reassuring or not, whether he should believe that his tactics would deliver him from pursuit or if the matriarchs had devised a more subtle trap for him than he could imagine.

Either way, he could not stand on the top of the hill, glowing his triumph like a beacon. His radiant colors would certainly attract the attention of any Kh!lict within his line of sight. He damped them down, coloring his carapace to match the duns and beiges of the earth and the dry grass. Starting off, he picked his way through the sparse grass with exquisite care to avoid calling attention to his passage. Somewhere there must be a cave or a tunnel or a cut bank where he could hide from aerial surveillance. Once he found that place, he could conceal himself and begin to make plans to overcome the enforcers that would soon be following him. He could not afford to let them find him; when they did, they would dismember him a joint at a time, trying to prolong his suffering as an object lesson to any other Kh!lict who had committed the same offense. His only hope lay in avoiding capture for a turn of the seasons, until the matriarchs decided his isolation had become a greater torture than the punishment to which he was originally sentenced.

Kirk gradually became aware of the flow of the grass and the chaotic patterns of loose rock passing his line of vision. What, exactly, had happened was still unclear, but this time he told himself to take things slowly and to analyze all the evidence before letting his grotesquely distorted perceptions trigger another violent reaction. He couldn't afford to act until he learned all he could about his situation.

His body was climbing a talus slope, carefully picking its way across the unstable surface. Kirk knew he could not perform such a complicated motor skill while on automatic pilot, especially not in an alien body. That meant that, as an initial postulate, he must assume another consciousness was also occupying this body. He could not detect any foreign presence directing his thoughts, so he decided that the alien was walled up behind its own mental barriers. That made things easier, since it gave Kirk a chance to observe the situation without worrying that his host would be distracted from navigating the treacherous slope, but it might create difficulties later when he tried to make contact with his host.

At first he concentrated on the visual information flowing into the alien's brain. The colors seemed oddly subdued and skewed toward the red end of the spectrum. Most life-forms evolved visual systems where the peak sensitivity of the visual sensors corresponded to the median wavelength of the incoming light from their planet's sun. That meant one of two things: Either his host had evolved in a much different star system than this one, or his race had died out before this sun had begun to dim. Normally the second hypothesis would have been extremely far-fetched, but given the antiquity of Careta IV's artifacts, Kirk decided that a cooling sun might have caused the death of his host's civilization. Massive climate changes, with the attendant disruptions in food supplies, had rung the death knell for many civilizations. Certainly this barren and unforgiving land seemed an unlikely place to support the civilization that had created the artifacts and the buried ruins they had found.

His next priority, he decided, was to figure out what kind of creature his host was. The obvious solution—to take control of the body's functions and experiment until he had his answers—was out of the question as long as his host continued on his present course. It was almost as if the creature expected pursuit, and Kirk wondered if he should worry. Presumably, none of the creature's people were left on Careta IV, but the *Enterprise's* sensors had suddenly reported two large life-forms after Chekov and Talika had fallen through the window. Even if, like Kirk, those life-forms were native hosts that contained the consciousnesses of his missing people, Kirk realized he had no way to determine what directives had been programmed into the minds that controlled the bodies. For all he knew, the artifacts could have been designed for alien war games, with the rules and allegiances programmed into the bodies when they exited the objects.

With direct experimentation temporarily out of the question, Kirk settled down to watch his surroundings. From the way the scene changed from wide- to narrow-angle views, he decided that his eyes must be mounted on stalks, allowing them to rotate freely. The narrow views gave stereoscopic vision, much like what Kirk was used to in human form. After he adjusted to the unfamiliar sensation of seeing up to two hundred and seventy degrees around himself, he began to appreciate the benefits of the panoramic views. The more directions a being could watch, the less the chance that something could attack without warning.

After a time Kirk was able to interpret the sensations from other parts of his new body. He had eight limbs, each ending in a pincerlike claw that could be closed tightly when walking or opened for fighting or to manipulate tools. All the appendages could perform most tasks, although Kirk sensed that the creature preferred using certain limbs for certain functions, much as Kirk favored his right hand.

While he had been analyzing his host's body, they had climbed off the talus pile onto a long, sloping ridge that led back the way they had come. The creature started climbing, following the crest of the hill until he found another talus pile. The rocks here were larger and more solidly packed than the precarious slope they had climbed earlier. However, when the creature started picking its way downhill, Kirk began wondering if this was any safer than their previous adventure. The rocks didn't look all that stable to him, and he wasn't sure why they didn't head back for the artifact. To his mind, but obviously not to his host's, the best solution to their predicament was to return to the object so Spock could reverse this unwelcome fusion of human and alien.

The thought of Spock brought up another problem. How was he going to communicate with the Vulcan? Unless Spock knew he was trapped inside this alien body, he would assume that Kirk had vanished into limbo—or, worse, been killed outright—when he stepped into the window. How did these creatures communicate with each other? He had sensed no effort on the part of his host to speak or to make sounds of any kind. If he couldn't find a way to control his host's body, he would be unable to let anyone know what had happened to him. The problem required thought, and since he dared so little else while the creature was traversing the talus, Kirk focused his mind on devising a way to communicate with his crew.

At the bottom of the talus slope, a wide, rocky channel meandered between the rolling hills. He approached the shallow stream and crouched to reach the muddy water, straining out the gritty sediment with his drinking filters. His thirst satisfied, he started upstream, hoping that any enforcers who had followed him this far would look for him in the predictable direction. He did not think the unit pursuing him would be large enough that they could divide their forces. At any rate, it was a gamble he would have to take.

The sun was nearing the zenith when he spotted what he had been looking for. The valley had narrowed to a tight canyon between yellowish dun walls, fissured and broken in many places. To his right, almost hidden in the sooty shadows, a narrow cleft opened in the rock face. He moved toward it, carefully picking his way across the rock-strewn stream bed to avoid leaving any tracks.

The gap opened at carapace level and was barely wide enough for him to squeeze through, which made it all the better for his purpose. The enforcers might check for him in such a place, on the assumption that he would go to ground in the smallest hole he could find. However, even if they thought this was a likely spot, most females—even the youngest ones—were larger than he was. In all probability they would not be able to wedge themselves through the fissure.

He pulled himself into the cleft one claw at a time, taking care not to dislodge the loose rock around the opening. It was hard work—far harder than he thought it should be—and again he wondered what had happened to his body during its passage through the transit frame. Strength, coordination, and memory had all been damaged by the transition, and the cumulative effect was beginning to wear at him. All the essential elements that defined him as a Kh!lict had been weakened or destroyed, leaving him with an identity as shattered as the cliffs that surrounded him.

That thought led to madness, he realized. With a shudder he pushed it aside, to be considered after he had protected himself from the inevitable pursuit. For the moment he was busy enough just keeping his balance on the treacherous footing. The narrow, twisting stream course acted as a trap for the loose rock that cascaded down from sheer walls above him. As he moved, the rubble shifted and turned beneath his pincers. Only his superior physique made it possible for him to retain his balance on the precarious surface. He rejoiced at the difficulty his pursuers would have in following him; the more massive females would find it almost impossible to negotiate the treacherous footing without having the rocks slide from beneath them.

The hiding place was so well concealed that he almost missed it. Sometime in the distant past, a large sheet of rock had fallen from one of the walls and was now tilted across the cleft. Talus had buried most of the slab, leaving only a very small gap to serve as an entrance.

He poked around the area for several minutes, trying to convince himself that no one was waiting to ambush him when he finally dared to tackle the opening. At last, knowing that he had nothing to gain by waiting, he circled to the uphill side of the slab and began to shift the rubble. In a surprisingly short time, he cleared away enough rocks to squeeze himself inside. He wriggled through the hole and into the space beneath the yellowish-tan slab of rock.

There was barely enough room for his carapace to fit inside, and he had to move more loose rock to get all his appendages safely out of sight. However, once he finished the work and his body was safely hidden, he began to relax. The small opening on the downstream side of his hideout gave him a clear view of anyone approaching from that direction. With surprise operating in his favor, he would be able to take out the first enforcers and arm himself with their weapons before they realized he was there. Even without scouting farther up the cleft, he knew his rear was protected. The matriarchs would not send enough enforcers after him to allow them the luxury of a multipronged attack. Secure in his choice of a hiding place, he shifted the colors of his carapace to match the shadows beneath the slab of rock. As long as he was patient and maintained his concealment, he would be the certain victor in the upcoming fight.

When he realized that his host had gone to ground and intended to remain where he was for some time, Kirk began phase two of his plan to explore the body he was trapped in. After passively watching how they had negotiated the uneven ground, he concluded that the creature's body greatly resembled an Earth-normal crab enlarged to human size. As best he could tell, the creature had four pairs of legs, which were coordinated by a complex series of rules Kirk's host did not consciously remember when he moved. Kirk, however, needed to learn those rules so he could control the alien's body, should he need to take over his host.

Don't force it, he told himself, although everything in him screamed for immediate and decisive action. As difficult as he found it, he needed to take a lesson from Spock, to be patient and work out his situation precisely before he tried to do anything. This creature was so very alien it would not be easy to establish contact with it. Besides, whoever controlled this alien body would probably not be eager to surrender its position to Kirk, and he would need to exercise caution.

With that idea firmly in mind, Kirk concentrated on the body in which he was imprisoned. At first he had little luck. It was almost as if his mind had been encased in an alien android with none of the sensory inputs connected. That thought was disheartening; if it were true, he had no way to sense his environment or to control events. Still, he couldn't be completely isolated, since he could interpret what the alien was seeing. That might mean that the artifact had only given him visual input, but Kirk rejected that idea for the moment. He stood a much better chance of learning something if he assumed that his host's physiology and anatomy were so alien that his human thought processes were not recognizing the information presented to him. That meant that the alien's mind probably did not recognize his presence, either.

He observed the view down the narrow canyon that was absorbing the alien's attention, noticing again how red the light appeared. That perception, at least, was not being reinterpreted for his benefit, and it gave him a place to start. The tumbled boulders and broken cliffs were monotonous and claustrophobic, but the alien kept at least one eye focused downstream at all times. That gave Kirk an idea.

Focusing on a location about thirty meters away and as far above the canyon floor, Kirk imagined something creeping down the sheer rock face and becoming visible at that spot. The alien twitched his eyes upward, then jerked his view downward to check the canyon floor. Kirk concentrated harder on visualizing someone climbing down the canyon wall. At first he got no response, but then, ever so slowly, the alien began scrutinizing the cliff from the base upward, studying each fissure and jutting boulder for hidden enemies.

Halfway through the search, Kirk sensed a growing irritation, as though his host did not believe anything could attack from that direction. Deliberately Kirk shifted his attention downstream, letting the alien check for the pursuers he obviously expected. When they saw no one, Kirk again focused on the canyon wall. This time the alien's eyes shifted upward more quickly, and Kirk worked to direct his attention to various spots on the cliff face.

The rocks were varicolored reds and browns and tans, with deep black shadows that could easily hide a man in dark clothing. As they searched the cliff, Kirk sensed a growing uneasiness in his host, as though the aliens could also hide themselves from sight like ninja. When he tried to focus on that thought, the perception slipped away, leaving Kirk with his own sense of disquiet. The multicolored rock face disturbed his host greatly, and Kirk realized that he would learn a lot about the alien if he could solve this particular riddle. However, he did not know how to get at that information, so he put the problem aside.

With a measure of control established over his host's eyes, Kirk tried to manipulate other parts of the alien's body. Wedged into the tiny space beneath the slab of rock, Kirk could not afford any energetic experiments, but he needed to know how this strange, crablike body operated. A human confined in such a restricted space would have been screaming from muscle spasms and pinched nerves long ago. Was the alien immune to such things, or did its physiology provide a filter that kept physical discomfort from interfering with its cognitive processes? And how would he be able to determine the answers to such questions?

Concentrating on a mental image of his hand, Kirk visualized closing his thumb against his forefinger and lifting his arm until the hand was in front of his face. Nothing happened, or, if it did, he could not detect it. *Is this what it's like to be paralyzed?* he wondered. It was disconcerting to give orders to his body and not feel any movement or tactile sensation from his extremities. It was even more disturbing to realize that he was at his host's mercy until he learned how to connect with the alien's nervous system, how to decipher the creature's reactions in a given situation, and how to control this strange, crablike body.

It would have been no small order to accomplish all that if he had known exactly how to do it. Unfortunately, he had never heard of anything like this happening before. That left him with no guidelines and no suggested procedures for making a first contact with a previously unknown race—from inside one of their bodies.

Chapter Eight

"SPOCK TO *Enterprise.*" It took all of his Vulcan control to keep his voice pitched to an absolute, flat tone. Around him he heard a ripple of dismay pass through the landing party. He could almost hear what the humans were thinking as clearly as if one of them had spoken the words aloud—the captain had disappeared into the artifact without anything registering on their tricorders, and Spock was acting as if Kirk had stepped out for a morning stroll. He debated lecturing them on the futility of squandering energy on emotional outbursts, but decided not to waste the time. Finding Kirk was a higher priority than educating humans on the virtues of controlling their passions. "*Enterprise,* has Captain Kirk come through the other side of the window yet?"

A long pause answered him. As the seconds stretched, Spock calculated the odds that something had gone wrong: equipment failure, unidentified ships dropping from warp just beyond the *Enterprise*'s orbit, the communications officer being away from her post. He had almost convinced himself that the problem was with his communicator when the device crackled to life. *"Enterprise.* This is Sulu, Mr. Spock."

"Report, Mr. Sulu. Have the captain and his party come through the artifact yet?"

"We don't know, Mr. Spock." There was a long, uncomfortable pause. "At the precise moment when the captain entered the window, something zapped the probes we had positioned around the second artifact. Besides destroying all our sensors in the immediate area, the energy beam—or whatever it was—scrambled the ship's sensors, so we haven't gotten *any* information about what's happening in the immediate vicinity of that artifact."

"Are you taking sensor readings of the area now, Mr. Sulu?"

"Negative, Mr. Spock." Sulu exhaled sharply. "Or, to be more accurate, our attempts to reestablish sensor contact have produced no information. Our readings are so garbled as to be worthless. We estimate the interference will dissipate in approximately ten minutes, sir. We are preparing a new set of probes to send down to the planet at that time."

"Very well, Mr. Sulu." Destroying the probes had not been a scenario they had considered. Since they could not detect any radiation from inside the artifact, it had seemed unlikely that something inside the object would recognize their probes. Since that assumption had been proven false, Spock realized that many—perhaps most—of their other inferences about the artifacts and their creators might be wrong. At the very least he would have to reanalyze their data until he found a way to penetrate the artifact's shields. He gestured for the men around him to give him their tricorders. "Mr. Sulu," he said, "beam me up immediately. Then commence transporting up the landing party, except for a pair of security guards, who will maintain a constant watch on this artifact from a discreet distance."

"Aye, sir." Spock had barely enough time to clip his communicator to his belt and pass the tricorder straps over his shoulder before the transporter beam took him.

Six hours later Spock was beginning to wonder why he had assumed that he could solve this problem quickly and easily. The readings from all the tricorders and sensor arrays had been fed into the computer, and he had analyzed the information so many ways that even he was losing track of the permutations. The results, though, were discouraging in their extreme lack of usable insights. Every time two groups of readings showed a correlation, the next data set contradicted it.

What would Captain Kirk do now? Spock wondered. Logic and scientific analysis were producing no discernible results; it was time for one of Kirk's leaps of intuition. The artifact operated by some disturbingly illogical rules.

As if to underscore Spock's lack of success, the bridge doors whisked open, and McCoy strolled over to the science console. "Well, Spock, how much longer are you going to twiddle your thumbs before you bother to locate Jim?"

Spock continued studying the data on the screen in front of him. "I am not 'twiddling my thumbs,' as you so picturesquely put it, Doctor. However, this device appears to have been designed by creatures nearly as irrational as you."

"I beg your pardon?" McCoy straightened, an expression of wounded dignity spreading across his face. "Since when does not thinking like some Vulcan machine make a creature irrational? Just because you're temporarily in command gives you no cause to insult those of us who don't follow your rules. The poor defenseless beings who built that artifact never did you any harm."

"I wonder at your definition of the word 'harm,' Doctor." Spock lifted his head from his viewer and fixed his most severe look on McCoy. "I submit that creating a device that causes any member of this crew to disappear constitutes 'harm' in the accepted meaning of the word. It is also a fact that our analysis has not revealed any rational pattern to the object's operation. Therefore, describing its operating principles as 'irrational' also does not constitute disparagement."

"I surrender, Spock." McCoy rolled his eyes toward the ceiling, as if seeking divine guidance for dealing with the Vulcan. "I don't suppose it occurred to you that the aliens might have designed their machinery to operate according to *their* idea of 'rational'? Unless, of course, you're going to tell me that Vulcan principles of logic are the universal standard throughout the galaxy, even for a race who died out millennia before your precious Surak was born."

"I had considered the idea, Doctor." Spock gave the computer a new set of commands. Indicators flashed red and amber in response to his orders. "A race as ancient and alien as this one probably did operate according to principles that we do not understand, although current anthropological research indicates that any sufficiently advanced civilization will converge on the Vulcan norm in matters of logic and moral principles."

"Sorry I asked." McCoy started toward the door, stopping at Uhura's station to talk with her.

After watching McCoy long enough to make sure the doctor was not coming back for another salvo, Spock turned back to his computer. As much as McCoy's irrational approach to life dismayed Spock, at times the doctor identified the essence of a situation. His questions had suggested that the artifact's shields might randomly shift frequencies. If properly done, the inevitable gaps in the shields would vary over time, making it nearly impossible to scan inside the artifacts and discover anything about their design, construction, and operation. While such protection methods were completely logical, a society that used them on their public transportation devices was not. In fact, Spock found the idea of so paranoid a society almost incomprehensible, even after his long association with humans. He wondered if the aliens were protecting themselves from outside invaders or if their security precautions had been directed against their own people.

The first ten formulas he tried failed to make any sense of the data they had recorded on the planet. As he studied the results, Spock began playing with the concept, trying to decide how he would create an absolutely invulnerable security system. Clearly, he should use a composite randomizing function, built from two or more standard formulas, so that a first-level analysis would not detect any pattern to the variations in field strength.

As he considered how many combinations existed for writing such a function, Spock realized the key question was *who* the assumed enemy was. An internal security system could be fairly simple; the ruling class would reinforce its control over the citizens by restricting education. However, if the security measures were to protect against an external threat, the security system would be extremely complex so as to defeat the enemy's best minds.

Which assumption was the most likely? Spock stared at his screen, searching for the pattern that the computer had missed. The problem, at its core, was that they did not have sufficient—or anywhere near sufficient—information on the people who had built these artifacts. They were an unknown race, and their civilization had disappeared so long ago that it no longer figured even in the legends of the successor cultures in this sector. Given that, had they encountered other civilizations? Or had these people lived and died isolated from other intelligent races, existing in the nebulous time period between the Meztoriens and the still earlier so-called orphan civilizations that some people believed had once occupied this sector of the galaxy?

The computer estimated that it would need seven hours to search the archaeological data banks for indirect references to such an ancient culture. He ordered the computer to start the search, knowing it would take too long to produce any useful information. However, since they needed a fast answer, Spock chose the simplest premise. If the security measures had been directed against the aliens' own people, the computer should be able to solve the shield frequency equations far sooner than it could locate possible references to this culture.

Spock programmed the computer to look for the simplest class of composite randomizing functions and then deliberately turned toward the main viewscreen. Built from the images from a dozen probes, an aerial view of the rolling hills around Site N4 filled the screen. Parts of the image were crisp and detailed, but other portions of the scene were degraded to a vague blur. Even after six hours they had not been able to eliminate all the residual jamming fields. "Status, Mr. Sulu."

Sulu swiveled his chair to face Spock. "No change in the last hour. We *think* there are six alien creatures near the artifact, but half of them are within the areas of maximum sensor distortion. There could be as many as eight creatures or as few as one in the areas where we're not getting good information. Another creature has gone to ground in an area of extremely broken terrain, and we're having trouble pinpointing its location."

Spock read the notations on the screen. The possible life-form readings were scattered over an area with a thirty-kilometer radius centered around the second artifact. That there were probably six aliens, and that their appearance coincided with the disappearance of the people from the *Enterprise,* suggested the two items were connected. However, the continued interference with their sensors left him with little solid information. The aliens could have been released from internal stasis inside the artifact when the humans entered the object, or they might represent a bizarre transformation of the missing people. With the poor sensor data they were getting, he didn't have sufficient information to decide what had happened. "What progress is being made with the sensors, Mr. Sulu?"

The helmsman shook his head. "We can't isolate the origin of the fields that are disrupting the sensors. It's almost as though something down there knows we're looking for it and is hiding to keep us from finding it."

"Please start a new search for the source of the disruption using that idea as your basis. Logic dictates that we choose a more complex set of assumptions once our initial premise has proven inadequate." Spock examined the viewscreen again, comparing the loci of disruption with those he had noticed earlier. The most distorted areas had moved—but was there a systematic pattern? "Mr. Sulu, please analyze how the sensor disruptions have migrated through time."

Sulu's eyes widened in surprise, then narrowed. "Right away, Mr. Spock." Scowling at his own slowness, he ordered the computer to replay the images at a high speed and reduced detail.

Three of the distorted patches had been moving since they first appeared. Evidently something on the planet was trying to keep their sensors from observing the alien life-forms. If he could decipher the design of the moving disruption fields, Spock thought, he would have a major clue to how it was that this ancient technology was more than a match for the best the Federation could send against it.

The computer took two hours to determine the equations for the shields that protected the artifacts. As Spock studied the result, making sure that *this* time they had gotten a real answer to their question, he couldn't quite suppress a flicker of satisfaction. The function was so simple that it could only mean one thing—the protection system had been designed strictly as an internal security measure. Whatever the race that had lived on this planet, it had been alone.

He turned his attention to the sensor distortions that had been giving Sulu so many problems. The first two aliens had appeared without any disturbances, but the *Enterprise* had not had probes stationed nearby when Chekov and Talika vanished into the artifact. When Kirk had led his security team through the window, the area around Site N4 had been saturated with probes and remote sensing equipment from the *Enterprise.* After the artifact had destroyed their scanners, the jamming fields appeared near the artifact, coincident with the arrival of several more aliens. The disruption was not total, and little effort seemed directed toward hiding information they already knew, but the distortions had prevented them from learning anything about the aliens.

Spock leaned back in his chair, his hands steepled in

front of him. It could hardly be an accident that the *Enterprise* was missing six people and that their best estimates showed six aliens on the planet. The question was—had Kirk and the others been transformed into these alien creatures, or had the artifact exchanged them for captives it had held in suspension for millennia? Spock wasn't sure how to communicate with the aliens once he met them, but clearly that was his next step. It was impossible to collect any information from the ship as long as the jamming fields remained in operation. He turned toward the communications station. "Lieutenant Uhura, notify Dr. Kaul that we will be transporting down to site N4 at first light in that area. Please advise him that among the personnel on the landing party I wish to include his languages expert."

"Aye, sir."

Spock resumed his study of the site. Which of the aliens should he contact? There were, of course, no guarantees that his efforts would be successful. However, it was the best option he could see on an extremely short list of ideas. He would have to search their sensor records carefully before choosing which alien to approach.

Chapter Nine

NEAR SUNSET, Kirk's host drifted to sleep, exhausted by the day's exertions. To his surprise, even though he had been a passive spectator on their strenuous trek, Kirk felt the drowsiness overtaking him as well. His last thought was that he must be more than a passenger here. There must be a physiological link between the alien's brain and his consciousness.

Later, although he was not sure how much time had passed, he became aware of random images drifting through his mind. Strange crablike beings with translucent shells floated and tumbled past the rock spire where he was sitting, watching a string of tiny moonlets rise in the east. At first he was content to observe the creatures—they called themselves the Kh!lict, Kirk realized without knowing where he had gotten the name—as they performed their aerial ballet for his benefit. The intricate patterns of their movements, carefully choreographed spirals and starbursts and other shapes he couldn't name, mesmerized him. He felt he could lose himself in their strange dance for the rest of eternity.

It was only after many minutes, in dream time, that he perceived that the inky black splotches on each dancer's carapace were tiny antigravity units. Once he spotted them, the devices stood out in stark contrast to the rainbow hues of the Kh!lict's shells, and he wondered how he had missed them before. Even in a dream, it was preposterous to believe that a crab who weighed as much as a full-grown human could fly on a world with nearly Earth–normal gravity. These creatures must have had a marvelous civilization, he thought, if they could devote even a small portion of their resources to such a beautiful art form.

As he watched the colors flicker over their carapaces, he began to see patterns that repeated themselves over and over. At first he thought the color sequences were an embellishment on the performance, with the changing hues complementing and enhancing the beauty of the dance. However, the longer he watched, the more he became convinced that the Kh!lict were singing. The color patterns and the timing of the changes formed the basis of the Kh!lict language.

Suddenly Kirk felt himself floating upward, his body drifting in lazy circles that brought him closer and closer to the other Kh!lict. Without a conscious effort on his part, he slipped into the dance as though he had been part of it all his life. In the language of movement and color, the history of his civilization unfolded around him—from the first proto–Kh!lict that emerged to conquer the land up to the mighty builders who had ruled the known universe.

The ancestral Kh!lict had been primitive creatures with few accomplishments and fewer needs. From the simple spiral movements and the neutral colors of the other dancers, Kirk sensed the distaste that the Kh!lict felt toward their beginnings; these memories survived in the Kh!lict racial consciousness only because Kh!lict hatchlings passed through a similar stage as they matured. As the history of the Kh!lict civilization unfolded, the dance became more complicated, the dancers' colors became brighter, and the tempo of the movements increased, reflecting the development of a highly complex and stratified society. To maintain the unity of their civilization, caste rules, language, and specialized motor skills were permanently imprinted on the lower brains of the young when they reached a certain size. For a brief moment Kirk was hypnotized by the terror and awe that each youth felt as his being was filled with the knowledge that bound him to the totality of his people. Shaped by that defining event, the unique elements of each Kh!lict personality emerged and were stored in the higher brain.

The interwoven patterns of color and movement carried Kirk into a universe where all things flowed from the Kh!lict totality. Stepping into the artifact had transformed his body into that of a Kh!lict, the only intelligent race imaginable to the device's programmers. At the height of their civilization, the Kh!lict had lived on over a hundred worlds. Some planets had been similar to the Kh!lict homeworld, warm and lush, filled with abundant food animals and ripe for serving Kh!lict needs. Other planets had needed much work—exterminating indigenous life-forms, reforming ecosystems, or altering climates. The dance became a flashing, swirling, twisting maelstrom recounting the glorious conquests of the Kh!lict people.

Sorting through the flood of information, Kirk realized that he owed his survival as an individual to the Kh!lict's unique bicameral brain. His human memories and knowledge were stored, separate and isolated, in the higher brain, while the lower brain contained the knowledge for functioning in a Kh!lict body and using Kh!lict technology. If he could access the information in his lower brain, he might be able to use the transit windows to return to his human form. It was a hope, and Kirk grabbed for it with the eagerness of a dying man reaching for a miracle cure.

Under the force of his excitement, his dreamscape fractured into a kaleidoscope of images that whirled and gyrated around him. He struggled to reassemble them into a coherent pattern, but before he could gather the fragments together, he was wrapped in a rising tide of mist and carried away, smothered in soft gray wool.

In the morning everything seemed clearer, more sharply defined. Kirk let his mind swim through the remnants of his dreams, sifting and culling the chaotic images for the truths beneath them. If he could master the linkage between the Kh!lict brains and find a way to cross the mental barriers at will, he could control his host body as he had in his dream. Moreover, if his guess was correct, his Kh!lict persona was little more than a housekeeping program for the creature's body. Yesterday's journey proved that rudimentary elements of personality and free will resided in the lower brain, but most Kh!lict believed those functions belonged only to their higher brains. The separation of instinct and intellect suggested that Kirk's extended flight across Careta IV's grasslands was a response to something preprogrammed into his host's lower brain.

That thought brought images of the Kh!lict justice system into Kirk's consciousness. For the most serious crimes against the Kh!lict totality, offenders were transported to a deserted location and hunted to death like animals by specially trained squads of enforcers. Given the deep understanding of crime and punishment imprinted on a young Kh!lict, Kirk decided it was almost inevitable that his host would panic at its unfamiliar surroundings. Deprived of direction from the higher brain, the Kh!lict mind had followed instructions encoded into the memories of its people two hundred thousand years ago.

With a start Kirk realized how many ways his personality went against the Kh!lict norm. All Kh!lict males were juveniles, and the Kh!lict matriarchs did not permit any male who challenged their authority to survive. The artifact would not contain an appropriate template for a dominant male and had apparently settled on the closest available model—a convicted felon. It was an unsettling thought, but it at least explained his circumstances.

His next step, Kirk decided, was to test his new insights by convincing his host to return to the transit frame. Although he still could not recognize the signs of physical discomfort in his new body, Kirk doubted that the Kh!lict had any greater tolerance for remaining motionless for hours than humans did. That meant his crablike body, which had been jammed into its hiding place for almost eighteen hours, was long overdue for some attention. He remembered seeing a weak trickle of water in the creek bed they had left to enter this narrow canyon. That would solve the first of his worries, but he had no idea what to do about food. Presumably his lower brain knew what he should eat, but that didn't mean he could find anything edible. His host's reactions told Kirk that Careta IV had changed so much that the computer that had created him no longer carried information that fit the conditions on the planet. From that alone Kirk knew the Kh!lict had died out a very long time ago.

Getting water would be the first test of whether he could order the Kh!lict body to do his bidding. If survival skills had been programmed into his lower brain, his host should have moved during the night, letting the darkness protect him while he got water, scouted for food, and made his hideaway more secure. That the alien had not done so told Kirk two things. First, his host was too young to appreciate the benefits of surviving at any cost and against all odds. Second, the information preprogrammed into the Kh!lict brains did not include such basic tactical skills as how to avoid surveillance and capture by one's enemies.

As he thought about his body's needs, Kirk became aware of a dry, chalky taste in his mouth. A feeling of satisfaction swept through him. He had been right, then, to assume that the Kh!lict lower brain mediated such activities without intervention of the higher thought processes. His next job was to take control from his host's instincts.

With the image of a refreshing drink of water firmly in mind, Kirk tried to move from his hiding hole. At first there was no response, and he began to wonder if he could overrule the deeply imprinted programming that constrained the Kh!lict lower brain. If a human had been trapped so long, he would have raced for water at the first opportunity. Kirk doubted that basic physiology would ever change so much that a thirsty creature would refuse a drink unless something was suppressing its survival instincts.

On the other hand, perhaps he had been here for so long that the body was unable to move. Considering how much warmer Careta IV had been when the Kh!lict ruled the planet, perhaps his host's physiology was unable to cope with the colder temperatures. If that was the problem, if he had been immobile for so long that his muscles had locked in their present position from the cold, then it would take extra work to escape from this rocky trap.

Remembering what it felt like when his arm fell asleep, Kirk shuddered at the idea of having pins and needles in eight legs at the same time. However, he could not let that keep him here until his host's body died of starvation or dehydration. Instead he returned to his experiment of the previous afternoon, concentrating on bringing his pincers together and slowly lifting an appendage to eye level.

This time he got a response, although the faint scritch of chitin-analog against rock as he twitched one appendage was *not* what he had hoped for. At that rate he would be there all day just trying to unlock his joints and limber up his muscles. He had envisioned a quick dash back to the artifact, followed by five minutes to readjust the equipment so that he would emerge from the window as he had started—James T. Kirk, human. Now, at the very least, his timetable would need serious revisions.

Kirk threw himself into mastering his Kh!lict body, imposing his will on nerves and muscles paralyzed by the long inactivity. Between fighting the basic Kh!lict physiology, which was so ill adapted to Careta IV's present climate, and wrestling with his ignorance of how to control the alien body, his progress was slow. It seemed a hopeless task to break down the barriers between his consciousness and the Kh!lict mind that shared the body with him. After fifteen minutes he could still move only one set of pincers or bend one joint, and he was beginning to fear he was trapped. He kept trying, knowing it was the only way he could escape, and finally his perseverance was rewarded. Extending one of his legs beyond the edge of the rock slab, he drew half a circle in the air, flexing and bending every joint through its full range of motion.

Progress came more quickly after that. Apparently his muscles needed to reach a critical internal temperature before they would work, one more proof that the Kh!lict had evolved in a much warmer climate. Once he could move one appendage, he loosened the others up quickly. With relief Kirk dragged his Kh!lict body from beneath the slab of rock and struggled to stand. His legs felt wobbly and uncertain, reminding him of a colt he had seen on his grandmother's farm when he was a boy.

I wonder if this is what that horse felt like? he thought as he took his first step. Only the fact that he had moved just two of his eight legs kept him from falling on his face. Why was he so shaky? Hunger? Thirst? The aftereffects of the long night? Whatever the cause, he couldn't wait for someone to rescue him. Presumably Spock would be looking for Kirk and the security men who had been with him, but the Vulcan would not be expecting to find his captain in Kirk's present condition. The alien life-forms would attract attention from the *Enterprise*'s search teams, but the crew wouldn't know who they were. They would probably assume they were an indigenous species not detected in their initial survey of the planet. It was up to Kirk to locate the search party and tell them what had happened.

He tried to walk again, going slowly and checking his balance with every stride. Again, as with his initial efforts to move, there seemed to be a critical point that he had to reach. In this case, he decided as he struggled over an unstable cone of loose rock, the difficulty was establishing control over the Kh!lict body. Yesterday's flight, directed by his lower brain, had occurred without any input or intervention from his conscious mind. Now, however, Kirk was trying to command the alien body against its instincts, and that required breaking through two sets of mental barriers to establish links between the Kh!lict's upper and lower brains that had not been present before. He was, in essence, training this body to do things no Kh!lict had ever dreamed of doing.

By the time he reached the mouth of the narrow

canyon, Kirk felt reasonably confident of his ability to manage the Kh!lict body. He was not up to fighting off a pack of Careta's master predators, whatever they had been, nor was he sure he could negotiate the steeply broken country that his host had clambered over yesterday. However, if he stuck with cross-country hiking and returned to the artifact as quickly as possible, he knew he could manage.

The stream was muddy and unappealing, but Kirk decided he didn't have much choice for available drinking water. Before he could act on the thought, his lower brain took over, bending his knees until his jaws were resting below the water. The water was tepid and bitter from dissolved minerals, but his sediment filters removed most of the suspended grit and clay. He allowed his body to drink until it could hold no more water.

Next he needed to get back to the artifact. Kirk looked around, assessing the canyon for routes to the uplands above. In his human form he might have been able to scale the steep, crumbling rock faces, although any experienced climber knew that it was foolhardy to risk your life on such unreliable surfaces unless your alternative was certain death. Trying it now, in an alien body over which he held only tenuous control, seemed uncomfortably close to suicide.

Reluctantly he started downstream, away from his goal. Somewhere the canyon walls would flatten out, and he could climb up onto the surrounding hills. As he searched for a way out of the canyon, he could feel the tension building in his lower brain. The Kh!lict programming was still functioning, and his lower brain believed the enforcers would spring up from behind every boulder.

As he moved along, searching for a route out of the canyon, Kirk considered what he had learned about the Kh!lict and their technology. He could not risk any more of his crew on this planet, he concluded. They had no way to recognize how dangerous a Kh!lict artifact might be until someone fell victim to the alien technology. As soon as he was changed back into his human form, the *Enterprise* was leaving Careta IV. It went against his usual desire to learn everything possible despite the risks. However, he felt a growing uneasiness about remaining here, and although he could not put his reasoning into words, he knew his conclusions were based on information he had learned from his Kh!lict host.

Kirk was still debating his decision to leave Careta when he reached a break in the canyon walls. A huge section of the cliff face had slumped into the canyon, forming a hummocky mound of rubble. Three smaller landslides disfigured the scar left by the primary slump; one of them was large enough to make a ramp that led almost to the rim of the canyon. Kirk clambered up the landslide, eager to escape to the freedom of the hilltops. The climb was easy going until he reached the canyon wall.

The Kh!lict form had not been designed for rock climbing, Kirk thought as he surveyed the last ten meters of cliff that separated him from his goal. The jointed and fissured rock offered dozens of hand- and footholds. In his human form he would have been over the top in less than a minute, but he had no idea how to clench his pincers inside a crack to anchor himself while climbing that vertical rock face. The smooth, inflexible shell covering his digits more than offset any advantage he might have gained from the extra limbs.

Still, there had to be a way to make the climb, and Kirk settled down to find it. In over an hour of walking, this was the first place where he had had the slightest chance of escaping the canyon, and it looked like it might be a lot longer before he found another place. He had no idea how far his host had come after descending into the canyon yesterday, but Kirk's impression was that he had a long way to go before he reached that spot. He could easily waste a lot of precious time exploring dead-end escape routes from this canyon. Spurred on by that thought, Kirk picked the most promising spot and wedged his pincer into a crack.

Chapter Ten

A SHARP WIND was blowing out of the east as the *Enterprise*'s landing party materialized on the hill at Site N4. Spock moved away from the beam-down point and began scanning the area. The security men fanned out, searching for clues that the remote sensors had missed. The hum of the transporter signaled the arrival of the science personnel from the *Enterprise*'s crew and from Kaul's archaeology team. The scientists began examining the artifact and the area around it immediately.

Signaling to a security guard to accompany him, Spock started downhill along a band of flattened grass. His night's work—analyzing the sensor data to confirm the presence of six aliens in the area—had turned up no definitive information about the crablike creatures or where they had come from. Even if he assumed that the artifacts had transformed the missing people into the image of their creators, he had found nothing to tell him which of the creatures was Kirk. In the end, Spock had decided to contact the individual closest to the artifact to learn if he could communicate with the aliens. After that he would attempt to contact the being who was hiding in the canyonlands to the northwest of the artifact in the hope that it was Kirk. Although the justification for this decision—that the captain would react differently than the rest of the crew—was weak, he had not found a better reason for choosing which alien to contact.

He started off, swinging his tricorder in wide sweeps to record his surroundings. One of the aliens was over the first hill, moving in slow, random zigzags that had kept it in the vicinity of the artifact. Spock and the guard with him approached the alien cautiously, giving it plenty of time to see them coming. At first it gave no indication that it saw them. Instead it continued to amble along as though it were the only living thing on the planet.

"Fascinating," Spock murmured, watching how the alien's eyes rotated on their stalks. "It appears to be looking past us as though we are not here."

"But it's looking straight at us," the guard replied. "Each eye is sweeping out a 180-degree arc, with overlap in the center to allow stereoscopic vision."

"That is correct." If his deductions about the aliens were correct, the human inside this body should be doing everything to attract his attention by now. This apparent indifference was not natural. "Ensign, cover me while I move in closer."

"Yes, Mr. Spock."

The guard trained his phaser on the alien while Spock moved beside it. Even this failed to produce a response until he stepped directly into the creature's path. Then, inexplicably, it froze, its limbs locking beneath it. Spock prodded its carapace and scanned it with his tricorder, but the alien remained motionless. Finally Spock reached for his communicator. "Spock to *Enterprise*. Lock on to the alien who is at these coordinates and beam it aboard."

He stepped back from the alien, and the transporter effect coalesced around it, dissolving the creature into golden sparkles. Spock waited for the ship to request additional instructions, but his communicator remained silent. A human would have been demanding answers, he knew, using the comparison to keep his curiosity at bay. Finally the instrument chirped to life. "Mr. Spock, we had a wee problem with that beastie you had us transport up. It went berserk the moment the transporter released it, and it cut up Mr. Kyle fair bad before we could hit it with our phasers."

"I presume Dr. McCoy will be able to tend to Mr. Kyle's injuries. What is the status of the alien?"

"Aye, the doctor will be having no problem with a few scrapes and gouges, Mr. Spock. But the critter dinna take too kindly to our phasers. It's dead, sir."

"Mr. Scott, your phasers should have been on stun setting." The alien's death, and its reaction to being transported, meant they would have to proceed with even greater caution than he had originally assumed. "We were hoping to study that alien alive in order to learn how to communicate with it."

An exasperated sigh came through his communicator. "The weapons *were* on stun setting, Mr. Spock. Unfortunately, we failed to 'communicate' what that meant to our 'guest.'"

"I see." Stun setting should not have been lethal to any being the size of the one they had beamed to the *Enterprise*. Why was the alien dead? He had better hope that his original deduction—that this alien was not the captain—was correct. By any reasonable set of assumptions, the creature should not be dead. "Have Dr. McCoy perform an autopsy on the alien as soon as possible. Perhaps he will find some clue that will tell us what happened."

"Aye, sir. *Enterprise* out."

Spock returned his communicator to his belt and started across the hillside to look for clues. The grass whispered and rustled beneath his boots. Although the vegetation ranged through the light and medium tones of grayish-green, it seemed dry and unhealthy, as though it found this cold and empty planet as hostile as the *Enterprise*'s crew had.

Spock shook his head, wondering where that thought had come from. True, the star in this solar system had been fading for millennia; such things were inevitable, and it was illogical to ascribe any emotional value to the event. Besides, the death of a star like the one in the Caretian system was a slow process, and the native plants and animals had had plenty of time to evolve with the changing climate.

Halfway around the hill, the display on Spock's tricorder began flashing random patterns. He adjusted the controls, trying to isolate the source of the disruption. Instead the display flickered more violently. Spock moved off the swath of flattened grass and continued to scan the area. The disturbance built, spreading until the air seemed to vibrate around him. A sound like the buzzing of a swarm of angry hornets enveloped him, starting softly and crescendoing to a deafening tumult. He pressed his hands over his ears to block out the noise, but it grew louder. The air turned massive and viscous with the weight of the sound, and Spock had to fight to drag the thick air into his lungs. Each step required a superhuman effort, as though his feet were encased in lead. Then suddenly the world tilted, and the ground rushed upward to meet his face.

Spock stirred and opened one eye cautiously. McCoy's face swam into focus, with color and detail spreading outward from his nose to encompass the worried look in his blue eyes and the concerned frown that wrinkled his forehead. With an effort Spock forced his other eyelid open. The soft humming and chirping of the medical diagnostic equipment told him he was in sickbay. He rolled onto his side and tried to sit up.

McCoy pushed him back onto the bed. "Not so fast, Spock. You fainted down there, and I'm going to know why before I let you out of that bed."

This time, knowing the move McCoy would use to restrain him, Spock ducked under the doctor's arm and sat up. The room was quiet and normal, with only the expected equipment noises in the background. No intrusive buzzing threatened to overwhelm him. Whatever had happened on the planet had been deliberate, an attack aimed at preventing him from investigating the artifact and the mysterious aliens. "I presume your instruments tell you that there is nothing wrong with me."

"Yes, dammit! You fall on your face down there, and this blasted equipment pretends that everything is normal." McCoy directed a poisonous glare at the diagnostics panel. "As if anything is normal about your mixed-up physiology."

"Your concern is noted, Doctor." Spock pushed himself to his feet, checking for any residual effects of the attack. He felt somewhat light-headed, as though an intruder in the back of his mind was waiting to attack again the moment he returned to the planet. Closing his eyes, he concentrated on the sensation, isolated it, and built a wall around it. Next time he would not underestimate the artifact's ability to bring novel weapons to bear against the *Enterprise*'s crew. "However, there is no need for you to exert yourself further on my behalf."

"Just what is that supposed to mean?" McCoy scowled, annoyed that Spock's Vulcan demeanor had never wavered. "I thought that you said that Vulcans never faint."

For a moment Spock stared at the doctor, one eyebrow raised. McCoy, who refused to learn the operating instructions for the newest equipment Starfleet issued him, could remember the most trivial facts when they served to score him points in an argument. When he saw that the doctor was winding up for a scathing denunciation of Vulcan inconsistencies and self-deception, Spock replied, "You are correct, Doctor. Vulcans never faint. Fainting is a human response to strong emotional stimuli. However, Vulcans can be rendered unconscious by virulent disease organisms or by the exercise of external agencies."

"Why, you pointy-eared—" McCoy stopped, blinking rapidly. His forehead wrinkled with a puzzled frown. "What did you say? What do you call that total collapse you experienced down on the planet?"

"I was rendered unconscious by the efforts of an external agency." Spock started for the door, knowing that McCoy would follow, if only to satisfy his curiosity. The door whisked open, and Spock started for the turbolift.

McCoy fell into step beside him. "Would you care to translate that into plain English, Spock?"

The turbolift door opened, and Spock stepped inside. "Bridge."

"Spock!" McCoy's tone was sharp with exasperation. "As your doctor, I want an explanation. Otherwise I'm declaring you unfit for duty until you submit to a complete physical."

Spock heaved a sigh. "Very well, Doctor. Something attacked me. It started as a faint buzzing noise, and the sound grew louder until it was a tangible force beating against me."

"No one else reported any such attacks." McCoy

glared at the Vulcan, daring him to stick to his story. "Why should you be the only one affected?"

"That, Doctor, is a very good question." Spock subjected McCoy to his most impassive stare, noticing the doctor's astonishment at the implied compliment. "I will entertain suggestions for determining the solution to that problem, since it may be a critical issue in discovering how the artifact functions. Perhaps Vulcans are more susceptible to its attacks than humans, or other factors may be at work. To date we have been unable to obtain any meaningful information on this technology, nor have we ascertained anything of importance about the beings who created it."

McCoy faced Spock, his expression incredulous. "And you're asking *my* help in solving this mystery?"

"At this point, Doctor, I would welcome any assistance, no matter how unlikely the source. We must learn what has happened to the captain and effect a rescue. We are at a singular disadvantage until we can discover how to operate the alien devices. I presume your autopsy results will give us some fascinating data to work with."

"No doubt they will, Spock, when I've gotten back the results of the lab tests." McCoy bounced on his toes, his chin thrust out at a truculent angle. "But as you well know, these things take a certain amount of time, no matter who needs the answers."

"I am all too aware of that, Doctor." The turbolift door opened, sparing him the need for further reply. Spock headed for the science station. Behind him the turbolift doors whished shut on McCoy's request to return to sickbay. Sulu, in the command chair, started to rise, but Spock signaled for him to remain seated. "As you were, Mr. Sulu. Status report."

"No change since you were beamed aboard, Mr.

Spock. Our security people have combed the area looking for clues to what attacked you. Three people reported momentary distortions in their tricorder readings, but the effect didn't last long enough for us to isolate it. Of the remaining aliens on the planet, four are approximately where they have been for the last twelve hours. The alien that was hiding in the canyonlands is moving, but we don't know why."

"Continue monitoring the aliens, Mr. Sulu. I shall analyze the tricorder and sensor readings to determine what I can about the force that attacked me." He slid into his chair, letting the familiar contours support his body. The sensation was so familiar, so expected, that for a moment he forgot the import of the last day's events. Solving the alien technology was a puzzle, an intellectual challenge of the type at which he excelled.

When Spock began reviewing the scanner data, the problem lost its abstract beauty and became again a matter of personal urgency. What had he been about to discover that had triggered the attack against him? How had he been isolated and rendered unconscious without the attack affecting the security guard with him? And, last but not least, what *had* happened to the captain? He knew the answers had to be hidden in the mass of data they had collected, but the noise-to-signal ratio was so high that they had not been able to glean any worthwhile clues from their sensor readings. What new techniques could they use to see through the distortions?

Three hours and countless dead ends later, Spock wondered what they had missed. The sensor logs contained more information than he needed, but he could not reduce the data to anything useful. Solving the randomizer function for the transportation win-

dows' shields should have let him penetrate the secrets
of the alien technology, but instead his results were
showing another layer of security measures that surrounded the internal mechanisms of the alien machinery. It was as if something was predicting his next
move and scrambling the data to make his analysis
worthless. Two days ago he would have dismissed that
idea as irrational. However, after spending so many
hours in fruitless research, Spock began wondering if
the artifacts' defensive system changed its tactics
according to its predictions of how someone would
analyze the data. Such a system would require a
pulsed scrambler beam to keep jumbling the data. The
effort Spock had put into unraveling this problem
implied that the aliens had used extremely sophisticated security measures. He ordered the computer to
analyze how such a defensive system would operate.

"Mr. Spock, look at this!" Excitement sharpened
Sulu's tone. Faces turned toward the main viewscreen,
which showed the wavering shape of a crablike creature attempting to scale the ten-meter scarp at the top
of a landslide. Silence gripped the bridge, broken only
by the chirps and whispered reports of various monitors.

The crablike body was not suited for climbing, yet
the creature chose its handholds with a caution that
spoke of much practice. Could it be Captain Kirk?
Spock thought, remembering how many times the
captain had asked him to go rock climbing. Spock had
always refused, citing the press of work or professional commitments as reasons not to go. In truth, he
could see no value to the sport. Humans had an
inordinate need to pit themselves against every haz-
ard the universe offered them, and they seemed to get
a thrill out of the danger. Spock found neither motivation compelling, nor could he find much to interest

him when he observed from a safe distance. However, watching the crablike being attempt to scale a cliff that it was in no way equipped to climb convinced Spock that Kirk was trapped inside the body of that alien.

"Mr. Sulu, I will need a squad of security men in fifteen minutes. We are beaming down to contact that alien at our earliest opportunity." He started to turn away, then realized he was overlooking the obvious— if he wanted to contact the alien, the most important member of his landing team was Dr. Kaul's language expert. "Also give our regards to Dr. Kaul and request the assistance of Nadia Hernandez. If we are going to talk to that alien, let us hope that she can translate what it says for us."

"Yes, sir."

McCoy marched onto the bridge and slapped a data tape onto Spock's console. "Preliminary autopsy report, just in case you're planning to rush back to that planet any time soon."

"Thank you, Doctor." Spock dropped the tape in a slot, hoping it would explain these creatures for him. He could have skimmed through the material faster on his own, but McCoy seemed determined to add a verbal commentary.

"Visually they look like giant king crabs, even though they're missing one set of legs. Also, the external ornamentation is completely different from anything that ever developed on Earth, and the claw structures are a strange mixture of delicate manipulator, walking surface, and lethal weapon." McCoy's shrug was eloquent with frustration. "For that matter, the skeletal structures and the ligament attachments in the limbs are unique to these creatures."

"I had noticed those particular differences, Doctor. The skeletal bracing and the tendon linkages give these creatures considerable striking power in their limbs." Spock slowed that section of the tape, confirming that the heavy exoskeleton on the limbs, ornamented in places with triangular spikes, had evolved as a fighting weapon.

"And did you notice that feeding nozzle, Spock? I don't think these boys had particularly elegant table manners."

"You may be right, Doctor." The creature had three triangular teeth that could have severed the spinal cord of a small animal or broken the carapace of an Earth–normal crab. However, instead of grinding or shearing teeth to break up its prey, the creature had a long, retractile proboscis with a serrated edge for piercing its victim's flesh.

"You could get a hell of a mosquito bite from that creature." Shaking his head, McCoy left Spock to examine the rest of the report.

By the time the landing party was assembled, the crablike being had almost reached the top of the cliff. Spock took one last look at the viewscreen and ordered his team to beam down out of sight near the top of the cliff. After their results with the alien they had beamed aboard the *Enterprise,* Spock was taking no chances. Even if Kirk was inside the creature's body, he would not expect a group from the *Enterprise* to greet him as he crawled the last centimeters over the lip of the canyon. It would be far better to remain hidden until he was clear of the unstable rim.

Spock and five security guards materialized about thirty meters downslope from where the alien would crest the cliff. The vegetation was sparse and dry, mostly ragged clumps of grass that rattled in the breeze. Even this close to midday, the air was cold, and Spock knew he would not be able to keep his people stationary for long. The wind brought the chill factor down to dangerous levels. Although their protective clothing helped, the humans needed to move around to generate enough body heat to prevent hypothermia.

The hum of the transporter told Spock that Hernandez and five more security men had materialized behind them. He signaled to them to fan out and crouch behind any convenient tuft of grass. Logic suggested that if Kirk controlled the crablike being, he would head uphill, away from their current position. However, Spock wanted the landing party to be as inconspicuous as possible, in case his assumptions were wrong.

Even after McCoy's autopsy report and after studying the probe records for hours, Spock found the first sight of the alien unsettling, like a dull toothache that did not seem to belong to any one tooth. Except for its size, the alien resembled a king crab, with an outsized body perched on top of long, stout, segmented legs. The carapace was translucent but blotched with purples and blues that shifted from moment to moment. The eyes were similar to human eyes, with central pupils surrounded by magenta irises, but they were mounted on stalks that allowed them to swivel independently. The terminal claws on each leg were closed into footlike units for walking, but the individual digits were capable of surprisingly delicate manipulation. Spock allowed himself a moment's admiration at the elegance and efficiency of the anatomical design.

The creature pulled itself over the edge of the cliff and staggered to its feet. For a moment it just looked around, its color shifting to a deeper, more uniform blue. It pivoted its body back and forth, as if scouting out the terrain, but did not notice the *Enterprise*'s landing party. Its examination finished, it turned away from the humans and started uphill, moving at a deliberate pace.

Spock extrapolated its heading. Unless he completely misjudged the alien's intentions, it was headed toward the artifact. He stood and followed the alien, gauging his speed to allow himself to overtake it slowly. The rest of the landing party spread across the hillside and followed him at a cautious distance. Spock was certain that the creature's eight-legged locomotion could attain far greater speeds than he was capable of reaching, if the alien desired. However, if his deductions were correct, Spock expected the alien to stop when it realized it was being followed.

Five minutes later it was clear that he had missed a critical factor in his analysis. Although he had partially closed the gap, the alien had increased its speed and showed no sign it had noticed him. Behind him Spock heard several of the security men struggling to breathe in the oxygen-poor air. Spock could continue the chase for several hours, although long exposure to the Earth-normal environment on the *Enterprise* had lessened his tolerance for such conditions. However, he did not wish to confront the alien alone, without the support of his security men. He hoped that their tricorders would record vital information about the meeting, but especially after the violent reaction of the creature they had beamed aboard the *Enterprise*, he wanted their phasers for safety. The creature might decide he was a gourmet meal.

Spock stopped to let the others join him. While he waited he pulled out his communicator. "Spock to *Enterprise.* Twelve to beam up, with the first contingent returning to the planet immediately. We wish to materialize one hundred meters uphill of the alien in a location where he cannot miss us."

"Aye, sir," came the reply. Spock selected four guards and Hernandez to accompany him. *This had better work,* he thought as the transporter beam formed around him. Because if it didn't, he did not know what his next course of action would be.

Chapter Eleven

KIRK DRAGGED HIS Kh!lict body over the top of the cliff. How he had made the last meter and a half, he wasn't sure, but somehow the tenuous claw holds had held his weight. Twice he had been positive that the rock was too weak, that it would crumble away from his outspread pincers before he could anchor himself in a more stable fissure. However, his luck had held, and he pushed himself over the rim even as he heard the rock fragments from his lowest claw hold cascading downward and bouncing off the rubble at the foot of the cliff.

He gave himself a moment to collect his wits after the climb. The Kh!lict lower brain, he sensed, was almost incapacitated from terror at what he had forced his body to do. When he had started the climb, the concept of scaling a vertical rock wall had been so alien to the Kh!lict mind-set that Kirk had negotiated the first meter or so before his lower brain had realized what he was doing. By then innate caution and the need for survival had forced the lower brain to leave Kirk in control, even though the Kh!lict's inborn instincts screamed against the unnatural act Kirk was forcing his body to perform.

Dragging himself away from the treacherous rim, Kirk stumbled to his feet. His legs were dangerously unsteady, partly from the stress of the climb, an activity for which the Kh!lict form was singularly unsuited, and partly from the physiological response of forcing the Kh!lict lower brain into conflict with its own programming. The best thing for this internal warfare, Kirk decided, was to keep his body moving, to use the familiar patterns of walking and scouting his surroundings to subdue the conflict between his human memories and consciousness and his alien physiology and instincts.

He checked the area for signs that the enforcers had been there. *Enforcers?* After a moment's confusion, Kirk realized the Kh!lict had originated that thought. His host was still convinced that his society's equivalent of the Gestapo was after him. The slope below him was dotted with scraggly clumps of grass and misshapen, odd-colored boulders, but there was nothing that could hide a Kh!lict large enough to hurt him. With a feeling of profound relief, he turned uphill and set out at a measured pace.

After a few minutes, as his host's brain decided that no enforcers—or any other Kh!lict—were in the area, it began to relax and to move his legs with greater coordination. To Kirk's relief, he doubled his speed, although he was heading uphill. The faster he could travel, the sooner he would reach the artifact and could return to his normal form.

When the bipedal creatures appeared directly before him, the Kh!lict brain seized with terror. His limbs froze in midstride, and momentum carried his body forward, pitching him ignominiously to the ground at Spock's feet. Mortified at this betrayal, Kirk struggled to reassert control over his body. It was like trying to unravel a pile of wet spaghetti. His appendages had snarled together, and his attempts to regain his feet produced random tremors that did nothing to improve the situation.

"Fascinating," Spock said, studying his tricorder readings with the familiar cocked eyebrow. "This creature's physiology shows it to be totally unrelated to any known species in the galaxy."

"I beg your pardon, Mr. Spock?" Hernandez stepped forward with a second tricorder. "Dr. McCoy's autopsy showed the bioparameters were similar to the dominant forms in the Selevai system."

"That's an interesting suggestion, Dr. Hernandez." Spock changed his tricorder settings. "We should consider the possibility that these creatures evolved in that sector, although the readings I am getting now clearly show this group of life-forms to have developed along independent lines for the last several hundred thousand years. If our estimations of the age of these ruins are correct, it is conceivable that they diverged far enough in the past to account for the large genetic discrepancies."

Hernandez nodded. "That would be consistent with our other findings. It's also probable that the groups who migrated from the home planet underwent genetic manipulation to survive the natural dangers of their new homes."

"I will analyze that hypothesis when we return to the ship. For the moment we must concern ourselves with why this creature is here now when our earlier scans of the planet revealed no large indigenous life-forms." Spock circled around Kirk, his tricorder clicking and whirring.

Kirk struggled to regain his feet but discovered that his Kh!lict brain had retreated from the reality facing it. His coordination, his motor functions—in fact, every physical action that might come under conscious direction from one of his brains—had been completely shut off. Struggling to remain calm, Kirk tried to tap into his Kh!lict awareness to discover the cause of this sudden catatonia.

At first the random images and chaotic swirls of color that surged through his mind reminded him of the Kelvás, the abstract art of Denaya 4. The rigid and stylized patterns of the Kelvás required a detailed knowledge of Denaya's culture and history in order to interpret the multiple layers of symbols incorporated in each design. And as if that wasn't enough, different combinations of symbols or different colors used together changed the meaning of the basic pattern. On his first visit to the planet, Kirk had tried to learn enough to avoid offending his hosts, but despite his best efforts, he had never been able to remember more than a few of the basic modulations.

Now, to his horror, he realized that the bright abstract images filling his mind represented the Kh!lict language. Somehow, if he was to interpret the store of information encoded in his host's brain, he would have to learn the distinctions between the varying shades and patterns. Humans processed massive amounts of visual information in their daily lives, but Kirk didn't think it was an accident that their most basic communications came through sound rather than from vision. Vision could be fooled so many ways, by changing light intensity or wavelength, that a language based on color and shape seemed doomed from the start. Still, if his impressions were correct, that was exactly what the Kh!lict had had.

He relaxed and let the patterns flow through his

mind, trying to follow the emotions that accompanied them. At first fear and confusion excluded everything else. The appearance of the *Enterprise*'s landing party had deeply disturbed the alien. As the thoughts repeated themselves, Kirk deciphered the gist of how the crablike aliens viewed the world.

The Kh!lict had evolved many grand cycles of eights ago, when Careta IV was a far different world. They considered themselves the pinnacle of life, the goal toward which the universe had been striving since its hatching. As they developed space flight and moved outward from their homeworld, their discoveries confirmed their belief in their superiority and uniqueness. Many planets in the sector had evolved life, but nowhere did the Kh!lict recognize organisms with even incipient intelligence. Any beings that interfered with their expansion or contradicted their worldview were thoroughly and ruthlessly exterminated. Kirk tried to examine that last thought in more detail, but the uncontrolled flood of Kh!lict history from his lower brain swept it aside. The further the Kh!lict explored, the more firmly they came to believe in their natural right to dominate all they encountered. That they were the only intelligent race that had ever evolved—or that ever *would* evolve—became the foundation of their collective view of the universe.

Kirk allowed himself a moment's amusement as he imagined what Spock's appearance would have done to a Kh!lict in its full minds. As it was, his host had been thrown into panic by the appearance of a lower life-form that controlled technological devices. Worse, the design of Spock's equipment implied a non-Kh!lict origin. Following that thought to its logical conclusion forced Kirk's host into an untenable position: It must either reject what it saw or deny the racial wisdom of its people.

Briefly Kirk felt sorry for the Kh!lict, even though the body he occupied was an artificial construct produced by the aliens' matter transport system. The artifact had reproduced the instincts and the racial memories of a genuine Kh!lict so well that it was hard not to think of his host as an authentic member of that long-dead race. With a surge of horror, he realized the implications of that thought.

The Kh!lict mind-set was so fiercely xenophobic that Kirk could barely comprehend the intensity of its faith. Even the most unreasonable beings the Federation had encountered conceded the possibility of other intelligent races, although a few granted outsiders no more credit than humans awarded their dogs. To deny that other intelligent beings *could* exist, even when staring one in the face, went beyond the most outrageous limits ever conjectured by anyone in the Federation. If Kirk had needed proof, this one fact was sufficient to tell him how isolated—and how fanatically closed-minded—the Kh!lict had been.

That knowledge, however, did nothing to solve his current problem. He had been trying to return to the artifact to contact Spock, and miraculously, Spock had found him. Unfortunately, his Kh!lict body, with its preprogrammed assumptions of how the universe worked, was not willing to let him communicate with the Vulcan. How could he catch Spock's attention before he decided that he had learned enough about the new life-form confronting him? How had the Kh!lict communicated with each other? And how could he convince the Kh!lict lower brain that the *Enterprise*'s crew was his own kind and that he needed to talk to them?

Kirk felt inspiration strike. Fighting to contain his growing sense of urgency, he concentrated on the thought that Spock was one of his own. Hot, angry zigzags of red and black—powerful symbols of rejection and denial—surged through his brain. The Kh!lict lower brain would not yield its prejudices so quickly.

"Fascinating!" Spock said, his eyebrow rising higher. "The colors and patterns on the carapace are changing with a rapidity that suggests this is a normal function of these creatures. However, there are only a limited number of uses in nature for such ostentatious displays." He ran his tricorder over Kirk's shell, with the sensors only a few millimeters above the surface.

Communication! Kirk thought with all the intensity he could muster. With a mind meld Spock could read his mind, but he would not necessarily be looking for his captain inside the crablike alien. Also, Kirk was not sure if the physiology of the Kh!lict brain permitted telepathic transmission. It didn't seem like a safe bet, and even if Spock had deduced what had happened, the Vulcan would begin to doubt his reasoning if he failed to make contact soon. Kirk had to establish communications quickly.

He concentrated on talking to Spock and explaining to him who and what the Kh!lict were. A soothing pattern of interwoven blues and greens washed across his vision. The Kh!lict word for "communication"? Kirk wondered. Even if it was and even if his carapace was transmitting the same motif, he had no way to translate that particular combination of shape and color for Spock. He was only guessing at the meanings himself, based on his dominant thoughts when each shape/color cluster appeared in his mind. With another Kh!lict or another human in a Kh!lict body, he might be able to communicate, but without a partner who shared his understanding of the language, he could not hope to exchange enough information to solve his problem. Adapting the Kh!lict language so he could contact Spock was impossible. The Kh!lict system of projecting shapes and colors on their translucent shells and the deep-seated imprinting of their language on their lower brains defeated his desire to write English letters on his shell for Spock to read. He needed a different approach.

Kirk took inventory of the Kh!lict's physical limitations. Surprised that he had not noticed sooner, he realized that he had no vocal apparatus and could not produce any sounds whatsoever. The Kh!lict had modified their visual language of color and form by clicking their claws in rigidly formalized patterns. It wasn't much, but it was worth a try.

Kirk tried to lift his foreleg, but nothing happened. A flare of brilliant white, as hot as his anger when he realized the totality of his failure, washed across Kirk's vision. The instinctual programming of his body would not allow him to do anything that ran counter to the Kh!lict's hard-wired directives. At the moment his body was frozen by the catatonia that had seized the Kh!lict when the landing party first appeared, and his host was trying very hard to reject Spock as a hallucination. How could he make the alien's instincts work *for* him rather than fighting every attempt to contact his crew?

"Most creatures with such conspicuous displays use them to enhance their desirability to potential mates," Hernandez was saying. "The shifting color patterns are usually a form of sexual display, although I am at a loss to see how that works for our current subject."

"An interesting hypothesis, Dr. Hernandez. However, I would recommend that you speculate less freely on matters of motivation until we have determined the basic physiology of these creatures." Spock ran his tricorder over Kirk's head and throat, concentrating on the areas where the vocal apparatus was found in most creatures.

"I beg your pardon, Mr. Spock?" Hernandez was a small woman with an aggressive, determined manner, but at the moment a nervous frown wrinkled her forehead.

Spock looked up from his tricorder screen. A sharp gust of wind ruffled his bangs before moving on to other mischief. "I presume that your tricorder reports no evidence of any vocal apparatus capable of reproducing a spoken language."

"Yes, but Dr. McCoy's autopsy report implied that we were dealing with an individual abnormality in the alien he autopsied." After a moment's delay, the light dawned for her. "You mean none of these creatures has the capability of producing a spoken language?"

"That covers the facts we have observed so far, Doctor. Have you discovered any relevant information that we have omitted from our analysis?" Spock circled Kirk, studying the Kh!lict anatomy.

A sense of relief, which washed his mind with a soft apricot haze, swept through Kirk. Spock had deduced how the Kh!lict communications system worked. That meant he had only to manipulate the alien's physiology long enough to tell Spock what had happened to him. With the colors and patterns being controlled by the Kh!lict lower brain, his prospects of bypassing the programmed responses seemed remote.

Suddenly he knew what to do. If his lower brain projected designs on his carapace in response to his thoughts, he could alternate between two contrasting ideas to produce a message in old-style Morse code. The question was, did he remember the signals well enough to get Spock's attention on the first try? If he didn't, he wasn't sure he would have a second chance. Unless he got past the obstructions created by the

Kh!lict programming soon, Spock would return to the artifact to work on the puzzle from that end.

Kirk tried to remember the games he had played with his brother when they were children. One vacation at his grandparents' home in Vermont, he, Sam, and the three McLaughlin boys from the adjoining farm had spent an entire month pretending they were Indians battling the invading white settlers. Their long-range communications system had been a set of talking drums they had built from designs Tommy McLaughlin had scrounged off the computer network. At the time none of them had considered that their parents, whom they had cast in the role of the invading British, were as capable of translating their messages as they were. Still, by the end of that summer, Kirk had been proficient at using Morse code, and he felt he should remember it, even if he had not used it much in the intervening three decades.

The next question was what would catch Spock's attention the fastest. The traditional SOS was a simple, repetitious pattern that would give him a chance to experiment with controlling the Kh!lict physiology. On the other hand, signaling his name would tell Spock what had happened, but the longer and less regular pattern to the letters spelling "Kirk" increased the chance that he wouldn't be understood. In addition, once he got Spock's attention, he could repeat complex messages until Spock understood them.

His decision made, Kirk concentrated on "communication" until the interwoven blues and greens swam across his vision. When the pattern was established in his mind—and, he hoped, reflected on his carapace—he summoned his anger and frustration at being trapped inside the Kh!lict body. As soon as the white flare crossed his vision, he released the anger and focused again on communicating until the peaceful blues and greens returned. Then he called on his anger again, relaxed into thoughts of talking with his crew, and finished the *S* with a final flare of anger.

The *O* was a little harder, requiring him to hold onto his rage longer and to time the intervals so that his dashes would be distinguished from the dots. After that effort it was a relief to return to the relatively simple task of putting out three dots for the final *S*.

Halfway through the *O,* Spock paused in his circuit around the crablike Kh!lict body. He stared at Kirk's upper back as though trying to remember some long-forgotten fact, and his expression didn't change while Kirk finished the second *S*. Dismay washed through Kirk as he realized that Spock had not deciphered his message. Since he was sure that the Vulcan remembered Morse code far better than he did, Spock's reaction could only mean that Kirk's attempts to produce dots and dashes by changing the colors on his carapace were not clear enough to be read.

Kirk started the message again, trying to make the transitions in his thoughts as sharp and precise as he could. It seemed to him that he was getting a feel for how the Kh!lict brains worked together, and that the shifts between the two contrasting concepts were cleaner and quicker, but Spock's expression didn't change as Kirk finished his second SOS. Discouraged, Kirk repeated the signal again, hoping that Spock would figure out what he meant and not reject the changing patterns as the Kh!lict equivalent of a facial tic.

"Dot-dot-dot," Spock murmured to himself as Kirk began the third SOS. "Dash-dash-dash. Dot-dot-dot. SOS." He moved to the Kh!lict's front. "Are you human? Is that you, Captain Kirk?"

The apricot haze flooded across Kirk's vision. Spock had figured out what had happened! *Dash-dot-dash-dash. Dot. Dot-dot-dot,* he signaled. *Dash-dot-dash-dash. Dot. Dot-dot-dot.* YES! YES! Now that Spock knew what had happened, everything was going to be all right.

Chapter Twelve

SPOCK FLIPPED OPEN his communicator. "Spock to *Enterprise*. We have located the captain."

"Sulu here," came the response. In the background Spock heard subdued cheering as the bridge crew reacted to his announcement. "What's the captain's status? We're not picking him up on our sensors."

"That is correct, Mr. Sulu. The captain is being held prisoner inside one of the alien creatures. At present our working hypothesis is that, when our people passed through the artifact, it gave them the bodies of its creators. We are attempting to learn more but are limited by the aliens' methods of communication."

"Do you know when you will be able to reverse the process, Mr. Spock?" Tension raised Sulu's voice half an octave, and the complete silence in the background told Spock that everyone on the bridge was waiting for the answer.

"Negative, Mr. Sulu. However, I wish to communicate with the other aliens in order to correlate their information with the captain's. Please direct Security to locate the other four creatures and guide them back to the artifact. At present I suggest that this be accomplished on foot, since these beings do not respond well to our transporters. If those four are our missing crewmen, they will understand what is being said to them, although they lack the vocal apparatus to answer."

"If they can't speak, Mr. Spock, how are you talking with the captain? Could the security men use your system with the other aliens?"

Spock mentally reviewed the personnel files, but very few contained any mention of Morse code. He and Kirk were able to communicate because both of them had at one time memorized that particular code. Unfortunately, he could not expect the other victims to have the appropriate information in their memories. "The aliens communicate by changing the colors of their shells, Mr. Sulu. The captain has discovered a way to display messages using an old-style system known as Morse code. Unless the other people trapped in the alien bodies remember a similar code *and* have the force of will to impose their wishes on the alien physiology, I fear that we must confine our communications to yes-or-no questions. At this time I see no way to bypass the limitations of the system."

"I understand, Mr. Spock. I'll pass that along to the security people and have them begin moving the aliens back to the artifact."

"Very well, Mr. Sulu. Spock out." He returned his attention to the captain. Kirk's crablike body was sprawled on the ground, its eight limbs jutting from beneath the carapace at awkward angles. The captain had lost control of his body at the first sight of the *Enterprise*'s landing party and had not moved since. Such a reaction suggested that the alien body contained preprogrammed responses that operated without Kirk's direction and that might interfere with his wishes. What information was stored in the alien's brains, and how much of it could Kirk access? Could they use that information to gain control over the transporterlike artifacts and change the *Enterprise*'s crewmen back to their human forms?

With so many unanswered questions, it was difficult to know what to ask first. Waiting for Kirk's responses in Morse code would make exchanging information exceedingly slow, but the captain was limited by the alien's physiology. Until they could circumvent that difficulty, they would have to work with it.

Resigning himself to taking whatever time he would need to get his answers, Spock lowered himself to the ground. Crossing his legs, he pointed his tricorder at Kirk and began asking questions.

The setting sun had painted the landscape with the colors of Vulcan's Flaming Desert and a frigid wind was slicing across the hills when Spock called a halt to the interview. For the last half hour, Kirk's answers had been slower and the distinctions between the dots and the dashes increasingly blurred. Kirk's alien body was tiring, and soon he would need to find food and shelter for the night, but Spock had balanced that against the need to learn all he could. The more he knew about the aliens, the sooner he could control the technology that had transformed Kirk into an alien.

Finally, seeing how far Kirk had pushed his body, Spock stood. "Captain, I shall analyze this information and discuss it with our science teams. By morning I hope that we shall have some positive recommendations for solving this dilemma."

GOOD, Kirk signaled back, his carapace flickering between mixed blues and greens and an apricot color that appeared several shades darker in the ruddy light. One front claw twitched briefly, reminding Spock of a farewell wave. It was the first time that Kirk had moved since the *Enterprise*'s landing party had materialized in front of him. Spock took the motion as a favorable sign, hoping it meant the alien programming was releasing its grip on Kirk's motor functions.

Pulling out his communicator, Spock signaled the ship. *"Enterprise,* beam up remaining landing parties for the night. Inform all scientists that we will hold a briefing at 2100 to analyze our data and to formulate a plan of action. Spock out."

He moved away from Kirk, and the security guard with him took up a position at his side. The transporter beam formed around them, dissolving the crimson-and orange-painted landscape and reforming the scene into the familiar hues of the *Enterprise*'s transporter room. Spock headed for the bridge, aware of the questions in the eyes of every person he met. Word of what had happened to Kirk and the other missing people had spread among the crew, and everyone was wondering if he had found an answer to the problem. Involuntarily his hand tightened around the strap of his tricorder. The answers, if he had them, lay in the mass of data he had obtained from his long interview with Kirk.

The turbolift door whisked open, and he stepped inside. "Bridge." Security had not reported the results of moving the other aliens back toward the artifact. That could mean one of several things; knowing what had actually occurred would enhance his analysis of the aliens' psychology and of how their world view governed the design of their technology.

Stepping onto the bridge, Spock saw that most of the day crew was present, still briefing their replacements and otherwise dawdling over the shift change that should have taken place fifteen minutes ago. "Status report, Mr. Sulu," he ordered, circling to the science station.

"All operations normal, Mr. Spock." Sulu's tone

said differently. Spock recognized the tension in his voice, which pointed out how worried everyone was about Kirk and emphasized how deeply loyal the crew was to the captain. Worry was a human emotion, Spock reminded himself, and it would not necessarily undermine the crew's efficiency—as long as it didn't cloud anyone's judgment. He would have to make sure that the crew did not work beyond capacity *before* a superhuman effort was required. If a crisis developed, he would need everyone in top form.

"Have the security teams been able to move the aliens back toward the artifact yet, Mr. Sulu?" Spock slid into his chair and pulled the data disks from his tricorder. Dropping them into the playback slot, he turned to hear Sulu's report.

"All teams reported failure in moving the aliens, Mr. Spock." Sulu reached across the board to call up the scanner logs. "Two of the creatures became extremely agitated and attacked our people. The largest alien completely ignored all attempts to contact it, as though the security men weren't even there. And the other creature went catatonic, refusing to move or acknowledge that anyone was in the area. In fact, you appear to be the only person who has had any luck in dealing with—well, with whoever is down on the planet."

"I see." Spock shifted the visuals to his display and ran through them, now in extreme slow motion, now speeding the replay to nearly a blur. He found no obvious flaws in the way the guards had handled the aliens, but only the captain showed any willingness to communicate with the *Enterprise*'s landing parties.

He could at least explain the catatonic alien, if he had understood Kirk's narrative. The creatures—the Kh!lict, as they called themselves—had evolved in such isolation that they were absolute xenophobes to whom even the *possibility* of finding other intelligent beings was so alien and so inconceivable that thinking about the idea sent their mental processes into hysterical disorder.

The two Kh!lict who attacked the security men were harder to explain, but their actions corresponded to the other half of the classic fight-or-flight response pattern. The first Kh!lict had retreated from a situation it found incomprehensible, but the second pair had tried to destroy the *Enterprise's* security teams in order to erase the unacceptable fact that other intelligent beings *might* exist. He wondered if that reaction reflected normal behavior for the Kh!lict, and that suggested another thought: What would have happened if the ancient Kh!lict had encountered other intelligent races? Could violent encounters with the Kh!lict explain the large number of so-called "orphan" cultures whose fragmentary remains were scattered around this sector? After a moment he set the computer to searching for data on the statistical distribution of sentient races through time for this quadrant, with particular emphasis on the areas where the Kh!lict might have traveled, and then returned to the immediate problem.

The last Kh!lict on the planet, the one who had completely ignored the security men, was the most puzzling. The ability to ignore certain discordant elements in one's surroundings was a trait shared by all intelligent races, but a species' survival precluded as total a denial as this creature displayed. Even with Kirk's explanation of the Kh!lict's xenophobia, Spock had trouble interpreting the largest Kh!lict's actions. It was as though the creature recognized the *Enterprise's* security team and dismissed them as unimportant.

Spock replayed the tapes of that Kh!lict, noticing

how it ignored the humans and how oblivious it was to every attempt to attract its attention. Suddenly, without being certain of every step in his proof, Spock *knew* that the largest Kh!lict was Talika Nyar. The combination of Kh!lict xenophobia and Djelifan racial self-centeredness led the creature that housed Talika's consciousness to dismiss the humans as irrelevant rather than attacking them or retreating from them as the other Kh!lict had done. It was as though both halves of her mind agreed that the humans were not intelligent. Apparently the artifact had based its choice of Kh!lict host persona, at least to some extent, on the personalities of the individuals who entered the artifact. What that meant for their mission Spock did not know, but he filed it away until he had enough facts to evaluate the hypothesis properly.

With his analysis completed, Spock turned his attention to the bridge crew. "Mr. Sulu, you and the rest of the day shift may stand down now."

Sulu opened his mouth to protest but reconsidered. While there was no absolute prohibition against the day shift remaining on the bridge to await further developments, the only benefit—being where they could hear news first—was psychological. "Yes, Mr. Spock." He and Uhura led the rest of the day crew from the bridge.

That settled, Spock turned back to his console. The computer had finished its first analysis of the data from his interview with Kirk, and now he could examine the results. The bizarre and mutable biological parameters required careful examination.

Because of the late hour, there were only five people in the briefing room. However, Spock had authorized anyone with a science rating above Tech One to monitor the discussion and, if they chose, to relay comments and suggestions to him. Given the complexity of the problem and the large gaps in their knowledge, it was the only way short of holding the briefing on the hangar deck to insure that everyone could participate. In conducting the meeting this way, Spock was following an old Vulcan precept: The time required to solve a problem is inversely proportional to the amount of knowledge brought to bear on the subject. The more scientists who reviewed the data, the greater the chance that someone would find the key to the puzzle.

Spock presided over the briefing from behind the computer station. Kaul, still looking washed out and shaky from his reaction to the suldanic gas, was fiddling with a stylus as he paged through the summaries on his data padd. Lassiter was at Kaul's side, her face pinched with exhaustion and her skin almost as pale as her white-blonde hair. McCoy sat opposite the two archaeologists, his mouth compressed into a stubborn scowl and his eyes glittering with more indignation than usual. The chief biologist, Lieutenant Dara Niles, completed the group. Niles was a quietly competent woman of medium stature with close-cropped dark hair.

"I presume everyone has reviewed our earlier findings," Spock said to open the briefing. "Therefore, I will begin by summarizing my conversation with Captain Kirk."

"Are you sure it was the captain?" McCoy's drawl was as thick as his skepticism. "It's an awfully big leap of faith for us to accept that Jim has been turned into an overgrown crustacean, even one as offbeat as the creature I autopsied."

"I realize that, Doctor. However, I conversed with the creature at some length and am convinced that the captain's consciousness is housed within the body of this alien." He punched the playback button, and the record of his conversation with Kirk scrolled across the screen. For those who were not fluent in Morse code, the computer supplied translations at the bottom of the screen.

"How was this accomplished?" Lassiter's voice was barely above a whisper. "Does Captain Kirk understand anything about the technology that made this alteration?"

"The captain's impression is that the windowlike artifacts are matter/energy transmission devices that function in a manner analogous to our transporters. He believes that the error detection protocols within the artifact caused him to rematerialize as a Kh!lict because their system's program reads absolutely that an intelligent being must be Kh!lict."

"Are you certain of this?" Niles asked. "How do we know the device didn't transfer his consciousness to an alien body?"

"That is a good question, Lieutenant." Spock forwarded the log of his interview with Kirk to where they had discussed that subject. He let Kirk's statements play across the screen as he continued talking. "First we have the basic Kh!lict assumption that *all* intelligent life must be Kh!lict. Given that, they would presume that any intelligent creature using their transportation system must be Kh!lict. Second, all matter/energy transmission devices require a source of matter to reconstitute at the end of the transport path. The simplest design for such a system—and simplicity guides most engineering solutions—is to convert the body of the transportee into energy, transmit that energy using a zero-loss protocol, and reconstitute the original body at the receiving location. The captain's analysis, based on knowledge contained in his Kh!lict brain, is that his body was altered during reintegration to that of a Kh!lict. This is supported by the fact that his mass as a Kh!lict is, within acceptable error limits, identical to his mass when he entered the artifact. In the morning we will measure the mass of the other Kh!lict to determine if this applies to them as well."

"Don't you think this is a little farfetched, Spock?" McCoy nibbled the end of his stylus. "I mean, we come halfway across the galaxy, discover a race of aliens that died out over a hundred thousand years ago—and their transporters don't work any better than ours. And how does all this theory help us get the captain back?"

Spock straightened in his chair, his back going as stiff as a bracing beam. "One cannot hope to decipher the intricacies of a complex technology without an understanding of the underlying principles. Even you should appreciate that fact, Doctor."

McCoy's expression hardened. "What I appreciate, Mr. Spock, is that Captain Kirk is missing and that you seem more interested in theorizing about the technology of these creatures than you are in retrieving the captain. Does Scotty have anything to say about all this?"

"As a matter of fact, Doctor, we have finally collected enough data to begin constructing models of the artifacts' internal workings. Mr. Scott is running computer simulations to reduce the number of possible designs. Once we have determined the most likely parameters, we will attempt to reprogram the devices and retrieve our people."

McCoy snorted his disbelief but said nothing further. Instead Niles rapped her stylus on the table for attention. She pointed to her screen, where different colors of text highlighted several messages. "My people have been analyzing the Caretian ecosystem, particularly with regard to the nutritional requirements of the Kh!lict. It is our conclusion that most, if not all, of the plant and animal species that provided food for the Kh!lict have either become extinct or have evolved, thanks to the fading sun, into something no longer recognizable. Since the Kh!lict rely heavily on preprogrammed information, we surmise that our people on the planet will face starvation within a very short time, particularly since we have no idea what these creatures ate."

Stunned silence, followed by an outburst of over-lapping questions and exclamations, followed Lieu-tenant Niles's announcement. Spock marveled at how so few humans could generate so much noise. Pitching his voice to be heard above the hub-bub, he asked, "Do you have the data to substantiate that, Lieutenant?"

"Yes, sir. The information is in master file alpha-three-two-nine-chi-omega. It will be accessible to everyone within ten minutes." Niles tugged on a handful of her dark hair. "Given what has been said about the Kh!lict rejection of outsiders, we may have difficulties providing food to our people. Even after we figure out what they ate, someone will have to devise a way to get them to accept the food from us."

"Understood." Spock tagged her files for further study. "Lieutenant Niles, please work with Dr. McCoy to determine how we can provide appropriate rations to our people. If no one has any additional information, this briefing is adjourned."

For once even McCoy was silent. Spock stood, signaling the formal end to the meeting, and headed for the door. Sifting through the files that the biol-ogists had compiled would make for another long night. However, somewhere in the mass of data that the *Enterprise*'s scientists had collected, Spock knew he would find the answers to getting their people back. Like any problem in the sciences, it was a matter of working long enough and hard enough to assemble the information in the proper logical sequence.

Chapter Thirteen

KIRK WATCHED SPOCK and the security guard dissolve into sparkling motes of energy. A cold breeze whistled across the hilltops, ruffling the dry, flattened grass where Spock had sat for the last several hours. The final rays of the setting sun skimmed the hilltops, emphasizing the immensity and the emptiness of the land around him. A land that had once been populated by millions of Kh!lict who had looked like he did now and who had thought and believed the same things as the being his host was patterned after. It was a frightening and a depressing thought to realize how totally the Kh!lict had vanished from the collective memories and histories of this part of the galaxy.

Even after Spock disappeared, it took half an hour for his host to recover from its catatonic retreat. The last rose tints were fading from the western sky when Kirk felt his Kh!lict lower brain convince itself that the humans were a hallucination brought on by the bad transition through the transit frame. With the internally imposed restrictions on his movements gone, he needed to find food and a place to spend the night. He sensed that the Kh!lict were normally less active after dark, but he could still make out his surroundings in shadings of lighter and darker grays that resembled the patterns from a translation algorithm for a night-vision scope.

Cautiously he sent a message to his limbs, hoping they would respond after the long hours of immobility on the chilly hilltop. At first nothing happened, and he was afraid he would be stuck where he was until the morning sun warmed his body. He was almost ready to give up when he felt one of his front pincers flopping loosely in response to his directive.

It wasn't much, but it gave him a place to start. Kirk flexed the joint, working it until the blood began flowing into the limb. Next he concentrated on the other joints in that appendage, twisting and bending them until they responded to his commands. Soon he was able to work the adjoining appendages, and finally all eight legs were under his control.

Kirk heaved himself to his pincers, thinking how tiresome it was to go through this warmup routine every time he let his body remain motionless for more than a few minutes. How had the Kh!lict ever managed? They must have evolved in a much warmer climate and, during the time when they ruled Careta IV, the planet must have had an unusually uniform distribution of diurnal and seasonal temperatures. Any creatures so thoroughly incapacitated by cold would quickly be exterminated by predators.

First he needed food, Kirk decided as he started uphill. However, he had no idea what the Kh!lict ate, much less what food he could find in this barren land. At the thought of eating, he felt a hollowness in his interior. His host should be hungry, he guessed, considering that it had been a day and a half since Kirk had eaten. He didn't know how that translated for a Kh!lict, but he had been making tremendous physical and psychological demands on his body since he had emerged from the artifact. If his host did not need fuel to keep going, its physiology was radically different from anything known to Federation science.

He concentrated on the idea of eating a good meal. Letting his imagination have free rein, he conjured up his memories of the ten-course Japanese banquet he had attended the last time he had been called to Starfleet Command. To his surprise, the image triggered no response in his host's brain. That puzzled Kirk; every civilized race he knew of placed a high value on the rituals that accompanied dining and food preparation. He doubted that the Kh!lict were so alien that what they ate was of no importance. The other possible explanation of the Kh!lict's disinterest was that it found nothing appetizing in the meal Kirk had remembered.

Recalling the quantity and the variety of food served at that meal, Kirk could not believe that there had been *nothing* on the menu that would interest his host. Clear soup, sashimi, a dozen kinds of sushi, tempura vegetables, chicken teriyaki, steamed rice, sukiyaki with more kinds of vegetables than Kirk had been able to identify, shrimp custard, a fabulous lemon-soy tofu salad—he let his mind dwell on each dish, savoring the details of aroma and texture and flavor.

Quickly, from the surge of revulsion that shook him at the thought of eating plant matter, Kirk realized that the Kh!lict had not been vegetarians or even omnivores. In fact, the Kh!lict's strongest criterion for identifying inferior—and presumably nonintelligent —species was that they consumed plant materials as food. By that standard, humans failed to meet the minimum Kh!lict requirement for sentience.

With that insight, Kirk concentrated on the sashimi

and the meat dishes. Even the latter, he discovered as he went over them in his mind, had contained more vegetables than meat, and the idea of slicing and cooking the meat seemed alien to his host. The sashimi—paper-thin slices of raw fish—provoked a little more interest from the Kh!lict lower brain, but Kirk sensed that the preparation method was almost as alien as the concept of a food source obtained from the ocean. In their prehistory the Kh!lict must have evolved from marine animals, but they had not looked to the sea for food within the collective memory of their race.

Given his host's reactions, and the lack of them, Kirk decided the Kh!lict had eaten their meat raw and with very little preparation. He found the idea unappealing, but he realized that the Kh!lict lower brain would overrule his squeamishness if suitable prey crossed his path. But what would his host find suitable?

Still thinking about the problem, Kirk continued his trek back toward the artifact. Once he got the hang of coordinating eight legs, he found that the Kh!lict body could move rapidly, even over rough terrain. He returned to his question about suitable prey for a man-sized crab. With the ability to summon brief bursts of speed, the Kh!lict would have been formidable predators. Furthermore, with millennia to develop the infrastructure of their civilization, Kirk realized that they could have bred their food sources to be docile and slow to alarm, much as humans bred their cattle to be easily managed.

A vision swam before his eyes. He saw this land crossed with a network of closely slatted fences enclosing lush pastures carpeted with a variety of herbs and grasses. Each enclosure was stocked with rabbitlike creatures that nibbled on the succulent forage until they were plump and their flesh was flavorful and juicy. A hungry Kh!lict walked out into the pasture and chose his meal by the herbs he wanted to flavor the meat. As one of the docile *nanthken* came within reach, it was impaled on a pincer that flashed out and swept the doomed creature into the air. The Kh!lict sheared through the animal's spinal cord with its sharp, triangular teeth, shaped much like a shark's teeth and equally useless for chewing flesh. Ducts in the upper tooth injected the still-living prey with a combination of fast-acting neurotoxins and digestive enzymes. Within minutes the flesh began to dissolve, and the Kh!lict sucked up the savory juices through its proboscis, much as terrestrial spiders fed on their prey.

Feelings of intense pleasure accompanied the Kh!lict's memories of catching and feasting on a squealing and twitching *nanthken*. Kirk was glad that he was not in control of his body at that moment, because he was revolted by the cruelty he sensed in the Kh!lict's thoughts. Eating animal flesh was one thing; torturing the animal before eating it was another. Kirk's sense of civilized propriety and his human squeamishness made starvation seem like an attractive option.

However, since he needed food to survive, Kirk hoped that his Kh!lict instincts would operate without conscious direction if he found appropriate prey. So far he had seen nothing in this barren land that even approximated the Kh!lict's memories of its standard fare. Until he did, he was worrying needlessly, since he was much more likely to starve than to reject a potential meal through squeamishness. For now all he could do was keep moving and hope to find something edible. The landscape around him faded into weaker, less contrasting shades as the heat leaked from the land and radiated out into space.

* * *

About midnight, Kirk's host began to stagger with exhaustion, and it became a struggle to move even one appendage at a time. Most of the heat was gone, making it difficult to see where he was going or to avoid the obstacles and pitfalls in his path. Kirk looked around, trying to find somewhere to spend the rest of the night. With the Kh!lict lower brain struggling to dominate his actions, he found it interesting that he had to actively change a directive that he had imposed on the reluctant Kh!lict instincts.

After half an hour of searching, Kirk discovered a spring hidden in a small grotto halfway down the hillside. Below the spring was a brackish pool covered with a thick mat of algae. Both his human and his Kh!lict programming agreed on how revolting the pond was, but Kirk steeled himself to ingest as much of the organic material as he could. The bulk of the *Enterprise*'s food was reconstituted from an algal base, so he knew that the basic nutrients his body needed should be present.

Beggars can't be choosers, he told himself sternly as he sucked the algae through his proboscis. Gourmet food it wasn't, but he hadn't seen anything larger than an insect in the last two days. Considering the energy he had expended, Kirk knew his body needed food, no matter how marginal or unpleasant the source, if he was to continue to function.

When he could not hold any more algae and water, he retreated into the grotto and settled himself into a sheltered niche. The ship's sensors had reported no dangerous predators on the planet, but he sensed that the Kh!lict slept only when their backs and appendages were protected. Such caution was fine with Kirk; the confined space would conserve his body heat and make it easier to start moving in the morning. He was beginning to realize how important that was and to appreciate how much conditions had changed on

Careta IV since the Kh!lict civilization had flourished there.

Morning brought, if not answers, then at least the outline of a plan for moving closer to a solution. Somewhere in the strange half-waking state where his mind absorbed memories of the Kh!lict world and the Kh!lict way of life, Kirk realized how deeply xenophobia was bred into the Kh!lict. Spock would never be able to contact the others who had passed through the artifact unless he changed himself into a Kh!lict. Only Kirk's overriding need to look after his crew and to prevent anyone else from becoming a victim of the Kh!lict technology had enabled him to surmount his host's denial that other intelligent races might exist. He doubted that Chekov had the experience to defeat the Kh!lict psychology, and he was sure the security guards' training wouldn't have prepared them to cope with the schizophrenic responses of a Kh!lict body inhabited by a human mind. In all probability the others had not been able to establish any contact with their lower brains or exert any control over their bodies. If that was the case, they were completely at the mercy of whatever programming the artifact had imprinted on their lower brains.

The best thing he could do to further their mission, Kirk concluded, was to locate the others, explain what had happened, and get them to return to the artifact. He didn't know what would happen after that, but by then perhaps Spock would know how to change them back to their human forms.

His decision made, Kirk set off to find the other Kh!lict. Locating them was easier than he expected, once he got near the artifact. The tall, dry grass yielded when someone passed through it and, once flattened, did not straighten again. The humans had combed the area close to the artifact, crisscrossing it with more trails than the best bloodhound could unravel. However, once he circled farther away, six wide swaths of broken stalks radiated away from the transit frame. After eliminating the one he had made, Kirk chose a track at random and set off.

The trail meandered across the hillside and zig-zagged into an adjoining valley, then wandered along an almost-dry stream bed for several kilometers. Judging by the spacing of the tracks, the Kh!lict lower brain had not felt an urgent need to be anywhere. That confirmed Kirk's guess that the human inside the body had not established a connection with the Kh!lict mind and had either gone along for the ride or had retreated from a reality he found too grotesque to believe. Either way, Kirk covered in two hours the distance the other Kh!lict had traveled in two days.

He approached carefully, his carapace blinking a bright/dark pattern for attention long before he thought the other was looking his way. As a human, he would have scuffed the pebbles with his feet to catch the other's attention, but when he tried that he could barely hear the sounds he was making. Considering how well he had heard Spock the previous day, Kirk decided that the Kh!lict hearing was highly selective. He wondered if that was because nothing in their environment had used those frequencies or if there had been so much noise in those ranges that selective deafness was a survival trait.

Finally the other Kh!lict noticed him and stopped, its carapace flickering a question in muted browns. <Parent?>

Kirk searched through his intuitive recollection of Kh!lict vocabulary. He could not remember any concepts analogous to military rank, but that didn't mean much. There were still immense gaps in his knowledge of the Kh!lict, although practice was making it easier for him to tap into the information stored in his lower brain. However, until he discovered what the Kh!lict pattern was that meant "captain," the word "parent" was probably as close as he could come to his true title. He relaxed and let the Kh!lict lower brain translate his thoughts.

<Yes, son. I am here.> The message was projected with an apricot overtone of reassurance that, while not strictly necessary, seemed to reach to the other person.

<Why am I hungry, parent?> the other Kh!lict asked, his question colored with the petulance of a very young child.

<There is food back the way you came,> Kirk told him. That wasn't exactly a lie, but Kirk knew he was shading the truth more than a little. After several hours to think about the question, he was convinced that there was no longer anything on Careta IV that a self-respecting Kh!lict would consider edible. Anything they ate, short of skimming more algae from scummy ponds, would have to come from the *Enterprise*. <You should retrace your steps until you find it.>

<Anything you say, parent.> The Kh!lict turned around and started back, his movements erratic from lack of food.

Kirk watched until the young Kh!lict disappeared over the crest of the first hill, thinking that convincing him had been almost too easy. This Kh!lict had been pathetically eager to take orders from him. His own Kh!lict lower brain had fought much harder to maintain control, and Kirk wondered why the difference between the two Kh!lict minds should be so great. Was starvation the sole reason, or was there some other, more satisfactory explanation for the wildly divergent behavior?

The only way to find out, he decided, was to locate the rest of the altered humans. Two individuals did not comprise a statistically significant number; any conclusion drawn from such a small sample had to be suspect. Even with data from all the changed people, they could hardly prove anything, but Kirk hoped they would not have any more data points for this experiment. He started off to find the next track, hoping it would be as easy to convince the others to return to the artifact.

It took him almost an hour to find the next track. When he found the broad swath of flattened grass striking across the rolling hills like a superhighway on Old Earth, Kirk felt a stirring of excitement in his Kh!lict brain. What it meant he wasn't sure, but a premonition tickled at the edges of his mind. Something was different about this Kh!lict, something that aroused his host deeply. Perhaps, Kirk thought, he should leave this track and its creator alone, at least until he discovered why his host was so interested in it.

He took a few steps past the trail, intending to search for the next Kh!lict, but his body veered around and started to follow the strip of flattened grass. Kirk tried to turn away, but each time he did, the Kh!lict lower brain reasserted itself as soon as Kirk relaxed his control. Finally curiosity overcame him, and he yielded to the mysterious pull.

This Kh!lict had wasted no time in its travels and had covered a considerable distance. Kirk's lower brain forced his body to move at a vicious pace, as if trying to make up for lost time. The longer he followed the trail, the more agitated and aroused his host became. With his mind no longer actively controlling his body, Kirk tried to reason out the cause for his host's sudden compulsion. Given the strength of his determination, Kirk knew he was either dealing with an intense personal delusion or an overwhelming biological imperative. The difficulty, as far as Kirk could see, was that he probably would not learn which it was until too late to forestall whatever the Kh!lict brain was programmed to do.

After several hours of rapid travel, the subject of his pursuit appeared on the horizon. A jolt of electrifying excitement shot through Kirk, and his Kh!lict lower brain forced his appendages to move even faster than before. The Kh!lict on the horizon was the most powerful, most beautiful, most terrifying creature he had seen in his life, and he could not reach her soon enough.

With a dawning sense of horror, Kirk realized what this entire chase had been leading up to. His mind howled a protest and struggled to assert itself, but the Kh!lict biology was in control. Like it or not, Kirk could only go along for the ride.

Chapter Fourteen

SPOCK FOUND the night of analyzing the biological data on the Kh!lict pleasantly restful after the day's turmoil. However, the intellectual challenge of piecing together the life cycle of a dead race did little to solve his more immediate problem. The captain and five other people had been transformed into creatures who had died out millennia ago, and one of those people was already dead. Worse, the creatures had left behind only a few mysterious and dangerous artifacts and no written records that the archaeologists had been able to find.

Leaning back in his chair, Spock let his eyes wander over the sensual contours of his Vulcan harp, hanging in its usual place on the wall of his cabin. The harp was an aid to meditation; the orderly precision of the musical scales directed his thoughts into crisp and logical channels. His eyes still on the harp, he steepled his hands and rested his chin on his up-pointed index fingers.

With what they knew of the Kh!lict physiology and anatomy, a written language using a conventional system of inscribed characters was improbable. Much of the Kh!lict's knowledge was imprinted directly on their brains, and such a procedure implied a repository for the knowledge that was passed down. Pretechnological Kh!lict would have been forced to transmit their heritage by mind-to-mind contact using methods analogous to the Vulcan mind meld, but Spock doubted that they had relied on such techniques once they could manufacture devices to perform the same functions. The clarity and precision of the hard-wired information that Kirk had accessed to answer Spock's questions implied an artificial repository; transmission by mind link was less faithful, with losses and shifts in the data accompanying each transfer. The Kh!lict at the height of their civilization must have used a more reliable system for disseminating the information than their own inadequate minds.

The question was, where was this insight leading him? They had found few Kh!lict sites on the planet, and none appeared more significant than the one they had chosen for their initial examination. If there were any major cities on the planet, they were well hidden. When he considered what they had found so far, Spock knew the Kh!lict must have made a much greater mark on Careta IV. The sophisticated technology of the transit frames implied a highly advanced civilization. The ruins they had explored showed no signs of outside destruction, but the shielding around the first artifact implied that someone had wanted very badly to keep it from *ever* being discovered. The archaeologists were still working to prove that the Meztoriens were responsible for hiding the artifacts, but as far as Spock was concerned, *who* was responsible was not as important as *how* or *why*.

How would one camouflage an entire city? Spock

wondered. The method would have to function for tens of thousands of years. Ruins springing out of nowhere on a supposedly deserted planet would attract more attention than if they had been left to decay without the protective concealment. That assumed the relics *could* decay, which was not yet proven. The Kh!lict objects that they had found were surprisingly well preserved, considering their great antiquity, and the power utilization curves on the transportation windows suggested they would be exceedingly difficult to destroy.

"Computer, display records of the magnetic flux readings for the major land masses, compression factor one hundred." If other shielded Kh!lict relics were hidden on the planet, subtle variations in the screening fields should mark the objects when one specifically searched the data for those effects.

"Working." The computer's response seemed sluggish, as though the machine were reluctant to carry out his orders. Spock's eyebrow lifted slightly. *Where did that irrational thought come from?* he wondered. Attributing emotions to a machine suggested that he had been around human illogic for too long, but the computer might still be developing a subtle malfunction. He ordered a full diagnostic of the system, then returned to his current task.

The data scrolled across his screen. To have escaped notice until now, any systematic variations in the magnetic flux had to be minuscule, little more than background noise. The question was, if every Kh!lict artifact was hidden by highly sophisticated force screens, would the *Enterprise*'s sensors have detected the energy leaking through those shields? Their data analysis programs had not been written for such situations.

He had finished skimming their first eight hours of data when his door buzzer sounded. Involuntarily he glanced at his chronometer. Only Kirk and McCoy presumed that he would be awake so early, and even they would not show up unannounced at his door at such an hour. A crisis serious enough to need attention before the humans had breakfast and their morning coffee meant the ship was on Red Alert. Putting the computer on standby, Spock cued the door release. "Come."

Meredith Lassiter stepped through the door, pausing as it whisked shut behind her. Her face was as pale as her hair, and she looked as though she had not slept in the last two days. "I hope I'm not intruding, Mr. Spock, but something has happened that has a bearing on the mission. I hesitate to report anything so subjective, but I feel that my knowledge may affect the success of this mission."

Spock gestured to the chair beside his work table, consciously imitating the gesture he had often seen Kirk use in similar situations. *What else would the captain do?* he asked himself. His ability to rescue Kirk and the others depended on his skills for managing humans, including the visiting scientists who were not bound by Starfleet regulations to obey his orders. "Please make your report, Dr. Lassiter. I have often observed that humans have a remarkable talent for reaching valid conclusions without considering every link in the chain of their logic."

Lassiter gave him a weak smile. "I guess that's one way of putting it. Another way would be to tell you that I am a native of Bendilon. Have you heard of that colony?"

"Affirmative." Bendilon, more often called Space Haven or Dreamtime by humans, had been settled in the early days of spaceflight. The colonists had used such diverse models as the Australian aborigines and the Amerind peyote cult for their society, and no outsider had ever figured out how it worked. People sent to study the culture either vanished into the social fabric of Bendilon, becoming more dedicated Bendiloni than the natives, or they never saw any of Bendilon's unique institutions. Bendilon was a classic Academy case study in how observers lost their objectivity when studying alien cultures. Several theories of how the Bendiloni subverted outsiders recurred in the student analyses, but Spock had not seen any solutions, either student or professional, that completely explained this perplexing society. "I presume that being from Bendilon has some bearing on what you wish to tell me."

Lassiter nodded. "Our people place a high value on subliminal perceptions, dream messages, and certain forms of extrasensory perception." She gave a diffident shrug. "Among our people I'm considered something of a cripple because I do not easily perceive the dream plane or observe events that occur beyond what I can see or hear. I can generally perceive only the very strongest messages from the shadow world."

Spock nodded to encourage her. As with many humans, when among strangers, Lassiter felt she must establish her credentials before presenting her data. Schooling himself to patience, he waited for her to make her point.

"When we arrived here, I felt something stirring in the dream plane. It was an incredibly ancient and malignant force, possessed of an indescribably cold and undying hatred. I didn't want to believe in anything so terrible, so inimical to intelligent life."

"I see." How did this relate to their mission? Was she sensing the Kh!lict racial consciousness? "Dr. Lassiter, what can you tell me about these mental emanations?"

She twisted her fingers through a lock of her hair

and brought it to her mouth, nibbling on the frayed ends. "The hatred, mostly. I'm not sure who or what this thing is, but it hates everyone and everything."

"Can you sense its physical nature or tell me to what species it belonged?" Spock was not sure how the answers to such questions would help him, even if Lassiter could isolate the information. After so long Spock could not expect the surviving remnants of the Kh!lict subconsciousness to be intact or fully sane.

"I'm not sure about any physical parameters." She flicked her fingers free of her hair and then recaptured the strand. Her forehead wrinkling with a frown, she chewed on the ends. "All I know for sure is that this entity hates all intelligent creatures, probably even its own kind."

"Fascinating. Can you sense anything more about it?" That she had perceived what she had was remarkable, Spock knew. Asking for more information was as illogical as praying for a miracle to restore Kirk and the others, but Spock would not reject divine intervention if it got the desired results.

Lassiter chewed harder on the ends of her hair. "Its projections have been growing stronger and stronger. The longer we are here, the more it hates us."

"I see." Spock studied her face. If he had learned to read humans at all, she was more relaxed than he had seen her since the archaeologists had come aboard the ship. "Can you tell me anything else, Dr. Lassiter?"

She dropped her hand to her lap. "I don't believe so, Mr. Spock. It's possible that something may have escaped my analysis, but I don't know what."

Spock stood. "In that case, Dr. Lassiter, I will not keep you from your duties. If you discover additional information, I would appreciate hearing it. Anything we learn about the previous inhabitants of this planet will be of enormous value."

"I'll be glad to tell you anything I learn." She stood

and moved toward the door. Just before she reached the sensor, she turned and gave him a short, formal bow. "I thank you for your courtesy in listening to my story."

Before Spock could answer, she stepped backwards into the sensor's range and then slipped through the door as it opened. He called up the results of his computer analysis, but his mind kept trying to fit this new information into the increasingly bizarre problem.

The bridge crew was unusually quiet, Spock thought as he glanced from his hooded viewer to the main viewscreen. Careta IV's largest continent lay directly below them, its irregular shape obscured by high wispy clouds and a dust storm brewing on the western edge of the land mass. He had been sifting through the reams of data the *Enterprise* had collected on the planet for so long that it seemed as though he knew Careta almost as well as he knew Vulcan.

By midmorning he had isolated thirty sites that might contain major Kh!lict artifacts. He chose the most likely anomalies and ordered intensive scanner observations while security teams prepared to examine the sites in person.

He was switching back to check Kirk's activities when the bridge door whisked open. McCoy left the turbolift and strolled toward Spock's station. "I thought you would be down on that planet asking Jim what we can do to help him."

"I *am* helping him." Spock bent his head over his viewer in an attempt to discourage McCoy. "I am analyzing the device that changed him into a Kh!lict."

McCoy perched on the edge of the console, one eyebrow lifted in imitation of Spock's favorite gesture. "Wouldn't it be better if you *asked* Jim about the technology? I mean, from what you said at the briefing last night, Jim is cohabiting that body with one of the alien what-you-call-'ems."

"They call themselves the Kh!lict, Doctor. And while you are correct that the captain is sharing a Kh!lict body with the lower elements of a Kh!lict intellect, it appears that his host has very little knowledge of the fields in which we most need information. This fact is disquieting, since we cannot acquire data about the Kh!lict sciences and technology except through the 'memories' of our crew who have been altered into Kh!lict."

"Well, now I've seen everything." McCoy shook his head in disbelief. "You're telling me you are waiting for someone else to tell you what to do?"

Spock exhaled heavily. "That is essentially correct, Doctor. Unless we can find a storehouse of Kh!lict written records and can translate them, we must rely on what our people report that they have learned from their Kh!lict memories."

"Which brings us back to my original question, Spock. Why are you up here talking to that dratted computer of yours instead of down there asking Jim to use his special knowledge to unravel the secret of those windows?" McCoy rested his thigh on the edge of the console and let one foot swing free.

Realizing the doctor wasn't leaving soon, Spock pushed the viewer aside. "I believe I just explained that the captain has very little information that will help us return our people to their natural bodies. Should you not be determining the Kh!lict nutritional requirements so we can supply our people with the appropriate foods?"

"I've already got a rough guess at that—as near as I can, anyway, using the sketchy information you gave me." McCoy drummed his heel erratically against the access panel, reminding Spock of the pseudo-random pattern used by the pythonlike Vulcan *pandree* to lure prey into its sand traps. "I still want to know why you aren't down there checking up on how Jim's doing."

Resisting the urge to strike McCoy's leg the way he would have attacked a genuine *pandree,* Spock flipped a switch on his console. Three views of the planet's surface sprang to life on the screens above his station. "Doctor, if you would turn around, you will see that I can monitor the captain's activities quite well. At the moment he is locating the other Kh!lict and directing them to return to the artifact."

McCoy glanced at the screens but refused to be budged. "I still don't see why you aren't down there helping him out."

Struggling against an all-too-human reaction to McCoy's perversity, Spock activated a fourth screen. This one showed a closer view of Kirk's host marching resolutely through the dry grasses. "Given the Kh!lict's xenophobia, I scarcely think that the captain needs—or even wants—our assistance. My interpretation of what he has told me suggests that he has a better chance of accomplishing this task if he is not hindered by our presence."

"Forgive an old country doctor his foolishness, Spock, but why do we want all those creatures herded into one spot?" McCoy's Southern accent had thickened noticeably as he assumed his "country doctor" role. "When we want to, we can just transport them to where we need them, can't we?"

Spock lifted an eyebrow. "Doctor, don't you remember what happened when we tried that before? The Kh!lict believe, as an article of faith bordering on fanaticism, that they are the only intelligent beings in the universe. The sight of us or of our technology drives them into hysterics. Only the rarest individuals retain sufficient mental flexibility to accept our presence. Even the captain is barely able to overcome the responses programmed into his host's brain."

"You mean to tell me that Jim doesn't want to talk to us?" McCoy's posture was too relaxed for him to sincerely mean the antagonism in his words. That suggested he was trying to generate a friendly game of "Insults" to distract himself from his own concerns; Spock concluded that the doctor's research was not progressing as well as McCoy would have liked. "Though I must admit, not talking to you is probably a step in the right direction."

Deliberately Spock lowered his head to his hooded viewer. "I am uncertain of the basis for your analysis, Doctor, although I, too, must confess to experiencing a touch of relief when I do not have to encounter certain levels of human irrationality. However, we were discussing the Kh!lict. Did you say you had determined their nutritional requirements?"

"Of course not!" McCoy scowled. "I've got a first approximation, for all the good it will do us. When I told the computer to run the last set of simulations and calculate the ideal Kh!lict field rations, it gave me a readout that looked like whole blood. Some of the element distributions were skewed, but in our opinion, the Kh!lict were carnivores who guzzled their food in a liquid or semiliquid form." A wicked grin crept over McCoy's face. "I'd be happy to provide you with more details on their table manners, if you like."

"No, thank you." Spock swallowed, disliking the idea of surviving by killing other creatures. "At the moment I am more concerned about keeping the five Kh!lict down there together in one area. When we discover how to reverse the transformation, we will return everyone to proper form and leave this system immediately."

"Well, it's about time!" McCoy shifted position, and to Spock's relief, his heel no longer rapped against the grille. "That's the first intelligent thing anyone has said since we came to this benighted planet."

Spock raised his eyebrow. "I doubt that it is the *first* intelligent thing anyone has said, but it is quite certain that we are not equipped to explore this planet. It is illogical to risk our people on a mission that requires greater proficiency with alien technology than even the crew of the *Enterprise* possesses."

McCoy's boots slammed onto the floor with a resounding thump. Bouncing on his toes, he leaned over Spock's station. "I thought that between the two of you, you and Scotty could do everything."

Spock tilted his head to one side, studying the doctor's face. To push so hard for no apparent reason, McCoy had to have something on his mind. Were the results he had obtained on the Kh!lict that disturbing to humans, or was it his *lack* of results that bothered him? "You are correct, Doctor, when you say that Mr. Scott and I are capable of solving most problems. However, there are perhaps four people in the entire Federation who possess the expertise needed to unravel this technology. I would be honored to assist them in their efforts, but I myself do not possess the full range of skills needed here. Unless, of course, your biological studies have revealed the key to these creatures."

As Spock was talking, McCoy's expression alternated between triumph at Spock's admission that he did not know everything and dismay that they might not be able to rescue Kirk. However, when Spock suggested that his biological studies might hold the necessary clue, consternation chased all other emotions off the doctor's face. "Are you out of your Vulcan mind? You can't seriously mean that the answers to those creatures' *technology* is hidden somewhere in their *physiology*. You'd better get back down there and have Jim talk some sense into that thick head of yours."

"Doctor, I see no need for us to continue this

discussion. You have your methods, and I have mine. I suggest that you pursue your research with a little more alacrity." As he turned back toward his viewer, a flicker of movement caught Spock's attention. It was on the screen that showed Kirk's activities.

Kirk was on his back, sliding down a long, steep slope using his carapace as a toboggan, his legs flailing the air in a vain attempt to gain control of his movements. A plume of beige dust rose behind him, spreading into a broad rooster tail in the stiff wind. As they watched he picked up speed, shooting over the dry grass as though his shell were coated with lubricant. "Oh, my God," McCoy murmured, his imagination telling him how hard Kirk was going to hit when he finally reached the bottom of the slope.

Chapter Fifteen

KIRK FELT the agitation mounting in his body as he raced toward the Kh!lict female, his legs extending to their maximum to attain the greatest speed possible. His host's reactions were so intense, so insistent, that Kirk could follow the Kh!lict's thoughts with very little trouble. He was pursuing the most seductive, the most provocative, the most desirable female he had seen in his short life. It would be a singular honor to lose himself to so commanding a mate. Perhaps, if he satisfied her sufficiently, he would be granted the rare privilege of fathering her other clutches and of being her acknowledged consort until the Change took him.

The intensity of his host's desire triggered a cascade of thoughts that flooded Kirk's mind with the details of the Kh!lict life cycle. With a growing sense of horror, he monitored the feelings, the needs, and the preprogrammed responses of his host, trying to find where he had misinterpreted the information. He *had* to have made a mistake somewhere; no intelligent race known to the Federation had such bizarre and transmutable biology.

The Kh!lict instincts forced his legs to move faster, pushing his body to its limits. The cold, dry air pulled every molecule of moisture from his gill membranes and parched his air ducts all the way to his lungs. Still his body tried for greater speed, although the ground was rough and littered with irregular chunks of rock. His guesses *must* be true, Kirk realized. Nothing else could explain the intensity of the Kh!lict's drive to reach the female ahead of him.

Shock surged through Kirk's mind, blotting out the Kh!lict instincts. His legs stiffened and skittered off the loose rocks beneath his pincers. He scrambled to regain his footing and overbalanced, pitching on his side. Kirk skidded, tried again to catch himself, and rolled off a low bank. His momentum flipped him onto his back, and he began to slide, picking up speed as his smooth carapace skipped across the dry, slick grass.

In scraps and snippets, images of the alien landscape registered on Chekov's consciousness. How he had gotten here, why he was here—or even something as simple as how he was traveling across this arid and unfamiliar landscape—seemed beyond his comprehension. It was as if he had been drugged and then turned loose to wander on an uncharted planet.

When the other creature had approached, he felt intensely relieved to know that he wasn't the only person on this desolate world. He was even more relieved to learn that food, shelter, and others of his kind lay back across the hills in the direction of the sunrise. Following the instructions of his elder, he began retracing his footsteps. Already he could feel the weakness in his body, the deep shakiness that emphasized his need for food and drink. And it would be nice to see others of his kind, to converse with them and exchange images of what they had seen and done in this wide and empty land.

He did not think he had traveled far, especially since the elder had reassured him that the food pens were very close at claw. However, time stretched, and he seemed no closer to his destination, even though his limbs were shaking from the effort of dragging his body across the rolling hills. It must have been much longer since he had hunted than he thought. Surely he must have had his sunrise *nanthken* yesterday—or was it the day before?

When he thought about it, he couldn't remember when he had last eaten. He knew the answer should be the first thing in his mind—the color of the *nanthken*'s fur, how much effort it had taken to capture it, what rituals he had observed in conjunction with his meal. If he could not remember that, he was losing the colors and textures that defined his life and gave it meaning. Suddenly he was no longer sure of anything.

When the transit frame appeared on the horizon, he almost turned around again. The elder had said that food and others of his kind lay in this direction, but even a fool knew that no sane Kh!lict put food pens near a transit frame. In the dim past thieves from competing cohorts had stepped through the frames, caught their meals, and disappeared before anyone detected them. In lean years such depredations forced the sacrifice of the younger males in the cohort to feed the matriarchs. Even in the present, more enlightened era, the ancient customs held and the food pens were several major eights of walking distance from the frames.

Perhaps the elder had meant the food pens were

beyond the transit frame, he thought as he drew closer to the black object. The elder's directions had been vague and somewhat confusing, especially in his present state of body. His thought processes were always confused and muddled when he went too long without eating.

At first he didn't even see the strange creatures swarming around the transit frame. From the barren and empty landscape, he had not expected any life except a few scrawny *nanthken* and the survivors of their exploration team. The only possible reason for him to be in such a desolate place was if he had been part of an exploration team searching for new places to settle. They must have seated the transit frames before the disaster. He wasn't sure what had gone wrong, but something had scattered their team and destroyed their food supplies. The elder must have tried to tell him, but both of them were too addled after the accident.

His next look at the bizarre animals stopped him in his tracks. Never within the lifetime of his race had anyone reported life-forms as deformed and appalling as these. They moved on two feet, like the arboreal fruit-catchers in the tropical jungles of the home-world, but there the resemblance ended. These animals were on bare ground, scouting as though for prey. However, nothing with so few appendages and with eyes pointed strictly to its front could succeed as a terrestrial predator in competition with the mighty Kh!lict.

He studied the beasts, wondering if they were the food the elder had said was near the transit frame. After a few moments he decided they were not edible. If the elder had intended that, Chekov's Kh!lict mind decided, the elder's thoughts were even more distorted than his own.

That left him with two choices. Their food supply was either beyond the transit frame or it was through it. Both alternatives meant that he had to pass the strange, deformed animals. His body rebelled at being near anything so repulsive, but in the end hunger won out. He needed that food quickly, before starvation further clouded his mind and destroyed his reason.

Having reached that conclusion, he regained control of his limbs. He started forward, picking up speed as he did. Going through the transit frame seemed the better choice. This was not the master frame, so most of their supplies and equipment were probably not in this area. Also, crossing through the transit frame would put some distance between himself and these bizarre animals and would give him time to puzzle out their significance and the role they fulfilled on this strange planet.

As he ran toward the frame, several of the beasts made noises and moved toward him. At each step their ungainly two-legged strides made them look ready to fall on their faces. How could anything designed along such irrational lines survive? he wondered. Chekov moved faster, his legs reaching for the distance-eating stride used by messengers in the dim past. If these animals were not food, he had no use for them. He should get past them quickly so that he could find the food pens and replenish his depleted energy stores.

He was only a few lengths from the frame when two of the creatures moved in front of him. Chekov could not have stopped if he had wanted to. He shifted his course slightly, aiming straight for the largest animal. The soft, deformed body went down under the impact, its alien flesh deforming satisfactorily beneath his pincers. The edge of his carapace brushed the other beast, knocking it toward the transit frame.

Chekov charged through the portal without waiting to see what happened behind him.

Once he quit worrying about his speed, Kirk discovered that sliding downhill on his back was not too bad. It reminded him of tobogganing when he was a boy, but this time he did not have to worry what would happen if he hit a bump. His sled covered his body and would not go flying in one direction while he went in another. His only concern was injuring himself when he reached the bottom of the slope.

Experimentally he flung out an appendage to see what would happen. His body wobbled a little, but his course seemed unaffected. He had started downslope with his head uphill, so he could not see what lay ahead of him, and the weight distribution in the Kh!lict body seemed to favor that position. If he worked at it, he guessed he could turn his carapace around, but he wasn't sure that was a good idea. This way, even though he could not see where he was going, he did not risk putting out an eye if he crashed into something head first. Until Spock changed him back to his human form, he needed to keep all the faculties of his Kh!lict body in prime working order. Also, he didn't know if any injuries he sustained while in the Kh!lict form would be carried back across the transition. That meant he didn't want to do something that would leave him crippled when he returned to his human form.

The slope flattened, and a flicker of relief went through Kirk before he returned to worrying about what lay ahead. If his luck held, friction would slow him down before he collided with something; any other outcome he would know about only when it was too late to prevent. His descent began to slow, and he reminded himself that the only way he could have kept out of this situation was to have controlled his reactions to the Kh!lict sexual cycle. After his human responses interfered with the Kh!lict's motor functions, he had earned whatever he got.

He hit a patch of gravel and started to spin. Once the rotation started, he couldn't stop it, and the uneven forces on his carapace sent him spiraling down the hill. As the scenery spun around him, he told himself that the rotation would further decrease his speed. The argument was firmly grounded in physics, but Kirk didn't find the thought very reassuring. Ahead of him was a dry stream bed littered with boulders and cobbles. It took very little imagination to know that he would be bounced around like a starship in an ion storm when he hit those rocks.

Kirk racked his brain for some way to stop himself, but in his inverted position he had no means for gaining leverage against the ground. The reduced slope and the spinning were slowing him down, but he still hit the stream bed with more speed than he liked. The water-worn cobbles slipped beneath his carapace like ball bearings. He skittered and bounced against the boulders, and the clatter of the impacts echoed and re-echoed in the confined space.

This is slowing my momentum, Kirk told himself. *Really. The physics books never lie.* Still, it was difficult to convince himself, particularly when his random collisions increased the illusion of speed. He began wishing for a larger rock, one big enough to absorb his momentum when he hit it head-on. A moment too late he remembered the adage about being careful in your choice of wishes.

A sharp spur of rock loomed ahead of him, its jointed cliffs of dark basalt forcing the stream into a sharp bend. With no control over his movements, Kirk slammed into the wall of rock, rebounded into the air, and flipped. He smashed onto the rocky stream bed with one appendage trapped underneath his body and two others twisted into unnatural positions.

The brutal landing left him disoriented. At first he couldn't remember where he was or how he had gotten there. As his mental numbness dissipated, he noticed aches and twinges everywhere in his body. The Kh!lict's heavy shell had protected him from the worst of the beating, but several of the impacts had caused internal bruising. Kirk shuddered, realizing how sore he would be when the injuries stiffened. Unlike a human, any swelling would be confined by his carapace, and the pressure on an enlarged joint could become intensely painful.

It was, however, too late for him to worry about avoiding the bruises and strains. His best hope was to keep his muscles loose by continuing to move and to hope that the cold air would keep down any swelling. One at a time he tried moving his appendages, flexing each joint to assess its condition. To his relief, nothing seemed to be broken, but several of his midlimb joints felt like they would be stiff from swelling around stressed connective tissues.

He levered himself to his pincers, testing each joint and appendage as he stood. At first his balance was unsteady, but after a few eights of steps, the black rocks and the purplish sky quit swinging around him. He staggered upstream until he found a gentle slope leading out of the stream bed.

The way was not difficult, but it took more out of him than he had expected. His Kh!lict body was reaching the end of its reserves. He needed to round up the other transformed humans quickly and then find himself some food and a place to rest.

An hour of climbing brought him back to where his foolish mistake had sent him for the long slide. He debated what to do next, but Kh!lict physiology decided matters for him. A gust of breeze tickled his gills with a whiff of something dark and mysterious. The Kh!lict's instincts took charge, and his body bolted in the direction the female Kh!lict had gone.

Chekov tumbled through the transit frame, his entry speed disturbing his balance as he stumbled through. The transition was rough, as though the maintenance crews had not serviced the mechanism recently, and it took a moment for him to regain control of his limbs. He looked for the base camp and the food pens that should have been waiting for him, but only a desolate, rust-colored plain stretched as far as the eye could see. Suddenly, as though someone had raised the curtain of fog that shrouded his brains, he knew where he was. Behind him, even before he turned around, his mind showed him the canyon with the narrow path cut into its wall. Halfway down, secure from outside attack, lay the caves and the city that controlled the world. Beyond, at the bottom of the canyon, safe from all depredation, lay the food pens with the fattest, tastiest *nanthken* any Kh!lict had ever slid its proboscis into. Some disaster greater than he could imagine must have occurred if his world had been turned into this desolate wasteland.

He started to turn, pulled toward the vision of a feast his mind was drawing for him. Distracted, he didn't realize another Kh!lict was coming through the transit frame. He shouldn't have had to worry; proper etiquette forbade following at such a short interval, but apparently this individual was trying to force a status battle. If that was the case, Chekov would be glad to oblige him.

The second Kh!lict charged through the window at full speed, crashing into Chekov's flank and spinning him halfway around. Chekov staggered but kept his limbs beneath him. He turned to face the threat. The pincers flexed on his second set of appendages, and glancing down, he saw that the claws were tipped with sharp, thick spikes that would pierce another Kh!lict's shell when aimed with sufficient force. His other pincers were also tipped with spikes, but they were not as strong as the second set.

His opponent attacked, his carapace flashing a chaotic design of reds and blacks streaked with every other color of the spectrum. Chekov read the other's rage and disorientation, but most of the patterns were chaotic, carrying no meaning. This one was crazy, with an inborn insanity that must be destroyed before he impregnated a female with his defective genes or—worse—sired his predestined quota of offspring and Changed into one of the females who ruled their world. Chekov's duty was clear: He must eliminate this one before his defects spread through the sacred Kh!lict genome.

The other Kh!lict swung a pincer at Chekov's eyes, trying to sever the basal attachments. It was so primitive and so predictable a move that Chekov could barely believe anyone, no matter how deranged, would try such an opening attack. Chekov swung his left second pincer in a sweeping circle, aiming for the vulnerable spot near his opponent's mouth, where the joint between the upper and lower plates of the carapace was thinnest. His blow connected solidly, and he felt the shell yield, but he did not penetrate deep enough for a decisive blow. The other charged past and turned, his pincers skittering on the gravel.

Chekov pivoted to follow his opponent's movements. The other was still flashing colors of hate and turmoil, now tinged with something else. The patterns changed too fast for Chekov to follow them, and he was afraid to take the time to puzzle them out. His opponent was strong, much stronger than Chekov had expected, and he needed all the skill he possessed to hold his own until he found an opening.

The next three attacks were the same as the first, down to the slices aimed at his eyes, and Chekov began wondering why his opponent was being so predictable. Even a deranged individual should know to vary his technique, especially when it hadn't worked the first time. To protect himself in case his opponent was setting up a subtle trap, Chekov varied his response, first attacking the other's limb attachments, then trying to flip the other Kh!lict on its back. He didn't believe either approach would succeed against a heavier, stronger opponent, but it made his actions harder to anticipate.

When his opponent started his run for his fifth attack and Chekov realized it would be no different that the previous four, he was ready. As the other Kh!lict approached, he pivoted to the side, moving his body out of its expected position. His opponent's stride faltered as he tried to follow Chekov's movement. Chekov rammed the spikes on both his second pincers deep into the other's carapace. The chitin yielded with an ugly, muted crack.

Momentum carried the other Kh!lict forward, tearing Chekov's pincers clear with a wet, ripping sound. Bluish-purple fluid spilled from the wound and splattered Chekov's pincers, the ground, and the dying Kh!lict. Instinct took over, and Chekov mounted the corpse, his carapace flashing an aroused and triumphant kaleidoscope of purples and oranges. His proboscis protruded from his jaws, its serrations erect and gleaming wetly as he inserted it into the gaping wound and gorged himself hungrily on the sweet, hot blood.

Chapter Sixteen

THEY BEAMED the wounded security guard up and rushed him to sickbay, bleeding from several deep puncture wounds. The Kh!lict's claws had penetrated deeply in two spots, one on the shoulder and the other on the leg, and sliced deep gashes across both arms. Shaking his head at the damage, McCoy refused to let Spock interview the patient and took the guard into surgery. Left with only the preliminary reports, Spock returned to the bridge to search for the guard who had followed the Kh!lict into the artifact.

The remotes near the sites he had identified that morning showed nothing new in those areas, and no one, human or Kh!lict, had recently passed nearby. That meant the Kh!lict and the security guard had materialized somewhere else. At least Spock hoped that they were somewhere else, although he would never admit to such an irrational impulse as hope. Diligent search techniques would find them much sooner than all the hope in the universe.

It took him fifteen minutes to sort through the *Enterprise*'s orbital-altitude scanner logs. The Kh!lict had materialized halfway around the world, in an area with no evidence of any Kh!lict transit frames or other Kh!lict ruins. By the time the *Enterprise*'s scanners zoomed in on the area, the two Kh!lict had fought, and the smaller Kh!lict was proclaiming his triumph upon the body of his defeated foe.

Spock was sure the Kh!lict's victory rite, with its ritualistic cannibalism and systematic disfiguring of the corpse, would fuel many hours of debate, but for now they had a more serious problem. Although both creatures looked *and acted* as though they were aliens, human minds were trapped in both bodies. The physical death of a Kh!lict body marked the death of its human resident, whether either of the two beings was aware of its own humanity or that of its opponent. The ethical and moral implications of the problem were staggering, even if no one considered the legal ramifications.

"Killed in the line of duty," the log entry would read, with nothing more explicit to tell what had happened. Spock hoped that whoever was involved would let it drop there. Delving deeper could become exceedingly unpleasant, both for the crewman trapped inside the surviving Kh!lict body and for the relatives of the man killed in the fight.

The only benefit was that they had another Kh!lict body to examine. From their meager scanner data, Spock thought the dead man was the guard who had been pushed into the artifact, but the information he had was not conclusive. When the victor wandered off, Spock had the body transported to the *Enterprise* and taken to sickbay for examination. Since the man was dead, the least Spock could do was wring the maximum amount of information from his death.

Perhaps his body would tell them how to prevent similar insanity from destroying the other altered humans on the planet.

"Spock, are you out of your Vulcan mind?" McCoy's voice exploded from the intercom. "You want me to autopsy another crab *and* to determine who he was? As if he was carrying his identification stapled onto his shell? I'm a doctor, not a marine biologist. I haven't a clue what to look for, Spock. Invertebrates are *not* my specialty."

"I am aware of that, Doctor." Spock heard McCoy draw in his breath to renew the assault. Before he could speak, Spock continued. "Seven people, including the captain, have been changed into these creatures, and two of them are already dead. We need all the information we can obtain about these beings. In particular, we need positive identification of this crewman to support our conjectures concerning his identity. I can send you help from the biology section. I am certain Lieutenant Jylor or Ensign Bovray will be delighted to assist you."

"I'm sure." McCoy's voice was heavy with sarcasm. "Don't do me any favors, Spock. McCoy out."

Don't do me any favors. The words repeated themselves in Spock's mind, underlining their difficulties on Careta IV. Although he relished the intellectual challenge of learning about new people and their worlds, Spock heartily wished that they had never heard of Careta IV or of the Kh!lict.

After McCoy signed off, Spock went back to searching for more Kh!lict artifacts. With the discovery of an operational transport window that had not been found earlier, the problem required more attention. He needed to know what factors signaled the presence of Kh!lict ruins.

With the deadly turn their mission was taking, Spock wanted every scrap of information as quickly as he could get it. The Kh!lict artifacts were dangerous, and the least of their threat came from his ignorance of their purpose and function. Without knowledge he had little chance of reversing the transformation process or of preventing the artifacts from accidentally changing more people into aliens whose behavior was as puzzling as their technology.

Half an hour later, a movement on the monitor caught his eye. Most of the remotes showed tranquil scenes of Kh!lict wandering across the dry, rolling hills near the second artifact. Kirk was hurrying after the largest Kh!lict as if it was the most important thing in his life. However, what had attracted Spock's attention was a different scene, that of a small Kh!lict trying to descend a vertical cliff.

Putting his data on hold, Spock broadened the scan and identified the fighter who had killed the Kh!lict McCoy was autopsying. Replaying the tape, Spock watched the small alien circle around the artifact and wander along the top of a deep canyon. Its movements seemed intent and purposeful, as though it was searching for something.

After ten minutes it apparently found its objective. With cautious movements the Kh!lict picked its way over a pile of rubble and crept across the treacherous surface of an ancient landslide. On the far side of the crumpled ground, a trail was carved into the canyon wall. The small Kh!lict started down the trail, its movements jerky from impatience and desperation.

Ordering the remote to show him the entire canyon wall, Spock began examining the two-kilometer-high rock face. From a distance the sharp line incised into the wall proclaimed its artificial origins. Up close there were gaps, some of them impassable. In many places erosion had tumbled great masses of rock and debris across the trail, while in others the rocks had been worn away from below.

The treacherous path and the small Kh!lict trying to negotiate it told Spock that a major site must be concealed nearby. He sent the remote closer to the canyon wall, scanning the layers of blocky red sandstone and fissured gray limestone. Most of the way down, nearly hidden beneath a massive landslide, Spock found the unmistakable signs of long-deserted alien habitation.

A small hole was the only part of a broad, arching ceremonial entrance that was unblocked by fallen rubble. Once he knew what to look for, Spock found remnants of the decorative carvings that had surrounded the entryway. Some of the vandalized scenes showed alien prisoners being slaughtered on low, blocky altars, while others showed graphic and violent depictions of Kh!lict in contorted positions. Spock decided that he could safely postpone examining that aspect of the Kh!lict civilization. He directed the remote to report what lay inside the opening.

At first the readings were confused. One moment the sensors reported a huge cavern, large enough to hold the *Enterprise* with room to spare. The next instant there was only solid rock from the cliff face back as far as the sensors could penetrate. Neither set of readings was logical, which suggested a third possibility. Inside the cliffs lay a major Kh!lict site concealed by a jamming field similar to the one that had hidden the first artifact. The landslide had probably been triggered to conceal the entrance.

Spock ordered a landing party to report to the transporter room in fifteen minutes. If his guess was correct, they might soon have the information they needed.

* * *

The ledge was so narrow that the landing party had to beam down two at a time. Spock and a security guard were first, materializing a safe distance from the rocks that buried the entrance. Spock tied a rope around his waist and gave the end to the guard to belay. If the caverns were booby-trapped in addition to the camouflage that obscured them, he wanted to give himself those extra seconds for the *Enterprise* to beam him to safety. Being thrown to his death by the security measures of a long-dead alien race was not the way he would choose to end his life.

As he started up the rock pile, he heard the whine of the transporter effect as two more guards materialized on the ledge. After that, if his initial report was as expected, three groups of scientists were waiting to beam down.

Spock edged his way across the rocks, testing each step before trusting the rubble to stay in place. Twice blocks of weathered sandstone crumbled beneath his weight, and the fragments skittered down the slope. However, despite its apparent instability, the pile did not begin moving as he had feared. He reached the opening and paused to examine the bas-relief on the massive stone lintel. Originally the figures had been exquisitely defined, and the detailing on some of the carvings still bore traces of bright pigment, but the sculpture had been vandalized. The fragments of the scene depicted a ritual sacrifice, but the brutality of the remaining icons penetrated even Spock's control. The eviscerated, flayed, and dismembered bodies of half a dozen non–Kh!lict races—including two known only from single, isolated occurrences—were spread across stone altars, reminding Spock of the Aztecs' brutal sacrifices of their captives. He knelt to examine the entrance before the guards realized how disgusting he found those images.

At close range it was obvious that someone had

blasted the overhanging rock wall to bury the caverns. The opening had once been completely concealed, but the rubble had since fallen away to expose the opening. His tricorder could not give him a definite age for the carvings or for their burial, although he estimated the site had been built over 250,000 years ago. That age was consistent with everything else they had found on Careta IV.

Pulling out his torch, Spock worked his way into the opening. Inside the rubble spread across the floor of what had once been a large cavern. Now fallen columns and slabs of rock littered the floor and clogged the space. Reflections off random bits of metal and assorted junk told him the cavern was not purely natural, as did the remnants of carvings on several of the columns. A thick layer of dust covered everything, as though nothing had ventured inside in millennia. Conceivably, the last people to enter the room were those who had blasted the entrance shut.

Spock eased himself back out and stood, pulling out his communicator. "Spock to *Enterprise*. Commence beaming down the science teams. The presence of a large cavern behind the rock slide is confirmed. We will investigate this site thoroughly. Inasmuch as this promises to be an archaeological find of some significance, please request Dr. Lassiter to join the landing party, along with anyone Dr. Kaul wishes to send down." He allowed himself a moment's relief that Kaul was not yet sufficiently recovered from his reaction to the suldanic gas to be able to join the landing party. Until the senior archaeologist accepted the importance of their discoveries, Spock did not look forward to handling the personality conflicts Kaul's disbelief provoked.

"Acknowledged." Relays clicked on Uhura's board as she passed on his orders. "Is there anything else you need, Mr. Spock?"

"Not at the moment, Lieutenant Uhura. I will keep you informed if the situation changes. Spock out." He replaced his communicator on his belt and descended to greet the new arrivals.

By the time he reached the stable footing of the trail, Lassiter and seven other science specialists had materialized. Tallieur, the ship's assistant historian, was huddled against the cliff, casting apprehensive looks toward the sheer drop a meter from his feet. On the opposite end of the spectrum, a security guard and the young man who had come with Lassiter were leaning over the edge and discussing the best technique for attempting an unaided descent.

"May I have your attention, please?" He paused. "We have discovered a major Kh!lict center. Unfortunately, someone has vandalized the site. Given that a later civilization, probably the Meztoriens, has taken great pains to conceal all signs of the Kh!lict, we should proceed under the assumption that there is something even more dangerous about the Kh!lict than what we already know."

Tallieur cleared his throat. "Mr. Spock, um, if the Kh!lict civilization or, um, its successors were so dangerous, shouldn't we know about them, even if they died out so long ago? Most races survive in, um, in the legends of their successors."

"That's one of the questions we hope to answer, Lieutenant. So far a computer search reveals no references to the Kh!lict, unless we assume that the vast majority of the so-called orphan cultures were destroyed by them. However, we are continuing the search in hopes of turning up definitive answers. Does anyone else have questions they wish to raise at this time?" When no one did, Spock hefted his torch and turned back to the talus pile. "In that case, let us proceed with our investigation."

Chapter Seventeen

THE INSIDE OF THE CAVERN was far brighter than Spock had expected. He moved forward, and with every step his boots raised clouds of powdery beige dust that turned golden when they caught the slanted rays of sunlight coming through the opening. Five meters from the door, he stopped to examine his surroundings. Details of partially destroyed carvings stood out in sharp relief, as though lit by direct sunlight, and the expected dust was absent from the incised designs, which showed more scenes of mass sacrifices and ritual murder. No light source was visible in the cavern, and the center of the room was heavily shadowed, but whatever system the Kh!lict had used to illuminate this area was still working.

Silence, broken only by the whirs of half a dozen tricorders, told him the rest of the party was also looking around, trying to decide what to study first. The chamber had once been as large as the *Enterprise*'s hangar deck, with elaborately frescoed walls and ornately carved columns. However, the blast that had piled tons of rock over the entrance had disrupted the room's buttressing and toppled many of the decorative pillars. The facings had sloughed away from the structural supports, forming piles of broken rock and plaster at the base of the metal columns. Fallen ceiling panels, smashed into rubble or flung around like cards discarded by a gigantic child, choked the area with debris. At the northern end of the room, where the blast had been strongest, all the supports had collapsed, and the roof and outer wall had been reduced to fragments little larger than Spock's fist.

"Comments, anyone?" Spock asked, wondering how many anomalies he had missed. The contrast between the areas of complete destruction and the bits of still-operational Kh!lict technology, such as the lighting system, was striking.

"All or nothing," Lassiter murmured, scanning the back wall with her tricorder. "Either it's destroyed or it's untouched."

"Some of these carvings are almost three *hundred* millennia old." Amtov Kordes, Lassiter's assistant, was a chunky, dark-skinned man with a thick Dindraed accent, broad on the vowels and burred on the consonants. "Yet their surfaces are as fresh as if the work was finished yesterday."

"I don't understand the lighting technology at all." A frown twisting her round face, the *Enterprise*'s alien technology expert, Ensign Temren Knealayz, pointed her tricorder overhead and scanned the ceiling a third time. "I should detect something now that we're past the jamming field."

Spock duplicated her tricorder scan. His readings showed nothing but solid rock over their heads. "Ensign, characterize the jamming field."

"The field is extremely directional and strongly focused outward to screen this site. I'm not familiar

197

with jammer designs that serve this specific function, but I'd certainly know more if we could locate the projectors for the field." She shook her head, sending a train of ripples through her golden brown hair. "From this side of the field, I've obtained a crude frequency modulation profile. I wouldn't call my data definitive, but the pattern resembles some Meztorien field generators I've examined in the past."

Lassiter referred to her tricorder. Keeping her eyes on the screen, she said, "Approximately half of all Meztorien devices, normally those from the last millennia before their disappearance, can be restored to working order. However, no devices have continued to operate to the present."

Kordes stepped forward, swinging his tricorder in rhythm to his strides. "The devices normally fail because they lack an appropriate power source. It has long been theorized that the Meztoriens were capable of creating a technology that would survive through the millennia, if they'd gained control of the required energy sources. Dr. Kaul will be gratified to learn that his hypotheses have at last been vindicated."

Lassiter's mouth tightened as though she had just bitten into a sour stonefruit. "What we're seeing here, Amtov, implies that the jamming field generators were tied into an older technology. It's hardly a vindication of anyone's theories. At least, not until we've traced everything to its source."

Interpreting human motivations was not his specialty, Spock knew, but no one could miss the hostility between Lassiter and Kordes. Kordes was trying to undermine Lassiter's authority, either with Kaul's blessing or because he thought it was the fastest way to promote his own career. To avoid an ugly confrontation, Spock directed the discussion toward their immediate objective. "Locating those devices is an excellent suggestion, Dr. Lassiter. We will begin detailed examinations of this cavern immediately. All personnel should pay particular attention to locating power conduits and possible exits to adjacent sites."

Tallieur tilted his head to one side. "Does that mean you think there's more here than just this room, Mr. Spock?"

Spock considered the question. Was there more to the site than this partially destroyed room? With great effort the Kh!lict had built the access trail down the cliffs and decorated the entrance and the walls with detailed carvings. When he added the fact that the small Kh!lict seemed very determined to get here, everything pointed to the significance of their find. "Indeed, Mr. Tallieur. The question is whether our technology and our powers of observation are equal to the task of penetrating the protective measures that someone used to conceal this place."

"Understood." Tallieur started to examine one of the undamaged bas-reliefs, which showed several Kh!lict butchering a group of avianlike humanoids. The others took their cue from Tallieur and began working. With the confrontation averted, Spock started on his chosen project, examining the ceiling to determine how the illumination reached the carvings on the walls and spread through the enclosed cavern.

"I'm a doctor, not a marine invertebrate biologist," McCoy muttered to himself for the tenth time since the body of the dead Kh!lict had been delivered to his sickbay. He knew the statement was illogical; the Kh!lict had not been sea-dwellers in more millennia than he wanted to think about. However, because it let him hide his uneasiness about this particular autopsy, the irrationality was comforting. Although the Kh!lict body plan bore a striking resemblance to terrestrial crabs, the physiology was radically different. To make matters worse, although the corpse was alien, he kept remembering that it had once, however briefly, housed a human consciousness.

"Christine, what did we get from that latest chemistry panel?" he called, catching the flash of her blond hair as she returned from the lab.

"It'll be another half hour." Chapel ignored the impatience in his tone. Each lab report suggested new tests, and McCoy had spent the entire afternoon demanding the results as soon as the samples were delivered to the laboratory. That they both knew why he was so impatient did nothing to lessen his testiness. Comparing the test results of the two dead Kh!lict was finally giving them a handle on their physiology, but the answers were still painfully slow in coming.

"If we don't figure out what makes these creatures tick pretty soon, they're all going to starve. How will it look to Starfleet Command if we let Jim and the others die for lack of food?"

"You have a point, Doctor." Chapel turned to her computer screen, where she was correlating the corpses' physical parameters with the records of the missing crewmen. "However, I believe we have a little more leeway than you think."

"The problem, as I see it, is that they'll start shrinking inside those shells, and their muscles will start pulling away from their attachment points." He switched the scanners to a different channel and waited for the enzyme readouts to appear on his diagnostic screen. "A man in a baggy pair of pants is funny, but I don't think any of these crabs are going to find anything amusing about walking around in an oversized shell. In fact, I think it might make them downright irritable."

"It may." Chapel entered the command for "Repeat analysis" into the computer, and a moment later the screen flashed, "Duplicate analysis confirmed." She turned the display toward McCoy. "Doctor, we have a confirmed identification for the second dead man. He's Ensign Bradford Nairobi, the guard who was pushed into the artifact by the crab's charge."

McCoy grunted. "Nairobi? Pull up his records and see if there's anything unique in his profile. Anything we can use to help us identify the rest of our people."

"Yes, Doctor." Chapel started back to the lab, the tapping of her boot heels receding as she left the room. McCoy glanced after her, knowing that the lab technicians must be as tired of his late-breaking flashes of inspiration as he was of having a new idea spring up every time he was ready to concede to the mysterious Kh!lict. Still, his real problem was that the people on the planet, however bizarre their present form and physiology, were human, and he had to keep them alive until Spock could return them to their proper form.

He returned to his study of the Kh!lict's bicameral brain, trying to unravel the nerve connections that led from each sub-brain. It was the strangest way of controlling a body he had seen since his school days, when his exobiology class had constructed plausible brain structures for the great brontosauroids of Earth's far-distant past. Because of the vast length of their spinal cords those immense beasts had needed secondary neural nodes to control their motor functions. Without the subsidiary hip nexi to coordinate their reflex actions, they could not have responded rapidly to emergency situations. The Kh!lict had evolved a similar arrangement for subdividing their neurological functions, but without the justification of extreme size.

The dead bodies gave McCoy few clues to how this arrangement functioned in life, although Spock's interview with Kirk provided some tantalizing hints. For Kirk's identity to remain intact, it had to be housed in one section of the brain, presumably the area that governed the higher mental functions. Furthermore, that sub-brain must function independently of the areas that controlled the Kh!lict instinctual behavior and contained the preprogrammed learning.

McCoy knew his speculations would be difficult to prove, but he couldn't be too far off base. Unless Kirk's identity was spatially isolated from the Kh!lict functions, the distinctions would break down, and the Kirk/Kh!lict composite would become dysfunctional. The evidence so far, supported by Spock's interview with Kirk, was that the dysfunctions they were seeing in the Kh!lict were caused by isolation of the two halves of the brain rather than conflicting spatial mapping of separate and incompatible identities.

That the Kh!lict programming could—and perhaps in most cases would—dominate the composite seemed clear, given Kirk's reports on the strong hard-wired component of their culture and biology. When McCoy added in the disorientation that the humans would feel on finding themselves in the bodies of aliens they had not even known about three days ago, he realized it was a miracle even one person had been able to communicate with them. His next job, after figuring out what the Kh!lict ate, was to reach the other human minds trapped inside Kh!lict bodies and reassure those people that help was on the way.

Chapel returned from the lab, carrying the summary tapes from the latest tests. "I think we may have something here, Doctor. At least Dennis thought there was enough to try constructing a usable formula."

"Let's see." McCoy flipped on the stasis field to preserve the corpse. Technically, he shouldn't need to worry about decomposition for several hours, but long experience with starship medicine had taught him that interruptions always appeared when you hadn't planned for them. The stasis field would hold the corpse if he did not get back to his autopsy immediately, although standard procedure called for cryostorage in addition to stasis. Certainly for such a unique specimen, Starfleet Medical Branch would want to examine the corpse, and McCoy wanted to give them both Kh!lict bodies in prime condition.

McCoy dropped Chapel's tape into his computer and began reading, pausing occasionally to refer to his autopsy notes. The Kh!lict had three triangular teeth set in the front of a tiny jaw. The arrangement of the teeth allowed the Kh!lict to puncture its prey or to shear through soft tissue, but was ineffective for chewing food. Without any grinding teeth and with most of the space inside the mouth occupied by the proboscis when it was retracted, the Kh!lict had to have survived on a liquid diet. The enzyme studies and the structure of the siphonlike proboscis suggested that they had injected their food with powerful enzymes. When the food liquefied, they sucked it into their gullets through the proboscis.

He shuddered, realizing what those digestive enzymes would do to a human body. Luckily for humans, Kh!lict biochemistry was alien enough that humans would not seem appetizing. In that the crew was fortunate, McCoy decided, considering the savagery portrayed in the last artifacts Spock had found on the planet.

Shaking his head, McCoy went back to the biochemical data on his screen. The Kh!lict were predators, he concluded, functioning like certain terrestrial spiders. That meant that their natural foods resembled blood or pulverized meat. All he had to do was create a nutritionally sound formula that appealed to the Kh!lict palate.

"We don't have to do much, do we?" Chapel

commented, her thoughts traveling on a course parallel to his. "Just invent gourmet fare for a race that died out a hundred millennia ago. No problem."

McCoy chuckled. "I'll settle for something they'll manage to choke down at this point. Whether it's gourmet dining or pig swill, I don't care, as long as it does the job."

"All things considered, even that's a tall order, I'm afraid." She called up the data on her console. "Why don't I figure out how to feed it to them while you work on the formula?"

"Just what I was about to suggest." He gave her the relevant section of his autopsy notes, even though she knew Kh!lict anatomy almost as well as he did. "Let's see how quickly we can get this done."

"Yes, Doctor." Her tone was grim, showing she, too, knew they were struggling to prevent their people from starving on a planet that could no longer support the life-forms they had become.

Their break, when it came three hours later, was so like a scene from one of Kirk's favorite cheap entertainments that at first Spock could not believe what was happening. Tallieur had been scanning a section of the wall decorations repeatedly in various spectral bands. Spock was about to ask him why those carvings were so fascinating when Tallieur pushed against the central medallion in the design. Without warning a section of the wall vanished, leaving a dark hole in its place.

"What did you do?" demanded Kordes in a tone that assumed he was in charge.

"Please report, Mr. Tallieur." Spock stepped forward and blocked Kordes without seeming to notice him. If he gave Kordes the slightest opportunity, the archaeologist would bully everyone around him into taking his orders. That Spock could not permit if they were to accomplish their goals. Kordes placed his career above all else, but their mission was to rescue the captain and the other people who had been changed into Kh!lict. Anything else was secondary.

Tallieur faced Spock, deliberately ignoring Kordes. "These carvings resembled similar work found on Belesov V. There the purpose of the carvings was to conceal the hidden passageways around the royal audience chambers. I wondered if similar considerations influenced these decorations, sir."

"So you tested your hypothesis. Did it occur to you that it might be unwise to do so in a room full of people?" Spock glanced at his tricorder, which confirmed that the weak flickers he saw in his peripheral vision were power surges in a force field that filled the opening. They were safe as long as the field remained in place.

"Yes, sir. It occurred to me. However, my readings indicated that, if the opening existed, the space could not be much larger than my tricorder." Tallieur blushed a deep crimson. "In future I'll remember that this technology is too advanced for us to reject any possibility simply because our instruments don't register its effects."

"A wise rule." Spock studied the opening. Experimentally he touched the surface. A tingling warmth, similar to the one that surrounded the transit frames, crawled up his arm. He reached in farther, waiting for the overwhelming pull that characterized the fields around the Kh!lict transporters, but it didn't come. Finally he withdrew his arm, nodding to himself. "This field is different from the ones we have previously encountered. Ensign Knealayz, do you have a preliminary analysis?"

Knealayz gave him an apologetic grin. "It doesn't

match the parameters for any class of field known to our science. I've got some theories, sir, but I'll need several hours of sensor readings before I can conduct the analysis."

"We do not have the time to wait." Spock glanced at his tricorder, but his readings made no more sense than their earlier data. The long-dead aliens had not wanted their relics to be found after they had gone. "Mr. Tallieur, would you put your tricorder through the field and see if it can tell us anything?"

Tallieur slid his tricorder into the darkness. Spock kept his instrument trained on the field, and Knealayz and Lassiter scanned on a broader focus around the opening. Unless they knew where the mechanisms were housed, any tricorder might record the information that would give them the key to the Kh!lict technology.

After several minutes Tallieur withdrew his arm. His tricorder was still working, its sensors whirring normally although it had just passed through a Kh!lict force field twice. Spock nodded. "This field is definitely not the same as the others. Did anyone observe something of note?"

A chorus of negatives answered him. Spock nodded again. Since their efforts to date had produced so little data on the Kh!lict technology, it would have been surprising if they had detected any changes this time. However, he had needed to be sure before making the next test. "Will someone volunteer to walk through the field?"

Tallieur's response was immediate. "I'll do it, sir. I activated the field, so I should be the person to risk its effects."

"Very well, Mr. Tallieur. You, Dr. Lassiter, and I will examine your tricorder readings for any pertinent information. Everyone else may return to his or her previous activities." He reached for Tallieur's tricorder. Tallieur and Lassiter closed on either side of him to read the data.

"I protest this procedure," Kordes announced in a loud voice, planting himself in front of Spock. "I should be the person to explore this new discovery."

"Request denied." Spock didn't look up from the tricorder. "If Mr. Tallieur's test proves that passage through the field is safe, we all will explore beyond this room. Until then you may resume your previous investigation."

"I refuse to accept your unlawful orders." Before Spock could react, Kordes ran to the opening and dived through. The force field flared bright gold, then returned to black.

Lassiter replayed the data for Kordes's disappearance on her tricorder. "It wasn't pointed directly at the portal, but it was running," she said in an apologetic tone. "And here, when I turned to watch him, we can see through the gap that opened for him. It looks like a corridor or a long, narrow room."

"Mr. Tallieur's readings show the same phenomenon. They also confirm that the atmosphere on the other side is identical to that on this side." Spock looked from the tricorder to the opening. "I do not believe we will learn anything more without sending someone through and trying to bring him back. Are you ready, Mr. Tallieur?"

The historian squared his shoulders. "As ready as I'm going to be, Mr. Spock." He took his tricorder from Spock and switched it back to "Record" mode. Crossing to the opening, he took one last look around and then stepped through the force field.

Once again the field flared to gold and then faded to black. One second, two seconds, three. The interval stretched to over a minute before Tallieur, still in human form, stepped back through the field. "There's an extensive system of corridors and rooms behind this entryway, Mr. Spock. I would guess this force field is here merely to keep the uninitiated from entering the heart of the complex."

"I hope you are correct, Mr. Tallieur, because our answers are not in this chamber." Spock called the ship, telling them of the discovery and his decision to explore further inside the mountain. He ordered Sulu to keep the transporter room manned constantly, ready to pull them out of trouble at a moment's notice. With the formalities taken care of, Spock lined up his team, and one by one they stepped through the Kh!lict force field and into the unknown.

Chapter Eighteen

THE FEMALE HAD TRAVELED farther than he thought, given the immediacy of her scent, and Kirk could feel the shaking in his legs by the time he once again approached her position. Reason told him to break off this pursuit and find food, but reason didn't seem to be high on the list of things that motivated his host. Once he sensed the female in the area, the Kh!lict's instincts would not let go until he had mated with her. All other considerations had been erased from his mind.

When the female came in sight, Kirk realized his host had made a serious miscalculation. *She* was on the next ridge. A deep, narrow canyon divided them, the vertical walls near the stream course making it as impassable as Earth's Grand Canyon would be to a human. His host could never make the crossing on his own, and Kirk briefly entertained the idea of aiding the Kh!lict, if that was the only way to ease the compulsion that drove his host. He could see dozens of hand- and footholds in the fissured rock below him, but he was reluctant to try any more rock climbing in a Kh!lict body.

That left his host with only one option, if he was determined to gain access to the female. He would have to retrace his course until he found a place where the canyon was passable. If Kirk was lucky, he would travel far enough that the Kh!lict would lose scent of the female, and Kirk could regain control of his body. Then he would resume searching for the *other* missing people. Logic told him the female must be Talika, since she was the only woman who had been changed to a Kh!lict, and his mind shied away from the diplomatic repercussions of the liaison his host was contemplating. Kirk wondered what the Kh!lict equivalent of a cold shower was, but the thought did not trigger any answering impressions from his host. He would have to wait until events returned control of his host's body to him.

The Kh!lict started along the ridge, forcing his legs to move as fast as they could. Kirk sensed that the creature would have pushed the pace even more, but his body was faltering. The long marches and the lack of food had drained his energy reserves, and even the bellyful of algal scum that Kirk had forced down the previous night would not keep him going much longer.

Even so, the mating drive overrode all other concerns, and the Kh!lict kept moving as fast as he could. The female was back there, and she could not wait; if he did not get there soon, some other male might impregnate her. He could not let that happen.

The sun dipped toward the horizon, and still his host struggled to return to the female. After three abortive attempts to cross the canyon, he reached its upper end. Circling around the splayed stream channels at the canyon's head, Kirk's host reached the ridge where the female had been. Kirk struggled to head back toward the artifact, but the Kh!lict's instincts were still in control. His host poured on the speed, finding reserves of energy Kirk did not know he had.

An hour before sunset he finally caught up with the female. She was standing on the end of a headland overlooking a small, muddy lake. Even through his thick carapace, Kirk felt the icy bite of the wind, and he shivered at the idea of spending a night on this point, unprotected from the wind and the falling temperatures. It had been many thousands of years since this desolate land had supported life as the Kh!lict knew it.

At first the female seemed unaware of his approach. She kept her back to him, and her carapace remained a neutral beige. Surely she should have recognized the arrival of so strong and eager a partner by now. If she was ignoring him, it meant either that someone had beaten him to his goal or that something catastrophic was preventing her from responding to the most basic drive a Kh!lict could know.

He moved closer, blinking a kaleidoscope of eagerness and submission, alternating with boasts of his skill and prowess. The latter, Kirk realized, were empty images, formed out of his host's biological imperative and not based on actual experience. As alien as the Kh!lict were, some things transcended all barriers. Young Kh!lict males told the same exaggerated stories about themselves as did young males from almost every known race in the universe.

His host moved forward, clicking his pincers and scuffing rocks to get the female's attention. She turned finally, flashing orange bars of irritation. <What do you want, boy?> she demanded. <Be gone and leave an Elder in peace!>

<Oh, most high Elder, I crave the honor of serving

your needs in any manner that pleases you.> Kirk's host moved forward, his bold movements contradicting his groveling words. Given the female's attitude, Kirk thought it would be wise to leave immediately, but his host could not read the rejection in her images. He moved closer, rubbing his carapace against her side.

<Be gone!> she flashed again, her images more forceful. <I have no need of soft-shelled babies like you!>

<Oh, most high and powerful Elder, let me prove my worth to you.> Kirk's host rubbed harder against the female's side, trying to impress her with his virility. The Kh!lict mind seemed unable to recognize that her refusal was sincere and permanent. How could he regain control of his body before the female retaliated against the unwelcome advances?

Before he could try again to overcome the Kh!lict's instincts, the female responded. Hooking her legs beneath his carapace, she shoved. He flipped over and landed on his back, sliding downhill. A warm glow surged through his host at the thought that this was the greatest, most powerful female that had ever existed. Oblivious to his admiration, the female gave him another shove, and he picked up speed.

Suddenly the ground dropped away from beneath him, and Kirk was sailing through the air, a hundred meters above the rusty surface of the lake. Kirk remembered wondering about the Kh!lict equivalent of a cold shower. He had a horrible feeling he was about to find out what it was.

It must be here somewhere, Chekov thought, scouting across the surface of the landslide. He knew the path to the hidden city lay on this cliff face, concealed behind enough obstacles to keep individuals from other cohorts from stumbling upon it accidentally.

The question was, had he missed it himself, given his dazed and weakened condition? The battle had taken more from him than he had thought, using energy reserves he knew his body couldn't spare, although he had fought a smart duel and had taken his fill of his defeated enemy.

To top everything off, the area had changed since he last saw it. The vegetation had withered and died, the weather had turned cold, and the camouflage had been redesigned. He was starting to feel like an invader in his own cohort's stronghold instead of the conquering hero returning against the odds from a difficult mission. What had happened? Why was his memory so misty about the significant images that surrounded his life?

He moved farther, clambering on top of the landslide in hopes of gaining a better view. Nine times out of ten, his lower brain reminded him, only a rock wall stood beyond the slumped debris. This pile of rubble showed all the earmarks of being just such a piece of camouflage, its presence intended to fool invaders into believing that it concealed the trail. There might even be a false path leading around the corner, tempting intruders to follow it onto a blind shelf.

Still, his memory insisted that this was the trail to the hidden city, so Chekov took the path when he saw it. Maybe the invaders had been so numerous that the Elders had concealed the main trail. He could not believe they had destroyed it utterly, especially when the Elder had not informed him of the change. The trail was here, and he would find out what had happened when he reached the city.

The danger must be severe if the Elder had been unable to tell him when they met. Chekov was sure that no one had been within seeing distance, which meant that the Elders suspected the destruction of his world and its life-forms was the work of one of the technologically advanced cohorts. Less than an eight of cohorts possessed scrying devices capable of watching someone's conversations without others being aware that their devices were nearby.

The longer he thought about his meeting with the Elder and considered how little his world matched his memories, the more Chekov realized the magnitude of the disaster that had befallen him. He should have remained on the other side of the transit frame, should have offered the Elder whatever assistance he could.

Still, the Elder had sent him to find food, which said that the Elder knew more than he did. The Elder wanted him to fortify himself for a great mission. He was being made ready to save his people.

As soon as that thought occurred to him, Chekov knew it was right. The wasteland around him, the drastic alterations that made his world almost incapable of supporting life—everything pointed to the need for a savior to redeem his people. He was the Chosen One, the mighty warrior who would save his cohort from the ruin visited upon it by their evil opponents. Now that he knew the truth he could not fail in the great assignment the Elder had given him.

The visions of his glorious mission carried Chekov across the next three landslides and inspired him to traverse the narrow gaps where rock falls had removed the support for the trail, leaving only open air and fissured rock to hold his weight.

With each new obstacle Chekov felt his confidence wavering, but he reminded himself that the Elder was counting on him. He had to reach the hidden city to see what his cohort needed from him. It was his duty to accomplish the great deed that he had been given.

Clambering over rock piles and inching his way along fissures that were too narrow by half for him was exhausting work. In addition, a cold wind gusted down the canyon, kicking dust in his eyes and threatening to slap him off the cliff. Chekov knew he must believe in his mission. Surely the Elder would not have asked the impossible from him.

Suddenly Chekov knew he had misunderstood the Elder. The trail was so bad that the Elder could not have meant for him to descend all the way to the canyon floor. Reminding him of the *nanthken* pens in the valley below was only the tool the Elder had used to start him in the right direction. There were other ways to reach the valley floor, and the Elder must have intended for him to use the lift tubes inside the city. Anyone with such a vital mission would have all the resources of the cohort at his disposal.

He paused, trying to get his bearings. The upper entrance into the city had always been well concealed. With the current modifications to the camouflage, it would be hidden even better than before. He hunkered down on the trail to minimize his exposure to the wind. He had to be close, but for several long eights he couldn't remember enough landmarks to tell how far he needed to go. Hunger was dulling his mental processes and slowing his reactions to an unbearably sluggish pace. The Elders would have to let him feed before he could do any important work. He only hoped they had a bunch of fresh *nanthken* waiting for him, their hind legs lashed together in the traditional manner of offerings given to his cohort's greatest heroes.

The late afternoon sun made it difficult for him to see where he was. Unbidden, the memory surfaced that his people only used this trail in the early morning, when the cliff was in shadows and the uneven light disguised their carapaces as they worked their way down to the city. Still, he didn't have much choice. Given the urgency of his mission, he had to gamble. His uncertain recollections told him the entrance was a few eights of paces farther down the trail. With nothing better to guide him, Chekov heaved himself back onto his pincers and started down the trail.

Chapter Nineteen

THE CORRIDOR WAS WIDE and its walls were a mottled rusty beige, the variations caused by color differences in the sandstone into which the complex had been excavated. The low ceiling, which fit Spock's predictions for Kh!lict architecture, was barely high enough for the humans to stand erect. At intervals broad portals pierced the walls, their doors deeply carved with violent and brutal scenes similar to the ones that had been vandalized in the outer cavern. Several panels depicted mass sacrifices, and among the victims Spock recognized several races known only from isolated artifacts that had survived their makers. The difference between this area and the outer cavern was that no one had disturbed these carvings since their creators had vanished many tens of millennia ago.

In fact, despite the immense age of the complex, everything was in pristine condition, and there was little dust anywhere. Only a light powdering on the floor carried the imprint of Kordes's footprints.

Whatever cleaned this part of the complex was still functioning despite its age. Spock lifted an eyebrow, thinking how many people in the Federation would kill for the resale rights to a still-working technology created by a people who had been dead so long that even the legends of their existence had been forgotten.

After everyone had come through the portal unharmed, Spock started down the corridor, looking for clues that would direct them to the control center for the complex. He had no doubt that it existed; the care with which the Kh!lict had concealed this location pointed strongly to its being the headquarters for all their activities on Careta IV. Somewhere nearby, Spock hoped, they would discover a still-functioning library computer that contained the information they needed. He would have to translate the data into a usable form, but Spock was certain his computer skills were more than equal to deciphering the Kh!lict's data storage systems. After that it became a race to change their people from Kh!lict back to humans before more of them were killed.

They stopped to look behind some of the doors, choosing at random which ones to investigate. All opened into square rooms with very low ceilings. The interior walls were plain and unadorned, although occasional piles of fibrous debris suggested that tapestries might once have covered the stone. Most of the rooms contained objects made of sandstone slabs, which resembled narrow, waist-high, backless benches that could have supported a Kh!lict's body while letting its pincers swing clear of the floor. In the center of about half the rooms were larger objects that looked like desks or tables made of blocks of gray limestone. Nowhere did they learn who had used the rooms or what function they had served, although Tallieur suggested that they had been used for ritual penance or indoctrination.

By the time they had gone a hundred meters, Spock realized that distances inside the complex were deceptive. The lighting was the same diffuse, indirect illumination that had confused them in the outer cavern. No apparent energy source provided the light, and no one had determined how it reached its targets. Patches of darkness spaced randomly along the corridor suggested that the system was failing, but that told Spock nothing, since he had yet to figure out how it worked.

A hundred and fifty meters from the entrance, they reached the first cross-corridor. It stretched in both directions, appearing no different than the corridor they were in. If they encountered many such intersections, Spock realized the humans would have trouble retracing their route. With his inborn sense of direction, he did not anticipate trouble, but the others were not so well-equipped.

The farther they moved away from the entrance, the more frequently other corridors crossed theirs. As he counted the number of intersections, Spock felt increasingly certain that this was the master complex. The landing party had started from the ceremonial entrance, which was designed to awe and intimidate anyone who came to the cavern. The rooms near the entrance, which seemed so uniform and so uninteresting, appeared to be meeting rooms for individual interviews, training, or indoctrination. If they had known where to look, they might have discovered the Kh!lict equivalent of two-way mirrors concealed in the walls overlooking the cavern. The Kh!lict priesthood had probably not stored much of value in the rooms closest to their temple for fear that the complex would be looted or, worse, that someone would subvert their followers into rebelling against their ruling class. In most highly repressive societies, Spock thought, the rulers displayed an extreme degree of paranoia.

Such speculations did not help him locate the main control center, however. Finding that depended on choosing the right path through this maze of rooms and corridors, and Spock's estimation of the size of the complex increased with each step. Their tricorders gave them no long-range information on their surroundings, which suggested that the walls incorporated shields that severely attenuated their scanning beams. Even knowing their location, the *Enterprise*'s sensors had been unable to distinguish the complex from the background noise. The ship was keeping its fix on their position only because of their communicators, and Scott refused to beam additional personnel inside the complex. However, he had locked onto Kordes's communicator and beamed him back to the *Enterprise*, fighting mad at having his personal expedition canceled by Spock's orders. Anybody they wanted to join them would have to beam down *outside* the cavern.

For the first half hour, they moved inward, checking rooms at random to see if they contained anything of interest. The Kh!lict did not seem like beings whose rulers would be easily accessible, and once they were away from the entrance, the choices became less obvious. If their tricorders or the ship's sensors had told them even roughly how large the complex was, Spock could have estimated where to look for their objective. As it was, they were hunting blind.

"Damn! I'm just not getting *anything!*" Knealayz pivoted, swinging her tricorder in a full circle. "No shielding should be so good that we can't find variations in the background magnetic flux."

"Or something to indicate which end is up," added Tallieur. He frowned, searching the walls as if expecting a map to be engraved in the stones. "It's not like everything is so deteriorated that what we're looking for vanished a million years ago. Most of this looks like it was abandoned yesterday."

Lassiter nibbled on a lock of her pale hair. "It's got to be so obvious that we're missing it completely. This is the place; this *is* their center. I sense that much, but I don't know where to go from there." She blushed a deep crimson, realizing how much she had revealed with those few words, but no one challenged her.

"The only things we know about the Kh!lict are what Captain Kirk has told us and what we see around us." Spock tried to see their surroundings from a Kh!lict perspective. This corridor, like all the others, had been cut from solid rock, and no effort had been made to alter the natural colors or textures. In the distance they had traveled, the rocks had gone from the massive rusty sandstone near the entrance to a finer-grained and lighter-colored sandstone to the buff siltstone that surrounded them here. If the Kh!lict had left the rocks unmodified, perhaps they had some significance. What was it?

"Mr. Spock, you said that their language was based on color and gesture, didn't you?" Tallieur was frowning at his tricorder. "And that most of the information is carried in the colors and the visual patterns?"

"That is correct." An image of the cliff face flashed through Spock's mind. The rocks were tilted at a thirty-degree angle so that a rock layer that started at the canyon's rim would eventually reach stream level. Also, since the canyon cut across the rocks in an oblique direction, the layers also sloped backward into the hill. A tunnel driven straight into the cliff would eventually intersect every different type of rock found in the canyon. "Can we correlate the types of rooms we've been in and their location along this tunnel?"

Lassiter flipped through the records on her tricorder. "We have sampled the rooms randomly and have found three basic plans so far." Her voice rose in surprise. "The room layouts appear to be constant within each rock type. However, given the percentage of the complex that we've seen, we haven't come close to sampling a statistically valid subset of the rooms available."

"I am aware that we do not have sufficient data to support a scientifically defensible conclusion, Dr. Lassiter." Her reluctance to speculate gave Spock new insight into Kirk's often all-too-apparent irritation with his own caution in similar circumstances. He promised himself to reexamine his own actions later, when he had time for such things. At the moment, however, they needed a premise for locating the center of this complex as quickly as possible. "In the interests of shortening our search, can we formulate a working hypothesis that we can test with our explorations?"

Tallieur lifted three fingers. "The outer rooms had benches of the same stone as the walls, and some had desklike objects of gray limestone. The rooms in the lighter-colored sandstone had more desks, but these were made of the same rock as the walls. And the last rooms we've checked contained nothing at all."

"The only thing that stands out is those limestone desks." Lassiter chewed harder on the ends of her hair. "We were speculating that those rooms might be audience chambers for the priests or whatever high officials ran this place. Would the limestone have special significance for them?"

"Do we have anything stronger to base a conclusion on?" Tallieur asked. "I'd prefer something more solid, but I'll gamble on just about anything."

Knealayz gave the corridor another sweep with her tricorder. "Why not? We've traveled far enough that I should be detecting differences in the e-m flux, if nothing else. After all, we can *see* that their equipment is still using power; otherwise the lights would have gone out. So anything is better than stumbling around waiting for a lucky break."

"Very well." Spock had not expected them to agree so quickly. "In that case, we shall proceed down this corridor with all possible speed until we encounter the limestone unit from which the desklike objects were obtained. Meanwhile, everyone is to consider the means by which the Kh!lict moved from level to level within this complex. What we seek may be above or below us, and we must discover a method for contending with that possibility."

To the chorus of acknowledgments, Spock started down the corridor at the fastest speed he considered the humans capable of maintaining. So far, despite the low oxygen content of Careta's atmosphere, the group was holding up well. However, he dared not push them too far, or they would not be fit to cope with the unexpected, should it arise.

Two hours later Spock was beginning to question the logic that had started this enforced march. They had crossed two fault zones, each of which thrust the lower section of rocks toward the surface and placed them back in the rusty sandstone. By his estimation they had covered almost fifteen kilometers of corridor without getting any closer to their goal. Spot checks of the rooms along their route continued to support the correlation between rock layer and the surrounding rock type but gave them no new information to work with. The humans had long since lost their enthusiasm.

Without a clear idea of what to do, he ordered a stop in the next wide intersection. With the additional open space afforded by the cross-corridor, Scott beamed down ration packs and freshly filled canteens for everyone. The food and a few minutes of rest immediately boosted the morale.

"I think Mr. Spock had it right before," Tallieur said around a mouthful of his ration bar. "These people were so paranoid they wouldn't trust their own mothers."

"Would you trust your mother if she let you put something like that on your door?" Knealayz pointed to a door opposite them, which showed another graphic scene of ritual torture and sacrifice. The victim spread over the altar would have made a good illustration for a textbook on Kh!lict internal organs.

"Just so." Tallieur took a gulp of water to wash down his food. "Anyway, we've walked and walked and still haven't got anywhere. Just when we think we're making progress, a fault shoves the rocks around, and we start over at the beginning of the section. I'll bet the geologists would love it, but I'm tired of seeing the same rocks over and over again."

"And I'm still not getting any flags on the background energy flux." Knealayz shook her tricorder in frustration. "*Why* aren't we getting anything? There has to be some band that they forgot to shield."

Lassiter pulled her legs against her chest and rested her cheek on her knees. "It's more likely that their shielding is *where* rather than *what*. I mean . . ." She paused, nibbling on her hair. "We're out here, where anyone who gets into the complex would be. If we're hostile invaders, they don't want us to see *anything*, so they shield against *everything* we might scan with."

Spock straightened, wondering how many times he was going to confront the obvious before he finally unraveled the mysteries of the Kh!lict. "That would be logical. It also means we must penetrate beyond the first set of rooms along these corridors."

Tallieur glanced pointedly at the red sandstone walls. "My recommendation, for what it's worth, is to

224

backtrack to the last fault and check everything in the immediate area. If there's any validity to our assumption that function correlates with color and rock type, we can examine the most alternatives in the smallest area."

"That does seem reasonable, Mr. Tallieur. I suggest that everyone finish eating quickly so that we may resume our investigation."

Groans and protests greeted his words, but within five minutes they were marching back toward the last fault zone. When they reached it and the group fanned out to make a preliminary survey, Spock examined the fault itself. Straddling the break, with one foot on buff siltstone and one on rusty sandstone, he noticed something he should have seen before. The difference in the two rock types implied that the rock layers had at one time moved several kilometers relative to each other. However, the floor of the corridor was as smooth as the day the Kh!lict had bored out the tunnel. Geologically, such stability was not impossible, but it was, to say the least, extremely improbable. Somehow the Kh!lict had stabilized the fault zone for many kilometers in all directions—and they had done it so well that the result had survived their civilization by at least a hundred and fifty millennia. From what they had seen, Spock had concluded the galaxy was better off for the extinction of the Kh!lict, but they were poorer not to know the secrets of their technology and science.

Twenty minutes of scouting narrowed their choices considerably. Most of the rooms were identical to the ones they had been examining all along, with the same types of furniture and only one door leading to the corridor. These chambers were discarded without further study. Half a dozen rooms, randomly placed along the passageway, had a second door that led away from the hallway. Spock chose teams to investigate, but the results were disappointing. Each chamber was connected to another much like itself, which in turn was connected to another, similar room. Eventually the last room in the chain opened onto an adjacent corridor on the same level of the complex. The exploration teams returned dusty, thirsty, and more aggravated with the Kh!lict than ever. When the connections were drawn out on a map, they resembled a drunkard's walk from one point to another, but the conclusion was inescapable. Those chambers led nowhere they wanted to go.

That left the last two rooms, which straddled the fault plane. They had been avoiding them, hoping that they would find their answer elsewhere. "It would figure," Lassiter murmured, scanning the doors while trying not to look at the carvings. In these panels the Kh!lict had depicted their scenes of torture, sacrificial slaughter, and ritual brutality with such precise and graphic detail that no one was eager to explore how these rooms reflected that aspect of Kh!lict society.

"I can't think of a more effective way of discouraging people from opening this door." Tallieur glanced at the images, then looked away, shaking his head. "I thought the Aztecs were over the edge."

"The Aztecs were amateurs compared to these characters." Knealayz swallowed. "Who wants to bet the transporter controls are right under the altar?"

Spock pushed at the door, and it swung open soundlessly. The room was long and narrow, with the fault line bisecting its entire length. Ghostly light flickered in the corners, leaving most of the room in deep shadow. The exception was a pool of brightness that surrounded a block of gray limestone. Splotches of purplish black stained the altar's sides and spattered the floor around it.

"Not possible," Knealayz muttered in dismay as she glimpsed the blood-splattered altar. "Not bloody possible. Besides, no stasis field is *that* good." She began scanning the closest wall, deliberately ignoring the anomaly at the far end of the room.

Activating his tricorder, Spock advanced toward the object. After so many failures, the probabilities were against their finding anything useful, but he had to try. Halfway down the room, the readouts began jumping too fast for him to follow. He switched the display to half speed but continued to record on all channels. Behind him he heard gasps of surprise as the others repeated his discovery. It was as though a barrier divided the room in half. Once they crossed it, their instruments detected all the information that had been screened from them before.

One by one the landing party reached the far end of the room, circled the altar, and stopped with tricorders pointed at the gray block of limestone. "That is the source of the anomalies," Tallieur said, saying aloud what they already knew. Given the Kh!lict fondness for repetition, rooms containing similar furnishings and equipment probably straddled every fault in the complex.

"Sorry I suggested it," Knealayz muttered. "These people are too appalling to contemplate."

Privately Spock agreed with her. Still, if you didn't want unauthorized individuals to use your intra-building transport system, the best location for the control mechanism was the last place any sane person wanted to go. The Kh!lict may have been brutal, disgusting, and loathsome, but they had not been stupid. Unless he completely missed his guess, no low-ranking Kh!lict would willingly enter a room such as this unless he *knew* someone—or something—else would be the sacrifice. Taking a deep breath, Spock ordered, "Mr. Tallieur and Ensign Nakamura, would you move the altar so we can see what the controls look like?"

The two men crouched beside the block of gray stone and put their shoulders against its splotched surface. Their first shove had no effect. Stepping back, they looked at each other and shrugged. "It's a lot heavier than I thought," Tallieur said.

Nakamura nodded, and they braced themselves for a second attempt. Sweat beaded on Nakamura's forehead and trickled off Tallieur's face. Finally, with a terrible screech, the rock began to move. The next instant, everything went black.

Chapter Twenty

CONSCIOUSNESS RETURNED SLOWLY. Spock allowed his surroundings to seep into his awareness before he opened his eyes, listening for the soft, uneven breathing of his people almost lost in the emptiness surrounding them. When he heard nothing besides the sounds he expected from seven unconscious humans, he cracked one eye to confirm his impressions. The *Enterprise*'s landing party appeared to be the only living beings in the area. Knowing he could not be sure while he was on the floor, he rolled to his feet, reaching for his phaser as he stood.

A quick circle revealed no immediate threats and no other living beings. The transport system they had triggered by moving the altar stone operated differently from the Kh!lict's main system. Instead of transforming the humans, this transporter had knocked them unconscious and delivered them—where? The mechanism had been preset to send them to this location, wherever that was.

Lowering his phaser, Spock began a second turn,

this one slow enough to take in the details. They were in the center of a huge amphitheaterlike room lit only by small, diffuse lights hidden among the rafters of the high, vaulted ceiling. Looking around, Spock had the distinct feeling that the last occupants, when they left so many millennia ago, had turned out the lights and walked away as though they expected to return. If he knew where the switch was, he could bring the room back to life.

At one end of the oval-shaped arena floor, a broad ramp led upward to an enclosed area. Unlike the rest of the complex, the doors to that room were plain and uncarved, as though the people expected here didn't need to be intimidated. The ruling class, if they fit the pattern found in ninety-nine percent of such civilizations, had reserved the vulgar intimidation for their followers. That also meant the humans had finally gotten the good fortune they needed. When they discovered where the Kh!lict had hidden their intrabuilding transport system to prevent its use by outside invaders or by the uninitiated, the system had sent them to the control center for the entire complex.

Spock turned away from the mesmerizing bulk of the enclosure. They needed to explore that structure, but the rest of the area demanded his attention first. The arena was encircled by wide tiers that stepped upward into the shadows. Squares, rectangles, and strangely shaped boxes filled the space on each level, although there was room to maneuver around most of the objects. Spock's curiosity stirred at the thought of exploring this room, but he had more important business to settle first.

Knealayz stirred, and he went to her, checking her pulse and respiration. Both were normal, and before he finished, her eyelids fluttered open. "It's all right," he told her. "Their transport system worked better than we had hoped."

She sat up, rubbing her neck. "I take it that means I'm still alive, sir?"

"Affirmative." Spock inclined his head toward the other members of the landing party, most of whom were stirring. "Checking everyone is our first priority."

"Yes, sir." She pushed herself to her feet, moving unsteadily, and started toward one of the security guards. Reassured that the others would come out of the strange transport experience as easily as he had, Spock started to help Tallieur.

A scream ripped through the stillness. Lassiter jerked upright, her hands shoved against her face and her fingers digging into her temples. Knealayz, who was closest, went to her and crouched at her side. Sensing a presence nearby, Lassiter swung wildly, catching Knealayz across the chest and knocking her to the floor.

Spock grabbed the emergency medical kit. Pulling out the hypo, he set it to deliver the combination tranquilizer and psi-suppressant he had insisted that McCoy include in their supplies. He shoved the injector against Lassiter's shoulder and triggered the spray.

The contact sent her into convulsions, her body jerking and twitching like an epileptic's. Spock grasped her shoulders and eased her to the floor. A flood of emotions and information inundated him when he touched her. Disoriented, he broke away and stumbled clear of the group until his thoughts settled.

They had indeed reached their goal, Lassiter's involuntary outpouring had shown him, the control center for all Kh!lict activities on Careta IV. In the dim past the Kh!lict High Elders had ruled from here with an absolute life-and-death dominion over their people that had never been matched, even by the most brutal dictatorships of the previous millennium. The equipment and information stored here had programmed, directed, and controlled the Kh!lict people with a completeness made possible only by the unique construction of the Kh!lict brain.

In the almost-forgotten past of the Kh!lict, they had passed information from generation to generation through a complex coming-of-age rite that imprinted crucial knowledge on the lower brains of the adolescent Kh!lict. Over time the ritual had become so detailed and so elaborate that most of the Kh!lict culture was programmed into the young when they were admitted into the adult world. From there it had been a short step for someone to invent machines to transcribe into the young absolutely faithful copies of everything the rulers wanted them to know, and for the rulers to entrench themselves through their control of what they taught the young. Just when the culture had descended into the ruthless savagery unequaled by any known civilization, Spock could not tell from the images he had received from Lassiter, but he understood why someone had tried to erase all signs that the Kh!lict had ever existed. From the earliest days of their space explorations, the Kh!lict had exterminated every alien race they encountered, leaving themselves as the only intelligent race within their sphere of occupation. Even now the brutality of their civilization, coupled with their indestructible and irresponsibly self-centered technology, made the knowledge that they had existed a threat to the galaxy. The idea of Kh!lict technology in the hands of a spacefaring Hitler or a latter-day Kahless the Unforgettable was horror enough to chill even Spock's blood.

He pulled himself back to the present. The drugs had calmed Lassiter, and the other members of the landing party were stirring, shaking their heads in groggy confusion. Going to Lassiter, Spock helped her to sit. "I apologize for the inadvertent intrusion, but I detected most of the images you were receiving. Is there anything else you can tell me about this place, Dr. Lassiter?"

She shook her head, her face ghost-white. Her expression showed more confusion than denial. "I seemed to be reading the massed thoughts and lives of billions upon billions of Kh!lict. Of every Kh!lict who ever lived." She shuddered. "How could such horrible people exist?"

"I do not know, Doctor." Spock stood, bringing himself to eye level with the lowest tier of the amphitheater. From Lassiter's images he recognized bank upon tilted bank of machinery. The controls, laid out on the sloping surfaces, were designed to be manipulated by Kh!lict claws, and in many cases several limbs were needed to reach all the appropriate contact points. Worse, there was no writing to identify anything. Instead the consoles were color-coded, and the only readout devices were small screens that displayed the colors of the spectrum on a two-minute cycle.

An unaccustomed sensation of frustration gripped Spock. If these machines contained the information that would let him change their people back to human form, only a Kh!lict could decipher the data fast enough to help them. Lassiter's reaction made him wonder how this place would affect a Kh!lict, even one with a human consciousness in control, but he saw no other way to unravel the mysteries of the Kh!lict technology soon enough to save their people. Given sufficient time, Spock knew he could crack the Kh!lict language, but time was the one thing he did not have.

He pulled out his communicator. "Spock to *Enterprise.*" When only static answered him, he boosted the gain to maximum and tried again. "Spock to *Enterprise.*"

"Uhura here, Mr. Spock. Can you boost your

signal? We can barely read you." Her voice, through the static, was almost inaudible.

"Negative, Lieutenant Uhura. I'm already at maximum." He glanced around him, calculating the interference generated by the Kh!lict equipment. "You'll have to compensate on your end. Meanwhile, please have Mr. Scott beam the captain to this location. We are inside a large facility with enough open space to give him considerable leeway on the transporter coordinates."

The crackle of the interference filled the pause. When Uhura returned, her voice was stronger, but the transmission was still poor. "Mr. Scott says he has grave doubts about transporting anyone through the electromagnetic disturbances that are localized around your coordinates. Can you suggest any alternatives, Mr. Spock?"

"Negative. We are in the Kh!lict control center, but we are not certain how we got here. The captain's assistance is urgently required to gain access to the Kh!lict computers and other devices located in this room." He looked around again to see if anything could be operated by humanoids, but the design was too alien. If he had several months, the intellectual challenge would be stimulating. Under the present circumstances, his paramount concern was finding how to change their people back to humanoid form. "Please request Mr. Scott to take appropriate care in enhancing the transporter signals, but to get the captain here at once. Spock out."

Returning the communicator to his belt, he started for the nearest bank of equipment. Although he could not accomplish much without Kirk to interpret the data screens, he wanted to examine the devices. He had reached the narrow ramp leading to the first tier of machinery when he heard a shout behind him.

Coming from nowhere, a small Kh!lict charged the landing party. Its carapace flashed brilliant, coruscating patterns that signaled complete madness, even if Spock didn't understand the Kh!lict language. The creature's limbs moved in rapid, staccato jerks, flipping its lethal claws in deadly arcs with each stride.

The landing party scattered, giving the Kh!lict half a dozen separate, moving targets. Spock fired his phaser, his shot catching the Kh!lict an instant before the security guards' shots hit it. Under the combined force of four light stun beams, the Kh!lict collapsed. Its momentum carried it forward, skating on its belly like a flat stone skipped across a lake. It grated to a stop where most of the *Enterprise*'s landing party had been sitting.

Spock approached the unconscious Kh!lict, giving himself room in case it woke up. The security guards remained in defensive position, their phasers trained on the Kh!lict. Circling the inert form, Spock compared it with his recollections of Kirk's Kh!lict body. With the endless changes in pattern and color that characterized the Kh!lict, Spock had to rely on more subtle clues to identify the person before him. This Kh!lict was smaller than Kirk, and the longer Spock looked, the more subtle variations he noticed in the bumps and scallops that ornamented the carapace.

Without accessing the ship's records, he could not be certain that this was the same Kh!lict that had been on the canyon's rim earlier that afternoon, although the odds favored that conclusion. He wondered if the ship's sensors had recorded where this Kh!lict had penetrated the complex and if they could retrace its path, should the landing party need an escape route. After studying the Kh!lict, he decided the body probably housed Chekov's consciousness. The security guards who had accompanied Kirk through the artifact had all outmassed the captain by fifteen or twenty kilos, leaving Chekov the smallest person to be transformed into a Kh!lict.

By the time Spock finished his examination, Chekov was still unconscious. He holstered his phaser and gestured to a guard to join him. "While he is unconscious, we will roll him on his back to prevent him from attacking us again."

"Do ye ken that be enough, Mr. Spock?" the guard asked. "That beastie were tryin' fair hard to spread our innards acrost the floor."

"I will entertain suggestions, Mr. McGaren. However, we are short of the necessary supplies to execute any of the ideas that immediately present themselves."

"Aye, sair. If that aren't the truth." His face settling into grim lines, McGaren clipped his phaser to his belt.

With Spock at the front and McGaren lifting in the rear, they rolled Chekov onto his back. Moving away, Spock studied the unconscious Kh!lict. Chekov might be able to rock himself back onto his feet with a determined effort, but not before someone in the landing party noticed. Given how agitated his attack had been, Spock considered it unlikely that Chekov could muster the necessary concentration to flip his carapace, and the first attempt would bring the landing party's phasers to bear on him. For the moment this problem was solved.

"Do ye ken the captain will be as much gone when he arrives, sair?" McGaren asked.

"Impossible to say." How would the Kh!lict lower brain that controlled Kirk's body react to the *Enterprise*'s transporter? The guard they had beamed up to the *Enterprise* had gone berserk, and they had no reason to believe Kirk would arrive in any better condition than Chekov. He would have to gamble that

Kirk's lower brain would be reassured when it found itself in Kh!lict-built surroundings. "Mr. McGaren, you and the other security men place yourselves where you have a clear view of the arena. We must be prepared for all contingencies."

"Aye, sair."

The guards positioned themselves around the perimeter, each with his back against the lower wall. The scientists fanned out to examine the equipment, although they could do very little without someone to read the Kh!lict language for them. As he climbed up the ramp, Spock felt his sense of urgency intensifying. If Chekov was an example of what happened when humans were trapped too long in a Kh!lict body, they needed to rescue their people fast.

Chapter Twenty-one

ONE MOMENT Kirk was falling, tumbling pincers over carapace toward the rusty surface of the lake. The water approached with alarming speed, and Kirk wondered how well his Kh!lict body would withstand the impact. It was an experiment he would have gladly avoided.

Twenty meters above the lake, as he watched the abridged version of his life superimpose itself across the orange froth foaming off the choppy waves, he felt the welcome tingle of the transporter effect envelop his body. He materialized briefly in the *Enterprise*'s transporter room. "Welcome aboard, Captain," Scott said as his hands worked to lay in a new set of coordinates. "Mr. Spock is wanting to see you immediately on the planet's surface."

Kirk felt the shock radiating from his lower brain, but the transporter engaged before the Kh!lict mind could respond. When he rematerialized, it was worse —far, far worse. He was on the arena floor in the Holiest of Holies, the place where a Kh!lict male was only allowed once in his short life. That he was here for a second time, and that he was surrounded by these inconceivable alien monsters, was more than he could handle. Once again Kirk felt his Kh!lict brain close down all the voluntary functions of his body. His legs locked, and he flopped on his belly on the hard stone floor.

"Captain? Captain Kirk, can you hear me?" Spock, approaching from beyond his line of sight, crouched in front of him.

After what seemed like forever but was only a few seconds, Kirk regained his ability to communicate. The terror at finding himself in his people's most sacred sanctuary had affected his host even more deeply than the initial trauma of confronting other life-forms who possessed the minimal attributes of intelligent life. The Kh!lict lower brain was trying to retreat far enough to avoid acknowledging these impossibilities. YES, I HEAR YOU, Kirk finally managed to signal. THANKS FOR THE RESCUE.

"That is good." Vulcan or not, Spock sounded relieved. Kirk felt a moment of sympathy for his first officer. If being a Kh!lict was hard on Kirk, Spock must be finding it harder to be responsible for determining the means of returning him and the other people to their human forms. "Captain, we need your help to decipher how these machines work. This is the central control complex for the entire planet, but we cannot ascertain how anything works. The data screens display information in the Kh!lict language, and we do not have even the most rudimentary translations for the colors and symbols."

NOR LIKELY YOU COULD GET THEM, Kirk signaled after sorting through the chaotic images that surged through his lower brain. THE LANGUAGE IS VERY CONTEXT SPECIFIC. MEANING CHANGES DEPENDING ON WHAT COLORS OR PATTERNS ARE JUXTAPOSED.

"Captain, we believe the answers to your problem are contained in these machines." The dim light in the room left Spock's face in shadow and deepened the gaunt hollows of his cheeks. "Can you translate for us so that I can implement a solution?"

Can I do it? Kirk asked himself. The Kh!lict lower brain, terrified as it was to be where no Kh!lict of its age and gender was ever supposed to be, would not make it easy. In addition, Kirk did not think his host knew much of scientific value. However, if Spock needed a Kh!lict to translate the data screens, Kirk was the only one available. Why, he couldn't say, but he knew that the other transformed humans were getting even less cooperation from their Kh!lict hosts than he was from his. It was as if they expected to banish the *Enterprise* and her crew from their world by refusing to acknowledge that they existed. Kirk, at least, had forced a small measure of cooperation from his host. While it wasn't much, it was more than Spock had to work with now. He would give it a try.

Kirk searched his host's brain, hoping to glean information from the Kh!lict's memories that would help Spock. To his dismay, the mere idea of telling these strange—animals—*anything* so disturbed his host that Kirk feared he would drown in the resulting maelstrom of horror and fear. For several minutes, the Kh!lict's reaction was so overpowering that all Kirk could do was ride out the flood of emotion, hoping that his host would exhaust its ability to react so violently.

When Kirk again became aware of his surroundings, Spock was reaching for his communicator. The Kh!lict's panic was subsiding, but Kirk could not force the creature's nervous system to transmit Spock's words. While he could perceive some frequencies clearly, the Kh!lict's hearing membranes were inadequate to distinguish the nuances of human speech unless he could focus his full attention on the sounds. With the Kh!lict's present mental distress, understanding Spock was an impossible task.

A few minutes later, while Kirk was still struggling to calm his host, the air before him shimmered, and something coalesced from the transporter effect. While Kirk was trying to figure out what the odd purplish fluid in the hundred-liter monopore pouch was, his host leapt into action. Throwing itself on the pouch, the Kh!lict stabbed its proboscis into it and began sucking greedily. From its reaction Kirk realized that the odor of the pouch's contents had triggered the Kh!lict's feeding reflexes. Mentally Kirk thanked McCoy for recreating a Kh!lict meal from the meager clues available.

As his host fed, Kirk felt a growing calmness settle over the Kh!lict. At first he thought it was from gorging after so long a period of starvation, but the Kh!lict did not descend into the torpor Kirk expected. Instead it was gripped with an odd sense of serenity, as though divorced from its surroundings. With a flash of insight, Kirk realized that Spock had ordered McCoy to drug the food. If they were lucky, with his host in this euphoric daze, Kirk could mine the Kh!lict's brain for information and relay it to Spock.

WHAT DID YOU DO? he asked, in Morse code, checking to see if he was right.

"Diazilyrion." Spock studied him with an air of satisfaction. "Your body should be quite inebriated for several hours. There is no danger, as long as you exercise caution while attempting movements that require a high degree of coordination."

I SUGGEST WE TAKE ADVANTAGE OF THE SITUATION. Kirk swiveled his eyestalks around to examine the room with more care than his host had permitted until now. He could feel the diazilyrion working its way deeper into the Kh!lict's physiology, erasing the

241

creature's inhibitions. It decided the humans were creations of its imagination, strange hallucinations sent to deliver a message that only it could hear. With profound relief Kirk felt the Kh!lict descend into a state of babbling lunacy in which all the information imprinted on its brain became accessible in response to the right questions.

His first look at the tiers of equipment was disappointing. Bank upon bank of sloped teaching machines reached from arena level to the back walls of the cavern. Every young Kh!lict was brought to the Holiest of Holies after he survived his rite of passage. An Elder tested each youngster and assigned it its adult position in Kh!lict society, after which the youth was led to the appropriate tier of machines. With elaborate rituals each young Kh!lict was strapped and wired to a machine, and all the knowledge it would need for the rest of its life was implanted into its lower brain, much of it guarded by subconscious triggers that would release the information when it was needed.

When the programming was complete, the young Kh!lict—who, at this stage of their lives, were all male—were turned loose on the planet's surface to fend for themselves until they had sired their predetermined quota of offspring. At that point the Kh!lict surviving males metamorphosed into young females.

After spawning several clutches of eggs, the females gradually shifted their focus from reproduction to scientific work or the outright pursuit of power. Much of this was determined by how the young Kh!lict male had been programmed, but individual aptitudes also influenced the occupation of a Kh!lict female. Kirk sensed that this aspect of Kh!lict society was a deep mystery to his host, who had not traveled far enough along the path to maturity to have accessed the appropriate information from his ingrained lessons.

The flood of information slowed, giving Kirk time to sort through it. While the Kh!lict biological cycle was the most bizarre he had ever encountered, knowing its details did not tell him how to change himself back to a human. The answers must be in the computers that controlled the teaching machines. That brought up the question of which computer directed the other machines in this complex. He felt as though he was in the antechamber with no signs to tell him which doors led deeper into the complex and which only led to the Kh!lict equivalent of the ladies' room.

Looking around again, Kirk felt drawn to the featureless enclosure at the head of the arena. His host had not been near that part of the amphitheater and, when he thought about it, Kirk realized that no male Kh!lict had ever been closer to that enclosure than the base of the ramp. The conviction erupted full-strength in his mind—*that* was where they should look for their answers. IT'S IN THAT PLACE, SPOCK. I'M SURE WHAT WE NEED IS THERE.

Spock lifted his eyebrow in surprise. "We considered exploring that structure, Captain, but our tricorders indicated that nothing was inside it."

I DON'T KNOW WHAT'S IN THERE, SPOCK. BUT THAT ENCLOSURE IS THE ONLY UNIQUE THING IN THIS ROOM. Kirk paused to collect his thoughts. Using the cumbersome dots and dashes of the Morse code to spell out every letter was draining him of energy at a far greater rate than he would have imagined. He wondered how much longer he would be able to force his Kh!lict body into the unnatural responses that talking to Spock required.

Spock's forehead creased with the ghost of a frown. "If you are certain that the enclosure is our goal, may I recommend that you ingest more nourishment before we explore that area? We have discovered that not all Kh!lict rooms are as they appear to be."

This is news? Kirk thought, wondering if anything on Careta IV was as it appeared. Certainly everything that the Kh!lict had touched seemed bent against its normal grain. I AM SURE, SPOCK, he signaled. THESE STATIONS ARE DUMB TERMINALS. THEY TRANSMIT INFORMATION FROM THE CENTRAL COMPUTERS TO THE BRAINS OF THE YOUNG KH!LICT. THEY HAVE NO OTHER PURPOSE.

"In that case, Captain, we will investigate the enclosure when you are ready." He conferred with Lassiter and the other scientists while Kirk ate. Given the energy he was expending, he figured his host would need to eat often; furthermore, increasing the amount of diazilyrion in his bloodstream would make it easier to get the information he needed from his Kh!lict lower brain.

Spock returned just as Kirk felt he could not force down another drop of food. Staggering from his full stomach and from how punchy the diazilyrion was making his host, Kirk followed Spock up the ramp. His tricorder held before him like a shield against attack, Spock circled around the structure. "The only openings are on this side, Captain," he reported. "Is there any difference between the doors?"

I could have told him the entrance was on this side, Kirk thought as Spock made his report. A detailed schematic of the enclosure wall flooded his vision. Acting on instinct, he moved between the doors and placed four of his pincers on the precise spots that he saw in his mind. The wall went transparent, and a whirling vortex filled the space beyond. Knowing it was the right thing to do, he stepped forward into the maelstrom.

Kirk landed in darkness, his head still spinning despite the solid stone beneath his pincers. His host retreated again, frightened by where he was. Kirk let the Kh!lict mind escape into oblivion while he sorted out what had happened.

Slowly the darkness receded. Bulky objects coalesced from the shadows, taking on definition and solidity as the light built in intensity. He was sprawled on the floor between two tilted, misshapen consoles that resembled the teaching machines in the Holiest of Holies. However, the complex control panels on these machines told Kirk that they were the master units that directed everything in the complex. Somewhere in this room they would find what they had been searching for.

His next step, Kirk decided, was to find Spock. He could not see the Vulcan anywhere nearby, and the room shifted perspective around him like an Escher drawing. Between the twisting perspective and the massed banks of equipment, Spock could be three meters away, and Kirk might not see him. He tried to stand, pulling his limbs beneath his carapace and forcing them to lift his body off the sooty gray limestone. Even with his bloodstream full of diazilyrion, his host was on the verge of dissolving into gibbering terror. With an unpleasant shock Kirk realized that only the oldest and most powerful Kh!lict females were allowed in this room. That his host knew of its existence and its functions meant that someday, with great age, he would have become one of the Elders who controlled Kh!lict society. However, at his present age and as a male, it was a capital offense for him to be here.

This is an exception, Kirk told his Kh!lict alter ego. *The Elders chose us to solve the mystery of these aliens while they work elsewhere on the problem. They don't want the aliens to see them. We're the only ones who can do this job.*

To his surprise, the specious argument worked, and

his host calmed. He figured the Kh!lict would see through the reasoning eventually, but until then it gave him control of his actions.

It took Kirk fifteen minutes to find Spock. The Vulcan had materialized less than a dozen meters away, but the shortest route between them was as snarled a maze as Kirk had ever seen. If the enigmatic floor plan and the shifting perspective were designed to discourage intruders, the Kh!lict architect who had designed the room knew exactly what she was doing.

Spock had just managed to push himself to a sitting position when Kirk found him, but even that movement had left him swaying dizzily. He glanced at Kirk when he came around the last corner but quickly looked back to his knees. "Captain, I regret to report that I am experiencing extreme sensory distortion. I am uncertain whether I shall be able to function in this place."

WHAT'S WRONG? Kirk's gills fluttered with agitation. They needed Spock's scientific expertise to solve the riddles of the Kh!lict technology. His host did not possess enough scientific knowledge to interpret the data.

"I think . . ." Spock squeezed his eyes closed. His face had turned the washed-out green of grass grown indoors and with insufficient light. "There seems to be a distortion field. It is affecting my vision and balance —to the point that I cannot—maintain my equilibrium."

Distortion field? As soon as Spock said the words, Kirk knew exactly where to look for the controls. Around the corner and three consoles from the end was a small gray unit that managed the security measures for the entire complex. Kirk retraced his steps, climbed up the sloping control panel, slid his pincers into the control sockets, and squeezed the activation bars. The screen cleared to a welcoming lavender, then requested his input.

Amazed that it was so easy, Kirk asked how to deactivate the security measures for the control room. The computer showed him the command sequence on its screen, and Kirk let his body act out the complicated dance of pincer movements and color displays. When he entered the last command, the screen informed him, <Sequence correct. Protective field deactivated until further command, Oh Bright One.>

Kirk withdrew his pincers from the sockets and rejoined Spock. Already the Vulcan's skin had returned to its normal sallow hue, and he was examining his surroundings with interest.

"Thank you, Captain. I presume we have reached our goal." He pushed himself to his feet, still moving a little unsteadily. In most things Spock's Vulcan physique was an advantage that often left Kirk envying his first officer's strength and endurance. However, the Kh!lict field had apparently disturbed the powerful links between his mind and body, turning Spock's strongest asset into a grave liability.

YES, SPOCK. THIS IS THE CONTROL CENTER.

"Which computer contains the information we need?" Spock's gaze lingered on some sets of controls and slipped quickly past others. His expression told Kirk how daunting he found the prospect of examining this massive array of equipment. From his mounting sense of urgency, Kirk realized that Spock was more concerned than he had let on about how much time they had left to solve this problem.

Kirk studied Spock's question, turning it around to look at it from several angles. No matter how he rephrased the words, his Kh!lict lower brain did not respond. TRY MORE SPECIFIC QUESTIONS, SPOCK. I NEED A CONCRETE TRIGGER.

Spock's eyebrow rose. "May I ask what told you how to eliminate the security measures?"

WHEN YOU SAID THE WORDS "DISTORTION FIELD," I KNEW WHICH CONSOLE WAS THE CONTROL UNIT. THE COMPUTER GAVE ME THE DIRECTIONS FOR DEACTIVATING THE FIELD. At the time he had been so concerned about Spock that he hadn't considered how remarkable it was for his Kh!lict lower brain to hand him the key to the entire planet's security system. In retrospect, it was frightening to think what else might be buried in his head.

"Fascinating," Spock murmured. He was quiet for several moments, as though analyzing *exactly* what they needed. "Can you show me how the transit frames work?"

At first Kirk felt no response. He wondered if he had misinterpreted the Kh!lict's reactions, or if he had misunderstood the Kh!lict term for their long-distance transportation devices. By rephrasing the question several ways, each time adding a slightly different twist and increasing the urgency of the request, he finally got something from his host. The transit frames were mere technology, a subject fit for underlings and technicians but too insignificant to interest a future leader.

Annoyed, Kirk informed his lower brain that aliens were secretly infiltrating their world by using the transit frames and that he had been assigned to prevent that from happening anymore. That satisfied his host, but the information he provided was vague and confused. I DON'T THINK HE REALLY KNOWS, SPOCK, Kirk signaled. I'VE GOT A ROUGH NOTION WHERE TO START, BUT I FEAR WE'RE GOING TO HAVE TO DO THIS BY TRIAL AND ERROR.

They started off, searching the maze for the console that matched Kirk's impressions. It took them almost an hour to find it along the far wall. Early in the search, Kirk had asked for directions from the consoles he and Spock passed, but he had been unable to access the information. Finally, after having to retrace their steps three times and begin afresh, they reached their objective. Sandwiched between two environmental control units and surrounded by the waste management computers for the major Kh!lict cities, it was the only active unit in a battery of equipment as dead as the people it had once served.

"Are those units permanently deactivated or merely on standby?" Spock traced his finger across the blank screen of a waste recycling computer. Even after being abandoned for the millennia since its creators died, this section of the complex was immaculate, with no speck of dust to mar the esthetics or the functionality of the control center.

When Spock asked the question, the answer floated to the surface of Kirk's mind. DEAD. THE LINKS BETWEEN THE CITIES THEY SERVED AND THEIR COUPLINGS TO THE GEOTHERMAL POWER GRID HAVE BEEN SEVERED. He paused, feeling more information coalesce in his mind. THEIR SUN ISN'T THE ONLY ENERGY SOURCE THAT'S FAILING. THE KH!LICT TAPPED THEIR PLANET'S GEOTHERMAL RESOURCES HEAVILY TO COMPENSATE FOR THE COOLING SUN. THAT LED TO THE COLLAPSE OF THEIR CIVILIZATION AND THE EXTINCTION OF THEIR RACE. THIS EQUIPMENT STILL FUNCTIONS BECAUSE THE UNITS NEED LITTLE POWER WHEN IN STANDBY MODE.

They set to work exploring the control systems for the transit frames. It was slow work, with Spock sometimes redirecting his questions five or six times before triggering any response from Kirk's host. Even then the information was so vague and confused that Kirk had to experiment for several minutes with the console's controls before he could get any data they could use.

When they stopped near midnight for Kirk to eat,

Spock said what was in both their minds. "This is not working, Captain. Your host does not possess the scientific programming we require to solve this problem."

TRUE. It was a frustrating and depressing thought. They were so close to the answers—he literally had his pincers on them. However, at the rate they were progressing, it could take days, or even weeks, to locate what they needed. Kirk did not think he could survive that long inside a body that had to be drugged almost senseless so that he could force his Kh!lict alter ego to give him the information he needed to free himself.

"There is only one solution." Spock reached for his communicator. "I shall go through one of the transit frames and then have the *Enterprise* transport me back here. Logic dictates that I will be given a Kh!lict persona with considerable technical expertise."

NO, SPOCK. IT'S TOO DANGEROUS. I ABSOLUTELY FORBID YOU TO TRY IT. It was bad enough that they already had five people to change back. Adding to the number only increased their problem, and there was no guarantee Spock's Kh!lict body really would possess the information they needed.

"Spock to *Enterprise*. One to beam up." He side-stepped Kirk's attempt to knock the communicator from his hand and moved behind him. Kirk, his pincers slipping on the stone floor in his haste, completed his turn as the transporter beam took Spock.

Chapter Twenty-two

SPOCK MATERIALIZED half an hour later with a communications rig adapted for Kh!lict pincers strapped to his carapace. Kirk knew immediately that Spock had drugged his Kh!lict body heavily with diazilyrion before letting Scott transport him back into the control center. Even so, the erratic flickers of color on his carapace and the skittering twitch in his movements told Kirk that Spock's host was even less comfortable being here than Kirk's was. Kirk suspected part of the uneasiness was caused by the newness of the transformation, and that, after Spock established his dominance over his host, much of the discomfort would disappear. However, they did not have the time to wait for Spock to pacify his Kh!lict lower brain.

Spock moved to the sloping console that governed the transit frames and fitted his pincers into the sockets. Within ten minutes he was shifting levers and twisting controls with a facility that made Kirk envious. After five hours he had not attained that much rapport with the unit. Feeling left out, he watched the patterns flicker across the screen, almost too fast for him to translate. Before long Spock had gotten so deep into the programming for the system that Kirk could not understand any of the images. With nothing more he could do, Kirk settled down on his appendages and drifted off to sleep.

A heavy thump close by aroused him from his nap. With an effort Kirk twisted his eyestalks around until he located the cause of the noise. Spock was sprawled on the floor beside the console, his carapace pulsing an unhealthy grayish green. <What's wrong?> Kirk asked.

<I—don't know.> Spock's words were distorted by random flickers of green. <I feel—dizzy. Faint. As if I can't breathe.>

<You don't look very good.> In fact, Kirk thought, he looked downright sick. The green color nagged at Kirk's subconscious. It was important, but he could not bring the reason into focus. <Are you making any progress with our main problem?>

<I believe so, Elder. However, I have reached a—restricted level—for which I do not have the access code. I believe we will need to locate a female Kh!lict—what the system calls a High Elder—to proceed further.> Spock settled his limbs around his body as though preparing to stay put for some time.

<Let me try it.> Kirk worked his way around Spock and slipped his pincers into the control sockets. It was easy to find where the system had rejected Spock's commands, but Kirk had no better luck in getting around the safeguards. Finally he dropped his pincers in defeat and turned back to Spock.

In the time Kirk had been working on the computer, Spock's color had darkened to a brighter green, almost the hue of Vulcan blood. That thought crystallized into a certainty as Kirk realized what the problem was. <Spock, did you run any blood chemistry

workups on the Kh!lict? Could the copper in your system be making you sick?>

<It is—possible—Elder. There may not be—enough iron in my system—for me to breathe properly. The copper—in my blood—may be poisoning—the Kh!lict physiology. I sense that I must—reverse the transformation—soon. Or I shall die.>

<You won't die if I have anything to say about it.> Kirk activated the communications unit and tapped in his message. There was one Kh!lict female on the planet, and it was time she helped them. Kirk wasn't sure how he would convince her, should Talika decide that the humans were on their own in this, but he had few options. Spock needed her assistance immediately.

Talika materialized in a high fury, ready to tear apart anyone who approached her. Her reaction was coming straight from the Kh!lict section of her brain, and Kirk was intensely grateful for the security team that Scott had sent down to control her. A calculated burst from their phasers immobilized her without rendering her unconscious.

<You must help us, Oh Highest One. We need access to the computer system so that we may change ourselves back to our human form. Only you can give us the access code we need.> Kirk had to struggle to keep his colors and his posture properly submissive, but remembering that Spock's life was at stake made it much easier.

Talika's carapace darkened to a contemptuous fuchsia. <Your blasphemy in invading this place merits death. No male has ever stood where you are and lived.>

<And I would like to be elsewhere, Most Magnificent One. I need the access code to remove my unwelcome presence.> Even to himself, that argument sounded weak. What could he suggest that

would get to her? Kirk wondered. Her rationale sounded purely Kh!lict, but he wondered how certain he could be of which persona was in control. In some ways there was little to choose between the self-centered Kh!lict world view and the Djelifan perspective, which was nearly as restricted.

<Why should I bother? I can rip you open with my claws and let the cleaning robots carry off the mess.> The fuchsia overtones gave her statement a more sinister meaning, implying that the death she intended for him would be both painful and slow.

Kirk decided to try a different approach. <You can kill me, Your Gloriousness. And the other male with me will die soon. That will erase the blasphemy you so detest, but it will also leave you with only three subjects to rule.> A slight flutter in her color told Kirk that his words were reaching her, although she was struggling to deny the truth of what he said. <And if you look behind you, you will see four aliens from a race unknown to any true Kh!lict. I guarantee they will kill you if you harm me.>

<Blasphemy! Heresy! Desecration! No self-respecting female should be forced to hear such vile insults!> Talika's words came through strong enough, but flickers of doubt punctuated each phrase.

Sensing how close she was to the edge of her reason, Kirk delivered the final blow. <You are as alien in this place as I am! Look into yourself, and you will know that you do not belong here!>

<Heresy! Blasphemy!> she repeated, her colors growing paler as Kirk's meaning reached her. <You are still inferior! You must acknowledge the natural order of life!>

He could not have explained why, but Kirk knew those last words were from Talika, not from her Kh!lict host. He delivered his clinching argument in gentle, supportive colors. <If you want to see your

sisters again, Elder Talika, you must give Spock the access code so that he may free you from your present form.>

<Yes.> One of her pincers twitched. <Yes. Tell them I need access to the console.>

Kirk tapped a message into the communications unit, telling the guards to let her move. By the time he finished, Talika was able to drag herself to the console that controlled the transit frames. Pulling herself into position, she slid her pincers into the sockets and shifted the levers in an intricate pattern that Kirk would have thought was beyond her in her present, half-stunned condition. When she finished, she withdrew her pincers and wandered away, her movements unsteady and wavering.

Worried, Kirk watched her leave but realized that Spock needed his help more. His gills were quivering erratically, their surfaces a dry and unhealthy green. Spock struggled to get to his feet after Talika left, but his strength was almost gone. Two of the security guards lifted him into position on the sloping console. With slow, hesitant movements, he entered a long string of commands into the system. Watching the screen, Kirk kept wondering when the computer would reject the overrides, which went so far against everything that had been programmed into the system by its builders. Even more, he feared that Talika had entered a trap code that would send Spock's programming back at them as a weapon.

Finally Spock withdrew his pincers from the sockets. <I believe—I have—done—it. The best—test— is that—I try it.>

Everything in Kirk cried out that it was too risky for Spock to be the first one through the reprogrammed transit frame. Talika's code could still be false, and the trap would spring when someone used the frame. However, Spock's condition was critical, and it was much too likely that he would die while they tried to check out the system. <Very well, Spock. You test it, and I will persuade the others to go through.>

He signaled the ship to transport him, Spock, and the security guards to the nearest transit frame. Although it took no longer than usual to beam them there, it seemed like the longest few seconds in Kirk's life. They materialized on the rocky ground where Chekov had fought his duel with the security guard. Spock tried to stagger through the frame, but he was too weak to stand, and his carapace was turning a ghastly, mottled green.

Unslinging the communications set from across his body, Kirk ordered the security team to carry Spock to the frame and push him through. On the other side, Kirk saw several security men clustered around the first artifact. As Spock's front pincers disappeared into the window's surface, the scene wavered and broke up. Kirk thought that he aged a lifetime before the scene from the receiving end of the transit frame reappeared.

An emergency medical team led by Dr. McCoy was clustered around Spock's inert but fully restored body. From McCoy's abrupt, impatient gestures, Kirk knew that Spock was in bad shape. The question he needed answered was whether the last passage through the transit frame had caused further damage or if Spock was suffering only from his inability to function in a Kh!lict body.

Hoping McCoy would have an answer for him soon, Kirk turned his attention to getting the others back through the transit frames. There would be fewer difficulties, he knew, if the Kh!lict saw no signs of the *Enterprise*'s crew or their equipment. However, if there were problems with the transformation process, he wanted medical teams standing by to give immediate emergency aid. Also, given how hard he had worked to get everyone back to the second artifact before he realized how traumatic they found the sight of their former crewmates, Kirk feared that the security guards would suspect a trap awaited them on the other side of the frame.

The thought of entrapment twisted through his brain, repeating itself in a dozen variations before Kirk noticed the mental loop. Something was happening to him, sending him off in a mental fugue that threatened to become a paranoid's dreamland. With that thought, the explanation unfolded itself. He had been feeding his Kh!lict body massive doses of diazilyrion to suppress his host's reaction to a situation the Kh!lict's programming considered impossible. His body was building up a tolerance for the drug, and soon the Kh!lict mind would go insane rather than obey Kirk's orders. He had to get the others to go through the transit frames before that happened.

The place to start was with the two people here, he decided. Hoping that both Chekov and Talika had ingested enough diazilyrion-laced food to tolerate the shock of the *Enterprise*'s transporters, Kirk ordered Scott to beam them to him.

Chekov arrived first, his carapace glowing with submissive golds and tans. <Oh Worshipful Elder, I am so grateful for the mercy you show in freeing me from the Forbidden Zone.>

<There is no need for thanks, Little One. Simply pass through the frame so you will be outside the reach of the Evil Ones who sent you there.> Kirk thought his speech was simple and his logic compelling. *If it's this easy,* he thought, *they'll all be safely back on the* Enterprise *in half an hour.*

<Your mercy in freeing me shows no bounds.> Chekov showed no sign that he had read Kirk's words. <I shall walk in your shadow forever.>

Kirk repeated his request for Chekov to enter the

transit frame, this time making his patterns simpler and his colors purer. Still Chekov did not see what Kirk was saying but continued to stagger drunkenly along a path only he could see, repeating his own message. After the fifth try, Kirk acknowledged that Chekov was too far gone in his fantasy world for him to reach. He considered ordering the guards to shove Chekov through the artifact but rejected the idea. Until he knew what had happened to Spock, he would not force anyone through the windows. Reluctantly he let Chekov wander away and waited for Talika.

When she materialized Talika was further out of touch with reality than Chekov. As far as Kirk could tell, she was completely unaware of her surroundings and his presence. Her carapace kept repeating the same patterns, but Kirk could only interpret about half of them. She was haranguing someone about female superiority, but Kirk could not tell whether her Kh!lict or her Djelifan persona was in control. Brushing past Kirk as if he wasn't there, she drifted off on a course parallel to Chekov's.

Fighting his frustration, Kirk ordered Scott to beam him to the other artifact and to clear away the signs of human occupation from around the transit frame. He materialized within sight of the two surviving guards. Immediately Kirk began flashing them a message of the fabulous food source he had discovered on the far side of the transit frame. As he had guessed, his images captured their attention, and they followed him eagerly toward the artifact.

It was a longer hike than Kirk had thought, and it took them almost an hour to reach the transit frame. During the last half of the trip, he sensed a growing instability in both his companions, and he was beginning to wonder about his own capacity for sane judgment. However, as the black rectangle grew on the horizon, Kirk's fears receded. These two, at least, would soon be safely returned to their human forms.

A hundred meters from the frame, the smaller guard flared to a bright crimson and jumped on his companion. The larger guard reared in the air, flipped his attacker, and bolted. His escape took him away from the artifact at high speed, and he was out of sight before Kirk could react.

The smaller Kh!lict went into convulsions, thrashing violently until he bounced against a spur of rock and caromed toward the lip of a nearby wadi. He tumbled over the edge and landed on the rocks below with a sickening crack.

Kirk felt the tide of insanity rising inside him, reaching for his mind with seductive, consoling arms. It would be a relief to surrender, to never make another life-and-death decision that affected someone else. With the last vestiges of his sanity, Kirk forced his limbs into motion and threw himself through the transit frame.

Chapter Twenty-three

HE AWOKE in a place of brightness and shiny equipment where panels of blinking lights and shifting patterns covered the walls and soft mechanical voices murmured a ceaseless lullaby. A woman's face, tired and drawn, framed by golden hair, floated into his line of vision. "Captain, how are you feeling?"

The words should have meant something, but they didn't. What was it she wanted from him? A worried frown creased her forehead when he didn't answer. "Captain, are you all right? Can you hear me?" Her voice was sharper, carrying a new sense of urgency. She turned away from him, raising her voice to be heard by someone farther away. "Dr. McCoy! The captain is awake, but he is not responsive."

Still not sure what he was supposed to do, he remained silent. Sooner or later someone would tell him what was expected, and then he would do it. When a man's face, older and more lined than the woman's but equally haggard from lack of sleep, floated into view, he was not surprised. The man gave him an affectionate smile that lit his rugged, kindly face. After a moment the worry slipped back in place, making the doctor seem more tired by contrast. McCoy surreptitiously pointed a small device toward his head. "Well, Jim, how are you doing?"

Since they still had not told him how he was supposed to answer those words, he again did nothing. Openly now the doctor waved the device over his body, paying special attention to his head and one of his knees. When he tried to move that leg, he discovered that the joint was painfully swollen. The doctor made a second sweep over his body, keeping his eyes on the wall over his head. Curious, he tried to sit up so he could see what was so interesting, but his body was strapped to the bed with wide bands of material.

"Total amnesia." The doctor snapped his hand closed around the device in his hand. "Complete inhibition of the nerve impulses coming from every area that affects memory recall. Christine, how long do we have?"

"He's been here for fourteen hours, Doctor," the woman answered. "Mr. Scott has been calling every half hour to find out when he can take over command."

"And there's no change in Spock's condition." McCoy heaved a deep sigh. "I hate to do it, but get the cortico-synaptic modulator. We can't wait for him to come out of this on his own."

"Yes, Doctor." Her boot heels rapped a staccato tattoo on the floor as she disappeared from sight. When she returned, she was carrying a small black object with a silver grille on one end and several controls on its largest flat surface.

McCoy took the object from her and did something to one of the controls. At the same time, the woman made some tapping noises on the console beside his bed. They finished their work at the same time. She looked at the doctor, frowning. "Current research indicates that the best results are obtained by starting at the threshold level and gradually increasing the intensity over a period of hours, until the subject's memory is restored."

"If we had a 'period of hours,' we wouldn't be using this gadget at all. I prefer to let nature take its course."

"Agreed, Doctor." She made a few more tapping sounds. "The captain's brain scans are on the screen, along with the cortico-synaptic results for several test subjects with similar brain-wave patterns."

"You've been busy, Christine." The doctor's voice held a warm note of approval. He left the bedside and went to examine the data.

"I feared this approach would be necessary, Doctor, after what you found on the first test series." She shrugged. "Besides, I didn't have anything better to do in between checking their readings last night."

"Well, it's saving us some time now." He adjusted the settings on the control panel. "Four point three should be enough, but I'm going a little higher. I'd rather not have to wait through the neurological rebound to take a second shot at it."

"Yes, Doctor." She stepped back. "He's ready."

McCoy passed the black object across his forehead and a blinding flare erupted in his brain. Everything he had ever seen or tasted or touched or smelled or felt seemed to be happening to him again, all at the same time. It was too much. He couldn't handle the flood of information that was clamoring for recognition. Then, mercifully, everything went black.

Kirk awoke with a splitting headache. The bleeps and pings of the sickbay monitors only intensified the pain. *Since when does Bones use one of his diagnostic beds for a simple headache?* he thought, trying to roll to his feet. The restraining band across his chest held him to the bed. "Bones, let me out of here!"

As if conjured up by his words, McCoy appeared at his bedside. "How do you feel, Jim?"

"My head hurts, but other than that I'm fine. Let me out of here!" A terrible sense of urgency gripped him, telling him that he was desperately needed somewhere else.

"Not so fast." McCoy ran a scanner over him and confirmed the report on the overhead monitor. "What do you remember about the last couple of days?"

"The last couple of days? Don't be ridiculous! We've been . . ." His voice trailed off as he tried to remember what he had been doing for the last two days. The *Enterprise* had been hauling a bunch of archaeologists around the sector, and they had discovered . . . Slowly the details of their investigations on Careta IV drifted into focus: an ancient and sinister race, inexplicable artifacts that still operated after two hundred thousand years, being transformed into one of the aliens. "How's Spock?"

A pleased grin lit McCoy's face, but he sobered immediately. "He hasn't regained consciousness, Jim. I was afraid to do too much for him until I knew what exactly had happened. He wasn't in very good shape when he came back."

"He wasn't in very good shape *before* he came back. We guessed that Vulcans don't have the right biochemistry to make good Kh!lict." He squinted his eyes against the light. "Can't you let me up and give me something for this headache, Bones?"

McCoy released the restraining straps and reached for his hypo. Kirk pushed himself to a sitting position, rubbing his forehead. The hypo hissed as McCoy pressed it against his arm. "Your guess about Spock is probably a good one. We'll let him recover a little longer on his own, then. You came through fairly well, except for your memory. We had to use the cortico-synaptic modulator to bring it back quicker."

"That explains the headache." Kirk eased himself to his feet, testing his balance and checking for minor injuries from his adventures as a Kh!lict. He found a few bruises and strains, but nothing that wouldn't heal within a few days. "What about the others?"

"You two are the only ones who've come back so far. Scotty said you were trying to herd everyone through those window things, but he guessed the others had gone pretty far around the bend. Anyway, we were waiting to hear from you or Spock before we tried anything more."

"How long have I been out?" Vaguely he remembered someone falling off a cliff and cracking something. He didn't know how well the Kh!lict withstood that sort of injury, or even how serious it had been, but he did know that the guard should have been treated quickly.

"Sixteen hours, all told." McCoy nibbled on his lip, reluctant to volunteer anything, but continued when Kirk gave him an angry frown. "For a while your readings were so erratic that we were afraid to do anything. Christine thought it might have to do with that drug that Spock was feeding you, so the best thing we could do was let your body flush it out on its own."

"I see." Kirk crossed to the intercom and called the bridge. He began issuing orders even before Scott could congratulate him on being back on his feet. "Scotty, I need the four strongest security men we have. Equip them with phasers set to heavy stun and give us one of your heavy-duty cargo nets. Have everyone meet me in the transporter room in ten minutes. Kirk out."

He turned back to McCoy. "Have your emergency teams standing by, out of sight, to assist our people when they come through. We'll find them and send them through one at a time."

"Are you sure you feel up to going down there, Captain?" McCoy's face was creased with worry. "The sensors can find them without your help, and I'm not sure you're fit for duty yet."

"I'm all right, Bones. Besides, it's not the general locations I'm worried about. It's what they'll do to hide from people on the ground." Kirk flashed him a smile and tapped his head. "At the moment I'm the only person who knows anything about the way a Kh!lict thinks."

McCoy looked ready to push his objections further, but instead he shrugged. "Good luck, Jim. I think you're going to need it."

"I'm afraid you're right." Giving the doctor a rueful grin, Kirk strode from sickbay.

Dawn on Careta IV was even worse than he remembered it. A cold, dry wind roared out of the sunrise, threatening to sweep them from its path. It smelled of dust and desolation, two things that Kirk knew he would always associate with this planet, and the rattle of the desiccated grasses sounded like the death knell of some ancient and withered being. Perhaps it was a fitting epitaph for the Kh!lict, he thought. Certainly his experiences here left him glad that their legacy had been as impermanent as the march of sand grains before the wind. The galaxy was incalculably poorer for the loss of the civilizations they had destroyed with their genocidal xenophobia. If he had his way, when the *Enterprise* left Careta IV, the Federation would impose as absolute a ban on this planet as they maintained on Talos IV.

The ship's sensors easily located both the Kh!lict who were near the third artifact, the one that stood on the canyon above the underground complex. Once she had been transported to the surface, Talika had wandered off and was hiding in a fold in the land. Chekov, however, presented a more dangerous problem. He had again started down the trail toward the subsurface city, and since they had not discovered how he had entered the first time, Kirk had no idea if he could get inside again. The sensors showed that he was stationary for the moment, but they had no way of telling how long that would last.

Kirk and the security guards started down the trail, picking their way cautiously over the loose talus and unstable slump areas that all but obliterated the trail in some places. That Chekov had negotiated the treacherous path as a deranged Kh!lict not once, but twice, was a tribute to the tenacity of living beings, whatever their physical form or societal values. Kirk found he was having enough trouble managing this trail in his human form, and he could tell the security men, with less hiking and rock-climbing experience than he had, were having greater difficulties.

It took them over an hour to find Chekov. When he had pushed his Kh!lict body to its limits, Chekov had pulled himself off the trail and crawled uphill across a landslide. Near its head a small ledge formed a den just big enough for his body. The fist-sized chunks of rock that littered the ground below the opening made a quiet approach almost impossible and promised treacherous footing when they tried to dislodge him from the hole.

After studying the hillside, Kirk heaved a sigh of frustration. "There's only one thing we can do. Stun him from a distance and then drag the body out into the net. At least we'll be able to beam back to the artifact instead of carrying him up the hill."

Stunning Chekov was easy, but extracting his body from the tiny hole proved a bigger challenge. He had chosen a hiding place that fit him like a second shell. Finally, after an hour of slipping on the unstable footing, struggling to gain a position where they could exert leverage on the inert Kh!lict, and swearing at everything in general, they got Chekov onto the net.

"Energize!" Kirk ordered, relieved to have finally retrieved one person. They materialized half a dozen meters from the artifact, carried Chekov up to it, and shoved his inert body through the window.

"One down, three to go," said Timmons, one of the guards. His voice was tense. If Chekov was any example, the rescue was going to take much more time and effort than they had hoped.

They walked past Talika's hiding place three times before Kirk spotted the deeper shadow of a pothole beneath the low cutbank. They should have located her sooner, but their tricorders had started giving them spurious readings when they entered the section of the canyon where she was hiding. Probably a Kh!lict graveyard, Kirk thought, promising himself not to mention the location to the archaeologists. It might be the only Kh!lict site on the planet that it was safe for them to explore, but he wasn't willing to take the chance. He had experienced more than enough of the Kh!lict to last him several lifetimes.

Talika was already unconscious when they found her. Even so, Kirk ordered the guards to stun her in case she woke up when they moved her. If their tricorders couldn't get a good fix on her at close range, they didn't dare trust that the ship's transporter would do any better.

Dragging her body out of the hole was hard, dirty work even after they used their phasers to cut a ramp. They had to crouch under the overhanging bank, and even before he had squeezed behind her to help push her out, Kirk's back was complaining. With him shoving from behind and two of the guards pulling from the front, it took them fifteen minutes to get her up to the level of the creek bed.

Timmons wiped his forehead, leaving a grimy streak across it. "You wouldn't think it would be so hard to move her, would you? My warmup weights start heavier than that."

The other guards nodded in agreement. Before they could carry the discussion further, Kirk ordered Scott to beam them to the artifact. With Talika sent through and returned to her own form, Kirk and the guards transported to the second artifact to find the men who had gone through that window with Kirk.

The country around the second artifact provided fewer good hiding places, but their search went much like the hunt for Chekov and Talika. The guard who had fallen into the wadi had managed to drag himself several dozen meters before finding a hole to crawl into. Knowing what to expect, they were able to rescue these two victims more quickly than they had retrieved either Chekov or Talika. Then, tired, thirsty, and filthy, they beamed back to the *Enterprise*. They were the last party of humans to leave the planet.

"What's the prognosis, Bones?" Kirk asked. The doctor was still in the transporter room, examining the last unconscious guard.

McCoy straightened and signaled the orderlies to carry the stretcher to sickbay. "The prognosis, Captain, is that you need a long shower, a hot dinner—and eighteen hours of sleep."

"Bones, that's not what I meant!" Exhaustion made his tone sharper than he intended. "What about the people we just brought back from the planet?"

With a shake of his head, McCoy relented. "They should be fine after they take a few days to recuperate. Even Jacobs, with the broken leg, should be back in fighting form by this time next week. But you won't be, unless you follow the prescription I just handed you."

"Yes, Bones." Kirk packed as much exasperation as he could into his voice, but he knew McCoy was right. He had pushed himself to his limit to rescue those people. Food and sleep sounded exactly like what he needed. He left orders that no one was to beam down to the planet for any reason whatsoever and headed for his quarters to follow his doctor's advice.

Chapter Twenty-four

FIVE DAYS LATER everyone was recovered enough to evaluate their experiences on Careta IV. Surveying the subdued group around the briefing table, Kirk decided they all needed a rest leave after this assignment. Spock, his complexion still a little greener than normal, sat in his usual place at the library computer. For once Chekov was not talking before the briefing started, and McCoy seemed fascinated by his stylus. Dr. Kaul was present, released from McCoy's care after an experimental treatment at last overcame his violent, recurring reactions to the suldanic gas. Lassiter and Talika flanked Kaul, and both women were as silent as Chekov.

Is it only two weeks since we sat here to decide the best way to explore this planet? Kirk asked himself as he waited for everyone to settle into the seats. It seemed more like half a lifetime. "All right, everyone," he said when he thought they were ready. "We're here to discuss what should happen with this planet and the Kh!lict artifacts. The unofficial consensus is to quarantine the planet. Does anyone wish to contribute any thoughts on this issue?"

Spock straightened in his chair. "Captain, I have been exploring options for severing the links between the Kh!lict devices and their power sources. At present there does not seem to be any possible way to do this short of destroying the objects themselves. I am uncertain whether even a direct hit with one of our photon torpedoes would be effective in obliterating the transport windows. The Kh!lict designed their systems to withstand all forms of tampering and, indeed, most forms of mass destruction.

"It would appear that we are not the first people to make this discovery. The jamming fields that surrounded many of the Kh!lict sites were the work of another civilization, which explored this system after the Kh!lict became extinct." Spock inclined his head toward Kaul to acknowledge the archaeologist. "Our analysis suggests the Meztoriens explored this system and discovered the Kh!lict artifacts. We theorize that they had similar experiences to ours and that they also concluded that the Kh!lict artifacts were extremely dangerous. We believe that their experiences so frightened them that they attempted to conceal or render inoperative all the Kh!lict ruins on the entire planet. The shielding mechanisms they placed around the transit frame at Site J3 functioned to inhibit much of the transport system. Coupled with the jamming fields that they installed at all the major localities, their efforts effectively prevented anyone from learning of the Kh!lict's existence for over one hundred thousand years. It is a remarkable tribute to both civilizations that significant components of their technology continued to operate up to the present."

"I have been assisting Mr. Spock in his investigations," Chekov added. "We have been unable to discover a way to operate these devices unless the operator is wearing a Kh!lict body. Since so much of their information was programmed into their brains, the computer systems assume that the operator knows this data. In some cases, as Mr. Spock and Captain Kirk discovered, specific information is programmed only in the brains of certain individuals. Without a Kh!lict body containing that programming, I doubt if we can ever determine how the system should work."

Talika lifted a massive hand to request the floor. "No one must ever again Kh!lict be. When Kh!lict I was, believed I that of universe sole ruler was I. God almost. Humans less than animals were. Of value none, since not even food were they. When again as myself woke I, realized I that Djelifans often others almost as badly treat. This to be wrong know I now. If persons must to study Kh!lict evil become, then study Kh!lict they should not."

Lassiter nodded her agreement, one hand twisted into her pale blond hair. "There is an evil presence lingering around this p-planet. I've sensed it ever since we arrived, although it took me several days to r-realize it. Mr. Spock found tangible evidence of this evil in the one underground city, in the carvings that decorated their temple. The Kh!lict gloried in every horrible activity we've ever heard of. From the references Mr. Spock has discovered in our computers and from the evidence of their own carvings, it is c-clear that the Kh!lict exterminated every intelligent race they ever encountered. We can n-now account for seventy-three p-percent of the 'orphan' cultures in this sector by d-direct reference to Kh!lict carvings that show these people being killed. The true horror of the Kh!lict's genocidal massacres is that they never c-considered that the other races they encountered might be intelligent. Their world view said that they were alone, and so all life-forms they encountered were b-by definition inferior.

"You have all seen the carvings they left behind, how evil and brutal these p-people were. By the time their civilization fell, their brutality permeated everything they touched. I can't—really—explain what I'm t-trying to say, but I'm sure that the evil was p-programmed into their computers along with all the other information that they stored there. And since the only way we can learn their language and study their knowledge is to become one of them, we c-cannot escape their evil, even though we tell ourselves we are searching only for the good."

"I protest." Kaul's face was rigid with anger. "This is the discovery of a lifetime, and you people want to bury it forever. Science deserves the chance to explore what the Kh!lict have to offer us."

Kirk looked around the room, seeing how Kaul's words sparked an answering fury in the others. *He wants his name in the history books,* Kirk could almost hear them thinking. *He wants the glory that would come from having made such a revolutionary discovery.* He shook his head to break that train of thought. Kaul's objection, no matter what his motives, was valid. "I agree in principle with Dr. Kaul that every discovery should be explored to learn how we might benefit from it. However, in this case, I don't see any way we can study the Kh!lict civilization from the outside."

Spock looked up from his computer screen. "Dr. Lassiter and I have given that question considerable thought, Captain. We have regretfully concluded that there is no possible way to gain access to the Kh!lict computers without a thorough knowledge of the Kh!lict language. And since the only way for the language to be learned is for the computers to imprint it on a juvenile Kh!lict brain"—he held out his hands, palms upward—"either the students must become Kh!lict, or they cannot study the society."

273

Kirk nodded. "When you add to that the fact that the Kh!lict brain is almost incapable of accepting the concept of other intelligent beings, you have a ready-made prescription for disaster. None of us was able to maintain his own identity all the time, and we have no reason to assume anyone else would have an easier time. Trying to coexist in a Kh!lict body with a Kh!lict lower brain is not an experience I'd recommend to anyone."

"Aren't you forgetting something, Captain? You're sounding awfully casual about this business of people changing into alien bodies." McCoy tilted his chin upward at the angle that said he was preparing for an argument. "I've had the privilege of trying to put the lot of you back together again after this-here little adventure. Now, you and Spock came out of it reasonably well, but everyone else has had more than a few problems trying to get some mental balance back. The problem is, I don't know whether I should help everyone regain his or her memories, especially considering what some of them have gone through, or if I should bury them so deep that they will never surface. So, Captain, I don't think two out of eight is particularly good odds, especially when *another* two out of that eight didn't make it at all. If anyone else was thinking about changing into Kh!lict, I sure wouldn't want to guess which people would come through it in any better shape than anyone else. It's much, *much* too risky an experiment to be trying ever again! And that's my official medical opinion."

Kirk looked around the room. Everyone but Kaul was nodding in agreement with McCoy's words. He made a mental note to have the doctor keep close tabs on everyone who had been transformed into a Kh!lict, particularly Chekov. However, unless Chekov's memories of his actions while in alien form surfaced in coherent form, Kirk thought it would do more harm than good for anyone to discuss the matter further. "That's it, then. Our official recommendation is to quarantine Careta IV and permanently ban all investigations of its surface."

"I protest!" Kaul jumped to his feet, slapping both palms against the table. "I protest most strongly at this refusal to examine a find of such significance!"

Taking his time, Kirk unfolded himself from his chair. Using his height to dominate the shorter man, he pinned Kaul with a steely glare. "We were down there on the planet, and you weren't. It is the considered opinion of everyone who had firsthand experience with the Kh!lict—including your own people—that we have had more contact with this civilization than is good for anyone's mental stability. The Kh!lict and their technology are too dangerous for us to meddle with, and we dare not let one of their genocidal crusades loose in the galaxy. Your objections will be noted in my official report, Dr. Kaul, but the quarantine recommendation stands. Briefing dismissed."

Before Kaul could collect himself for further argument, Kirk made good his escape. The bridge seemed wonderfully clean and peaceful and orderly after his experiences on the planet. Settling himself into the familiar contours of his command chair, Kirk gave the order they had all been waiting to hear for the last five days. A subdued cheer went around the bridge in answer to his command.

"Take us out of here, Mr. Sulu. Warp factor two."